Unmistaken Reality

Unmistaken Reality

by

KINGDAWUD MUJAHID BURGESS

SIMMS BOOKS PUBLISHING CORPORATION

SBPC

SIMMS BOOKS PUBLISHING CORP.

Publishers Since 2012

Published By Simms Books Publishing

Jonesboro, GA

Library of Congress Cataloging in Publication Data

Kingdawud Mujahid Burgess

UNMISTAKEN REALITY

Part 1 of 3

ISBN: 9781949433050

Printed in the United States of America

Book Arrangement by Simms Books Publishing

Edited by Mary Hoekstra/Jeirnear Barr

Cover by Kingdawud Mujahid Burgess

I would like to recognize all of those who made this book possible.

My sister, Yolanda Burgess, who raised us the best she could after our mother died; even after having done six years herself in a state prison. You also did 9 years in federal prison and never budged. You are truly more gangster than most men I have met who claim to be.

My Uncle Gator, who has served most of his life in jail for four homicides; in D.C and the state of North Carolina, you are a legend in the streets. My cousin, Kevin Motley, who survived being shot three different times and who also did a 10-year federal sentence and still is in good spirits.

My cousin Dwight "Whitey" Young, who was murdered way before his time to shine.

My cousin Kay, who was brutally murdered by The D.C Police Department. My hommie Redds, who lost his life to gun violence. My hommie Gus, who lost his life to gun violence. The men of Green Valley in Virginia and

Valley Green in South East D.C, Cheez, Joe Joe and many others.

My hommies from around 1000 and Potomac Gardens R.I.P. Lil Ron Ron, R.I.P. Apple Jack, a true tyrant in the streets of South East.

Shout out to Dutch from 21 and Maryland Avenue...Shout out to Wayne Wayne Mercer of Linda Pollen... My cousin, Guy Young, who just finished 10 years in the feds. My cousin Tiffany, who I love very dearly. Sorry for all of the losses in life you've taken, rest in peace to your husband who was murdered.
My cousin Dre of Barry Farms. The hommies from Wellington Park; Elmoe, Devon, D.C, Bud and Lil Marvin. Y'all will make it out of jail; they can't keep good men down.

The Kings of Uptown, the Notorious Mahdi men, Musa, Farad, Chief and Salahudeen; the whole family.

My hommies down in North Carolina on the Murc, Mingo, R.I.P. Lil Johnny, R.I.P. Draydee, Drat, Boota Boot, Sunny Boy and so many others. My brother

Walter " Mac One" Burgess, who taught me everything I know about women. My brother, Terrel Danner, who is finishing up two ten-year sentences after a twenty-year sentence for a triple homicide. Stay focused brother.

My Lil brother, Christopher Thomas, who survived being shot on three separate occasions. The whole R Street Crew; Mac, Steve Williams and Derrell Williams. The hommie Moon Man, the whole South Side As-Salaam-Alaikum to all my Ahks, the brothers from my city and all over the world stay deenen. Sifullah brothers of Philly, Pops of Nappa Street in Philly, the hommie whose last name is Jordan who's always wilding out.

R.I.P. Angel Marie Coleman from 751; I love you so much and wish you would have never been killed...

Lil Anthony R.I.P. Lincoln Heights, R.I.P. Twin, R.I.P. Dog...Lil Loudie, Derrick Motley, Ralph Nelson, Lafayette Nelson, my Aunt Birdie, Kewi, Tammy, and R.I.P. Eric.

My Aunt Ree, Aunt Vanessa, Aunt Linda, Uncle Birdie who made it sucka free down in Lorton for twenty years and my Uncle Guy; both of them. My Uncle's Randy and Buck, we gotta stop meeting up in these federal and state prisons.

My Aunt Portia, who supported me non-stop since forever. Faatima Abdullah, who is my personal Sheikha. 1000 Charles, Ron, Kuff, Chapellem, Gorgeous Parida, Keisha Nolan, Big Nolan, Red Head, Lil Jr., Kool Aid, Lil Eric, Mad Ball, Cunningham, Lil Omar, R.I.P. Shawn, Escobar Garcia from Capers. My cousin Swole from 18th and Death Row and the many others I haven't mentioned. There are three books; I'll get you your shout out.

The men make the city, so without so many men I'd have never written this book. My cousin Vinny and Shareef Muhammad from High Street South East, R.I.P. Black Pookie, Lil Kevin, and Tone Capone also R.I.P. Lil Eric. The whole 16th and W, Jihad, Bunny Man, and Ahmed, R.I.P. Leslie Burgess.

Part 1

Chapter 1

To a child looking into the sky, a shooting star is an amazing thing to see. It is something wonderful and mysterious. In its beauty and intensity, one could even say a shooting star is magical. Such a sight speaks to the soul of the watcher, speaks of the power life, and of a god-like immortality.

Eight-year-old Brad wasn't looking up at the stars in the sky. No, he had his eyes set upon the stars that were not too far from his reach. He was looking at the type of stars that lived on earth and were considered legends to the world in which they existed.

In a lawless land, they were bosses and millionaires among the poor; where many had failed, they had managed to succeed. Their names were well-known; to some they were even considered to be kings... stars in the street life, a world where very few ever lived long enough to shine. They were ballers in a game that unremorsefully retired its players to federal prisons for the rest of their lives and made winos, prostitutes, bums and crackheads out of so many others, simply leaving the rest dead in the streets.

Through the black steel bars of the gate and fence that surrounded the 1000 Building and incarcerated all other inhabitants who visited or lived in the Potomac Garden neighborhood, Brad watched attentively as one of those stars, known to the streets as Moe, yelled insults at the gorgeous, brown-skinned, supermodel-looking diva who stood beside him.

Her perfect, long, caramel legs were to die for; her body was so fine that it looked as if the Creator of Heaven and Earth had sculpted it. Her face was so opulent with beauty that anyone blessed to look upon her, found it extremely difficult to look away; even though she stood beside a ruthless man whose jealousy was unparalleled. From the hood of his black and beige Aston Martin Vanquish, upon which he sat, Moe continued to curse at the lovely creature beside him. She dared not speak up in an attempt to defend herself.

Moe was a true product of the ghetto and his actions and speech were testament to that. Though he was always dressed in Armani, he was no more than a hoodlum, a gangster, who was as bitter as the environment that had bred him.

At the same time, he could do two things most men in Chocolate City had failed to do themselves, survive and make millions of dollars while doing so. For those two reasons alone, he was put upon a trophy stand. It was those two reasons, and the fact that he could pull the classiest women the streets he came from would ever lay their eyes upon.

His women were so gorgeous that even the politicians of the city had to pay top dollar to be in their presence. They were women powerful men tried to marry, based on their looks alone; but to Moe, those women meant no more than sex and they were disposed of for good, unless they willed their souls to please him.

The way he treated women was looked at as admirable in the world he ruled with an iron fist. To show love was to show weakness, and weakness got a man killed in the

3

streets. It was not unheard of or uncommon for a man to be set up by a beautiful woman; Moe knew that, so he dogged every woman he came across before they got the chance to dog him. To his rivals and his homies, he had been very clever not to have slipped so far, but the same way some cheered him on, others prayed for his downfall. Not too many men were considered in the streets to be a jack-of-all-trades, but he was the American Dream to many on so many different levels.

Brad continued to watch as Moe gestured towards the woman with his hands. All of a sudden, a figure dressed in all black emerged from the alley on the opposite side of K Street Southeast, DC, parallel to where Moe sat on his Aston, accompanied by the woman. The figure, whose identity was concealed, due to the darkness of the block, moved unimpeded towards Moe. Though they saw the figure, none of the gangsters dared to intervene or stop him from making his approach.

The man, whose birth name was unknown in the streets, was known as Gutter, a name that matched every aspect of his character and savage mentality. Everybody knew him to be Moe's enforcer, hitman, bodyguard and cousin. He was a very arrogant individual who carried himself as if he were the Grim Reaper. He was never seen smiling and he didn't talk much. It was said that he expressed himself by way of gunfire. Those who were unfortunate enough to hear him speak usually never heard anything else after that.

As Gutter entered the circle in the dim glow from a once shot out streetlight hanging overhead, his jet-black face became more visible. It was a face few could look upon without looking away. A scar above his right eye had come from a knife fight he encountered while doing a year in the DC jail.

Two small holes could be seen above and below his lip on the left-hand side of his face. The holes were the result of him being shot five times by Pappy, another one of DC's notorious killers. Gutter was reluctant about crossing paths with him ever again.

A single 10-millimeter slug from Pappy's gun was still lodged inside Gutter's skull, and the streets declared it to be the reason he had a death wish. But others said he was just naturally burnt-out, like mostly everybody else in the Chocolate City. Whatever it was that was driving his madness, Gutter was on a crash course collision with death, a fate that would find him soon enough.

The battle scars on his body spoke volumes to those in the streets who considered him incapable of being murdered, while the mere mention of his name was enough to frighten the hell out of so many others. If it was rumored that Gutter would be in a certain place at a certain time, some chose to avoid that area altogether. He had the eyes of a man who had been dead for years but refused to remain in a casket long enough to allow himself to be buried. Looking into his eyes was like looking into a cold soul that seemed to be remaining alive just long enough to conquer its next victim. They were the eyes of a soldier who had been trapped in battle his entire life and wished to see no more war, murder, mayhem or chaos.

Upon reaching Moe, Gutter extended his hand and the two men embraced. They both were dressed in all black, but what Moe wore was of a finer quality than Gutter's. Moe wore a black, silk Versace shirt, black Ferragamo slacks, and a black chinchilla coat. Each article of his clothing seemed to fit his powerful form with ease.

6

Young Brad continued to watch in amazement as the two most powerful men, outside of his own family, stood in the middle of the Murder Capital's most violent neighborhood. They were like two old stone monuments in the middle of a graveyard, surrounded by zombies and goons and without the slightest hint of fear. Moe was the last of a quickly dying breed that seemed to vanish just as fast as they came. Brad heard stories in the morning of the men who died at night, while he was sound asleep, but Gutter and Moe were never among the dead.

In the streets of the nation's Capital, tomorrow wasn't promised to anyone, especially to men like Moe and Gutter. They were considered to the underworld what Michael Jordan and Larry Bird were to the National Basketball Association. However, unlike basketball, which was a game played by men, the street life was a game that played men and murdered its players as quickly as it drafted them. It was not a game to be taken lightly; those that balled in it usually got rich, murdered, or put in jail for the rest of their natural lives.

This was a game that kept score by adding up the lives it ruined. It was a game that had no rules and was home to the scandalous and lawless. A home to the most shiesty individuals the world would ever breed. With no rules to play by, it made one wonder why some managed to play by the rules. It made one wonder, *how could something so lawless have rules?*

"Brad!"

His mother's voice rang down to him from the balcony of the third floor and he snapped back into reality from the fantasy he was imagining. He was the youngest of Ms. Linda Staten's four sons. As the "baby boy" of the family, he was the one his mother and other siblings were most protective of.

His oldest brother, Mel, was 22 years old and had had such a rough life that he was already addicted to booze and pills. It seemed all the dirt he had done in the streets had come back to haunt him all at once. To his peers, he was no more than a junkie, a walking dead man who was simply being kept alive by the intoxicants in his system. He had no ambition at all. He hustled just enough to get by from day to day, but that was as far as his efforts went. If he had enough money to buy his food, drugs, liquor, and gas for the day, he was content with life. Every now and again, he went out of his way and spent $50 on a night with one of the local crack whores.

After Mel, was Kevin, but almost no one knew him by his real name. Those in the streets simply called him, "L," which was short for "Lunatic." At the age of 19, as wild as L was, people said that was the word that described him best.

Despite possessing an arsenal that included nearly every gun ever made by man, L had still managed to get himself shot on four separate occasions. That proved the philosophy of the streets correct; it wasn't about who had a gun, it was about who had the chance to successfully use theirs first.

L still walked around with a .22 caliber bullet embedded in the palm of his right hand, a bullet he refused to have removed until the man who had put it there was dead. That was the same man who had wounded him three of the four times he had been shot. No matter how much weed L smoked, and jokingly the people in the hood referred to him as a walking chimney, he could not and would not be at ease until the demise of his assailant.

For a man who had cheated death thus far, L seemed unhappier than one would have expected for a man who had survived several attempts on his life. With a constant look of disappointment on his face, L let it be known that he was anything but happy. He had 13 children by as many as12 fine women who were willing to sleep with him, even if they didn't want to be with him. Still, he was always unhappy and angry.

L once had a dream that would have provided a way for his entire family to eat without worry and probably for the rest of their lives. He had been the All-State leader in points, rebounds, assists, and passes in the DC-Maryland-Virginia region, with first round draft pick headlining over his photo in the sports section of the *Washington Post*.

He was headed out of the ghetto and it seemed as if there was nothing that could stop him. He would be the mill ticket that would provide a better life for people who had known nothing but struggle and mayhem for so much of their lives.

The great men who had founded his family had died before successfully securing such a way of life for their bloodline, but L was certain that he would not fail. And he knew it would have been glorious, if he'd kept his goals firmly focused. But L was a young man torn between two worlds. Basketball was only one of the many passions that burned at his soul, and it was overshadowed by the awe he felt for hope in the street life, and the gangsters who had carried the torch before him. He had something to prove and he would not be able to rest until he had fulfilled his purpose.

By his sophomore year, L had learned that he had a gift for controlling the minds of others and he worked at it, honing that talent like a fine-edged sword. By the time he was a junior in Georgetown University, L realized he possessed other talents as well. He could make millions selling drugs to school kids, while also controlling the streets of the ghetto's, that even the most treacherous men weren't able to control.

His ability to manipulate people into doing whatever he wanted was a gift and a curse that would almost destroy him. All the time he was excelling in college and on the court, L was building an empire in the streets. By doing so, he lost the focus of his true dream of going to the NBA and nearly lost his own life in the process.

His love for his siblings, children, and other relatives was fanatical and he vowed he'd never let them down in any way, or allow anyone to hurt them, even if it meant losing his own life. That had been the code of the men in his family before him and he would not falter in upholding it to the "t."

Just as his great-grandfather had believed, L believed, too, that if he allowed anyone to get away with harming any of his loved ones, the entire family would be considered vulnerable. Then soon they all would fall victim to being preyed upon. Weeks before he would be drafted into the NBA, L was playing the last game of basketball he would ever play in the ghetto.

L was in the middle of Lincoln Heights when his little cousin, GY, walked up to him, crying loudly. With a frown on his face, L reached out and pulled the crying boy closer.

"GY," he asked, "what the hell happened to you?"

GY tumbled over his words as he sniffled, trying to catch his breath. L stared at him, frustrated.

"Come on, little nigga, what the hell is the matter?" L demanded again.

GY took a long, ragged breath, and then said, "Bang Bang and PJ…"

"Bang Bang and PJ what," L asked.

"Bang Bang and PJ jumped me after school," GY finally managed. "They ganged up on me, L…"

Bang Bang was only 10, PJ was 11. They were not a part of the bloody street life, but L felt a rage building up in him that he was unable to suppress. He decided that he would not let their treachery slide. No! An example had to be made of them both, in order to send a clear message that the Staten family was never to be played with… and L would send the message himself.

An hour or so later, as the sun was sliding down the city sky, L spotted the two boys leaving a convenience store. He stomped on the gas. He flew across the parking lot of the store, slamming on the brakes briefly as the car came crashing into the boys, sending them both flying up against an old Buick idling while its driver waited for someone to exit the store.

The impact sounded worse than it was. It was a double "bang" as L's car smacked one boy, then the other, when they hit the side of the Buick and collapsed onto the concrete. They were hurt; both had broken legs, broken ribs, and were twisted up in ways that their bodies should never have been. L looked down from his car window at both of them, with mean mug on his face, making sure the two of them got a good look at him. He spat out the window, laughed sadistically and then drove away.

The message had been sent, he knew, but unfortunately L had made a mistake. He had forgotten that grown men never minded the games that boys played. The street did not respect what he had done. Many said L was more of a lunatic than they had thought, saying he would spare nobody, be they a baby or a 90-year-old woman, while others said he was simply a coward for trying to kill a couple of kids.

With his ribs taped up and his leg in a cast held up at an angle by ropes and pulleys, PJ was going crazy as he lay in his DC General Hospital bed. His anger was roiling through him like waves crashing against the seashore. Every time he closed his eyes, he saw L looking down at him from his car window, laughing hysterically.

When PJ turned to look at Bang Bang, bandaged and in the bed next to him, his hate for L grew deeper. As he lay there, PJ fantasized about ways to murder L. First, he would torture him by yanking out all his teeth. Then he would carve L's pretty boy face like a piece of meat.

As PJ stared at the ceiling, imagining L lying at his feet bleeding, the door to his room flew open. He expected it to be a nurse or someone from his family, but it was neither.

"Why the hell is this happening," the unbelieving, familiar voice asked.

Bang Bang looked toward the door, while PJ took a deep breath, uncertain of what was about to happen to him and his man. It was Gutter himself, standing there beside Bang Bang's bed, looking down at both of the boys with a face that could have melted steel.

"L ran us down with his car," Bang Bang declared quickly.

"What the hell ya'll little niggas do to him to make him do it," Gutter asked.

"Didn't do nothin," PJ shrugged.

Gutter was instantly at his throat, choking what little life PJ had left out of him.

"Don't lie to me, you little piece of shit! L hit you in retaliation for something. Now tell me what it was!"

"We were roughin up GY, L's little baby cousin," Bang Bang said. "We jumped him real good and took a lil money off him. That's all, I swear."

Gutter, who was listening to Bang Bang while still choking PJ, released his hold and stepped back from the bed.

"Ain't right what he did, at least not for that, but had it of been me, you both would already be dead somewhere," Gutter declared. "The next thing is this... Do you niggas got the nuts to get back at him before he gets back at both of you? Again."

PJ and Bang Bang nodded their heads.

"That's good," Gutter said. "Now when you get outta here, I'll send for you and I'll supply you boys with the proper tools you'll need to do the job successfully."

And then he was gone.

The third son in the family was Derrick. At 14 years old, he had already given the streets hell. He was hell-bent on living up to the reputation his predecessors had established, but he intended to turn up everything they had done to 1000 degrees. Derrick ran with a crew of young knuckleheads that consisted of local bad asses from Potomac Avenue to as far away as 37th Street and Minnesota Avenue. Although each of the boys was ruthless in his own right, they didn't have the balls to go as far as Derrick did with everything he did. That put him in the position to call most of the shots for the crew.

By street standards, which were really high, he was as wild as hell. Like a mad ball on fire, he was uncontrollable, and that got him the nickname, "Madball." Not only did he have a treacherous nickname, but he was also determined to live up to it as well as he could.

Due to his family's reputation in the street for being tough, Brad was constantly being pressured by his peers to toughen up. As far as he was concerned, it was tough enough living up to the standards of being a kid in the ghetto.

After being told so many times that he could grow up to be whatever he was meant to be, he was confused when people insisted that he be the next gangster in the Staten lineage.

Brad had dreams to one day be the President of the United States. That was definitely a man in a position to change the lives of so many others, for the better. Brad admired his brothers and the other guys in the street for being brave enough to overcome their situations by any means they saw fit, but being a child in the inner city was hard enough.

Being a gangster would be much more of a challenge, a challenge he himself wasn't up to facing. For the moment, he knew that starting a new school year was enough to think about and the morning would come soon enough. He went to bed with his thoughts still on the stars in the street, and the brothers whose shadows he would always be under.

Chapter 2

"Brad! Get your ass out of that bed right now," his mother yelled, rousing him from his sleep.

"I'm up, Ma," he called back.

He quickly jumped out of bed and joined the other kids who were all rushing to get ready. His sister, Tebetha, took a shower while Madball sat on the toilet, stinking up the entire bathroom.

Without complaint, Brad walked into the bathroom, past Madball, and to the sink. He began brushing his teeth. He looked at his brother on the toilet; Madball was making all kinds of weird faces as he struggled to relieve himself.

"What the hell you staring at me for, little nigga?"

"You better hurry up before Momma come in here and start yellin."

20

Brad just shook his head and wished that one day he would be able to buy his family a house that had more than one bathroom. For now, it was not gonna happen. The rule in the morning when getting ready to start the day was, *You do you while I do me.*

Ms. Linda was frantic; it was the first day of school and Madball was refusing to go. His closet was packed with boxes of new sneakers, but he was still demanding the "Dub Zero" Michael Jordans that would have cost Ms. Linda $350 she didn't have to spare.

"You little punk nigga," she screamed. "Do you know how hard I had to hustle to buy you them other four pair of Nikes you got?"

"I ain't even hearing none of that, Ma," he shouted back. "I been telling you all summer that I had to have them Dubs or I wasn't steppin' foot on the school yard."

"Boy, you gonna get your ass out of here and go to school or Ima knock sparks from your sissy ass," she threatened.

"You ain't gonna knock nobody nowhere, so stop doing all that faking!" Madball yelled, as she got up from where she was seated at the table and got in his face.

They both stood toe-to-toe in the middle of the floor, challenging each other to see who would back down first. Suddenly, the front door opened and L walked in with a huge bag in his hand. It seemed he had come just in time, catching his mother's wicked backhand she had begun to swing as a blow to Derrick's face.

"Hold up, Ma," L said, stepping in front of her and up into Derrick's chest.

"Lil boy, if you don't get cha ass out of my mother's face, Ima put that table over there up your ass!"

Derrick stepped back, then said, "Man, she be acting like somebody is supposed to be scared of her or something."

"Little nigga, you better be scared of her, cause

Ima be the one throwing the punches for her. You got that?"

Derrick, was still eyeing his mother, who was not grinning.

"Ya," he said.

"Here," L said, handing Derrick the bag he had in his hand.

Derrick quickly reached inside it and pulled out the black and silver box that contained the "Dub Zeros." He looked at Ms. Linda and smiled sadistically.

"Damn, man, this all I was asking for," he said.

He quickly took the new Penny Hardaways off his feet and replaced them with the Dub Zeros. Ms. Linda glared at him.

"Boy, you better get cha ass on somewhere before I sling you and them damned shoes off of that balcony. I brought your lil tail in this world and I'll take your ass out of it, and I'll do it whenever I get good and god damned ready!"

Tebetha walked into the living room and the sight of her calmed everybody down. She was amazingly gorgeous; she was a little girl whose body had out-aged her by at least 10 years. Tebetha was not just a beautiful face and a tempting body, she was a straight-A student, the entire family was very proud of.

She had the entire family eating out of her hand, because she was clever enough to play the innocent role so well, that everybody assumed she was the heavenly angel she so shrewdly appeared to be.

She was followed by Diamond, Ms. Linda's youngest, who seemed to be the only perfect child she had. Diamond never complained and she never had to be asked to do anything, whether it was her chores around the apartment or her homework.

"You look so beautiful," Ms. Linda said, smiling.

She knelt down and gave seven-year-old Diamond a hug.

"You already finished your cereal," Ms. Linda asked.

Diamond nodded her head. "Yes, Mama," she said, as she put her arms through the straps of her book bag.

Brad and Derrick were gobbling down frosted flakes, while L and their oldest sister, Butterfly, sat on the couch watching them.

"Ya'll need to hurry up," Butterfly said, frowning at Madball who was eating like a pig.

As he got up from his seat at the table, Ms. Linda started in on him again.

"Derrick! You lazy, fat muthafucker! I know your trifling ass didn't sleep in them clothes you got on!"

Derrick froze, silently, with an evil look on his face. He was about to start arguing with her again when Butterfly interrupted.

"Ma, leave that boy alone! You should be glad that his bad ass going to school after being suspended nearly all of last year!"

Tebetha walked up to her mother, looking like *Ebony Magazine's* model of the year. Her hair was in micro-twists, pulled to the back, and without a drop of makeup, her beautiful face was flawless. The skin-tight pink and purple Moschino top made her small ripe breasts look bigger and fuller than they actually were. Her tiny waist curved down to a perfect set of hips, firm thighs, and a plump behind that was always getting her second looks from everyone she passed by. The Prada stretch pants she wore fit her so perfectly that they appeared to have been painted on.

Ms. Linda was proud of her daughter's beauty, and often enough, she let it be known that Tebetha reminded her of herself when she was that age.

"Where the hell you think you going like that?" Derrick demanded.

Ms. Linda rounded on him. "Boy, you shut cha damned mouth! You ain't nobody's father around here," she said, beaming at the sight of all her children.

"Ya'll come here and give me a hug," she said.

One by one, Diamond, Brad, Tebetha, and finally even Derrick gave her a brief hug then headed out the door. The building stairwell was packed with kids, each of them looking and smelling like they just left a clothing store.

Like all kids, returning for a new school year was more bearable because of the nice clothes they got to wear. Likewise, most parents in the ghetto would buy their kids the most expensive clothes they could, to show that they weren't nearly as poor as they really were, or everybody figured them to be. Clothes were a symbol of wealth in DC, for jewelry only attracted the cops and stick-up kids.

It was much safer and acceptable to wear expensive designer clothes because no stick-up kid would wanna wear a pair of shoes somebody had already worn, unless times were extremely hard.

In the Chocolate City, you could look at a person's clothes and tell whether they or their family had money. If a person's family couldn't afford to buy them nice clothes, it was certain they couldn't afford to buy them anything else.

Many of the ghetto children's parents were either strung out on heroin or crack and the rest were weed heads or PCP users, also known as boat or swamp water smokers. PCP was embalming fluid in chemical portions used to embalm dead bodies. It also had elephant tranquilizers and 12 or so other deadly chemicals mixed with it that could easily fry a grown human being's brain in no time.

A lot of these kids had no father to financially support them or their families because their dads were either in prison, dead or too selfish to claim them.
Once out on the terrace, Derrick spotted Shawn Escobar

28

and like always, he began joning on him. Escobar wasn't Shawn's real name, but since he was mixed with black and Spanish, and looked like a photograph they had seen of Pablo Escobar, the other kids began to call him Escobar or just plain, old Bar.

"Nigga, I know you ain't take them boots you got on off that bum Leroy who be sleeping out front of the White House," Derrick said, pointing to Bar's feet. "It look like Carl Lewis ran three marathons in them B Zoots."

All the kids began to laugh. "Look like cars been using them boots for speed bumps. Naw, I know I seen them boots somewhere; that's them boots that been up on the telephone wire since before I was born. Ya, that's the same boots the Feds beat off Pipe Head Willy feet two years ago."

All the kids were laughing hysterically.

Bar fired back, "Oh ya? You over there looking like you just got finished having sex with Marge Simpson. All that toilet bowl crust all over your lips.

You the only French nigga I know rockin them tight ass butt huggin pants."

All the kids were still laughing like crazy. "That's why you got five different haircuts and three different shape ups," Ball shot back. "You look like somebody just snatched all 12 of them baby corn rows right out cha head."

Suddenly, the laughter ended, as a large group of kids bent the corner. Bar recognized one of the boys he knew was Psych, who was from around Arthur Capers Housing Projects where they both lived.

Bar and Psych knew each other well, having grown up around Arthur Capers Projects together, but Psych never got to know Escobar because he hung around the Gardens too much. For that reason alone, there was a question as to where his loyalty would lie if a war broke out between the two.

As the two groups came together, the tension in the air thickened. Some of the kids were smart enough to continue moving, while the pride of others, or their wanting to see a fight, kept them there.

"What's up wit ya'll, Psych?" Bar asked, being the first from among the group to speak up.

"Ain't shit up with us! What's up with ya'll niggas," said Psych, as his eyes slid away from Bar, over to Madball.

"What the fuck you mean, what's up nigga! What you want to be up," Ball said, stepping up so close in Psych's face that he was able to smell his breath, which reeked of stale cigar smoke and weed.
Psych retrieved a flip knife from his pocket and opened it, then held it up to Ball's chest. Ball glanced over at the blade and sneered.

"I'll make you eat that knife, Joe. You pulled it, now push it, you fake ass killer."

"Derrick! Stop," Tebetha screamed from the other side of the street.

The entire crowd of boys turned at the sound of her lovely voice.

"Damn, she fine," said Deejie, the boy standing to Psych's left.

Everybody else was thinking the same thing as they just stared at her in awe.

Psych, who was too busy himself, staring at Tebetha, never even saw Ball's three-punch combination coming. He was on his way to the ground when the fourth and fifth punches found his temple. He lost his grip on the knife and it fell to the ground.

Ball stood over top of Psych, pounding away at his face; with punch after punch that didn't seem to lose strength or miss their mark.

Deejie grabbed the knife and began swinging it wildly toward the group, but a hay-maker threw him off balance and made him step back. As he stumbled backwards, he grabbed Escobar's jacket and swung the knife, slicing Bar in the chest.

Everyone standing around watching began to join in the fight. Before long, it was an all-out brawl. Ball scrambled through the crowd to Bar and lifted him up from the ground where he lay.

"Come on, Slim, you gonna be alright," he said, looking over at Tebetha, who was crying. As he carried Bar to a parked car he yelled, "Get everybody to school, Theba!"

Ball removed his shirt, wrapped it around his hand, and punched the passenger side window, shattering it. Quickly he opened the door then pushed the button on the panel that unlocked the rest of the doors. He put Bar inside, hurried to the driver's side, and climbed in. Without wasting time, he pulled a screwdriver from his coat sleeve and jammed it into the ignition, turning with all his might. The engine roared. Ball threw the car into drive and raced away from the curb.

"Hold on, Slim, hold on," he said, looking at Bar.

From the look on his face, Bar was in excruciating pain.

The knife was still sticking out of his chest. Ball thought about removing it but didn't want to damage his friend any more.

In no time, the car swerved past DC Jail into the DC General Hospital parking lot. Without slowing down for the speed bumps, Ball flew through the lot towards the entrance of the Emergency Room. Once there, he braked, threw the gear into park, and hopped out. He ran around to the passenger side and quickly lifted Bar from the seat. He began walking with Bar toward the ER entrance.

"Hey! A kid is dying here," Ball screamed.

Two nurses rushed toward the sound of his voice and saw the other boy, covered with blood, in his arms.

"Sorry, ma'am, but I can't stay," he said, letting Bar transfer to the nurse's arms.

Then Ball sprinted from the hospital as the nurse called after him. He jumped into his stolen car and raced off like a madman, before the hospital police came.

The last thing on his mind was going to school or being arrested on a humbug. He decided to go to Lincoln Heights, a place he could chill for a while, until he figured out his next move. He looked down at his Dub Zeros and saw blood on them.

"Damn!"

He wasn't sure if the blood was from Escobar or Psych but the sight of it on his new shoes made him mad enough to kill them both. He shook the bloodstained shoes from his mind when he saw a police cruiser approaching behind him. He made a quick left off Benning Road, knowing it would be easier to run on the cops from the back streets.

Lincoln Heights, he thought to himself. The Heights was the second biggest dope strip in the city, next to Potomac Gardens and Arthur Caper. Dope fiends came from every corner of the Tri-City to buy the heroin that the dealers around the Heights supplied. The Heights wasn't just a dope strip though, crack, powder coke, Hydro, Ecstasy, and more could be copped from any building in the Heights.

The Heights was also known as "Baby Baltimore," because of its heroin; but unlike Baltimore, Maryland, which was a city, the Heights or the "heights of hell," as it was known to the rest of the city, was no more than a neighborhood that was home to a bunch of killers and at least six self-made millionaires...six the streets knew about anyway.

There was never a dull moment in the Heights. If somebody wasn't getting money, they were spending it. It was nothing to find a crap game whose pot was over a million dollars in property and cash, or see a circle of men fighting pit bulls for even heavier wagers. Sometimes, just for the hell of it, the hustlers would gather up the strongest dope fiends and crackheads from around the city and throw a couple bindles of heroin, or a couple grams of crack, into a circle and watch them tear each other to shreds for the drugs. At times, they would even bet on who would win the bloody brawls.

From Fitch Street, he could see the Heights, which looked like a great, enchanted beast just sitting quietly, lurking for its prey. Kelly Miller Junior High School was to his right. He slid down in his seat as he passed the crossing guard who just laughed to himself at the sight of Ball. Surely in any other city, a kid driving a car with its passenger side window busted out would have put up a red flag, but not in the nation's capital. The police weren't big on stopping crime or attempting to apprehend those who committed the crimes.

The city was full of law-breakers and law-breakers, so who was gonna be the one to uphold the law?

DC's ex-mayor had gotten himself caught smoking crack in a hotel with a prostitute and the President had got caught getting some head from a woman. With such examples to follow, how dare the country wonder why it's Capital had the highest murder rate in the nation?

As he made his way up 50th Street into the Heights, he heard gunfire erupting. *Probably someone getting killed or somebody's just testing a weapon they just got,* he whispered out loud to himself as he turned into the alley that ran along the back of 50th Street.

He pulled up next to a dumpster and hopped out of the car. He began wiping it down, making sure he removed his fingerprints from the vehicle. He looked over the car one last time then walked up the alley, which took him to the edge of the building surrounding the basketball court.

He walked up the cut as far as he could before he was stopped by a huge crowd of men in a circle. The men were gambling and their crap game was blocking the entire back entrance. Ball understood why. Most stickup kids snuck up inside the Heights from the back, so the men wanted to watch their backs.

"Man, ya'll niggas need to get the fuck out of the way," he said, pushing through the crowd.

A man who was known by the hood as Dogg looked up at Ball and said,

"Boy, what the hell your little ass doing out of school?"

"Ain't no money in school. Besides, I'm chillin like a villain, laid back in my style, doin' me!"

"Hey, Buck! You see your bad ass nephew," another man named Fruit called out from the crowd.

Buck looked up from where he was kneeling and spotted Ball.

"Nigga, your mother know you didn't go to school?"

"Come on, Uncle Buck, you know better than that. If my mother knew I was out here chillin with you, she'd be ready to kill the both of us," Ball said, smiling.

"Look here, shortstop, I ain't gonna turn you in, but you damned sure ain't about to be hanging around this crap game."

Buck quickly peeled seven $20 bills off the stack he had in his hand and handed them to Ball.

"Here, now make yourself disappear."

Ball took the bills, then said, "I'll this, too" removing a Backwoods cigar full of hydro from behind

Buck's ear.

"Hold up. Come over here," Buck said, watching as Ball speed-walked away.

Knowing he couldn't leave the huge pot of money he had sitting in front of him, Buck just nodded his head.

Ball walked down the sidewalk until he reached the basketball court off 50th Street. He spotted L on the court, crossing somebody over with his dribble, then finishing it with a slam dunk over his opponent.

"That's game," L said, dropping down from the rim and adding, "Ya'll can't fuck with me out here," as he collected his money from the four men. "Ya'll would have had a better chance at winning if ya'll would of helped each other," he said, smiling as he walked towards the side of the court.

He reached down and lifted his jacket from the ground, revealing the chrome .45 ruger automatic and the miniature AK 47, or the "A Kick," as the hood called it. He grabbed the strap of the assault rifle, slinging it around his shoulder to his back then he picked up the .45 and placed it down in his waistband. He looked over at Ball but remained quiet as he walked to the money-green CI 550 Benz.

"Wassup, lil brother," he asked, as he opened the car door and tossed the assault rifle onto the back seat.

Without saying a word, Ball went around to the passenger side of the car, opened the door, and climbed in. After closing his door, L turned towards Ball and just stared at him.

"Look, I ain't gonna assume nothing because assuming makes an A-S-S of U and ME, so go head, here's your opportunity to tell me why you ain't in school, like the rest of the kids in this country. Especially after you made all that fuss about them damned shoes you got on your feet."

Ball looked into L's red eyes. "Man, niggas from around Capers jumped us on the way to school this morning. They stabbed Lil Escobar and shit."

"Where's he at," L demanded.

"DC General. I took him to the hospital."

"How the hell you take him to the hospital," L asked sternly, making Ball look down at his feet. "I'm waiting," L said, mean mugging him.

"I stole a car," Ball said, expecting to get smacked with a backhand, but it never came, which caused his confidence to grow. "Man, I had to or that nigga would have bled to death."

After he remained silent for a while, a huge smile came across L's face.

"Damn, baby brother," he said. "Your little ass wild as a pack of hyenas. When the hell you learn how to steal a car?"

"Man, I been stealin cars since last summer," he said, letting out a sigh of relief. "I can steal anything with wheels, except a 747, and soon I'll be taking one of those bitches for a joy ride."

L laughed and then said,

"Here, hold this," passing the nickel plated .45 automatic handgun over to Ball.

He picked the gun up out of his lap and just stared at it in awe.

"Man, this jont sweet. How many bodies does it have on it?"

L looked at him without a word, grabbing hold of a blunt he had sitting in his ashtray; it was as big as a number two kindergarten pencil in size and width. He fired up the joint, took three long drags, then passed it over to Ball, who was still admiring the weapon he held in both his hands.

L started the engine and began cruising through the Heights as the marijuana smoke filled the air, nearly smothering them both.

"You wouldn't even know what to do with that if you had to use it," L said, referring to the handgun his brother couldn't take his eyes off.

"Nigga, know about my work. My victims be getting famous."

"Ya, like who?"

"Shit! You don't be reading the paper? All you gotta do is read the Metro section of the *Washington Post* and you gonna read about my work."

L blew the smoke that was buried in his lungs out through his nose as he looked at Ball.

"So you been putting in work?"

"Ya, I be puttin that work in all throughout the DMV. I do overtime and graveyard shift hours. If you need niggas chopped up, bagged and tagged, just holler at me. Hell, I enjoy the job so much that I won't even charge you."

L passed the blunt that he had resting between his lips back over to Ball.

"It's about time," he said.

He placed the cigar in his mouth and inhaled deeply, then he began to cough.

L laughed, "look little young'un, you gonna do whatever it is you wanna do out here in these streets, no matter what I say."

"Every man is responsible for their own destiny but those around us have a responsibility to try their best to guide us away from mistakes," L added.

"Unfortunately for you, the clowns that you are surrounded by have no idea what the hell they doing or who they doing it to! Half of them will end up getting killed before this year is up and the others will become dope fiends, crackheads, bums, or homosexuals, once they go to prison for the rest of their lives."

"How you gonna say that about my friends," Ball demanded. "Man, you don't even know my niggas!"

"I know the streets, and it's the same on everyone that takes it to be some sort of game. Men more thorough than your little block niggas have fallen victim to the beast," L replied. "You just wait and see and while you waiting, keep your fingers crossed and hope like hell that you don't become a victim of the streets yourself.

"This street life ain't no joke. Like I said, this shit ain't a game at all. You can yell 'time out' when a killer catch you by surprise and press that thing to your head with the intentions of blowing your brains out.

"Don't nobody get to push reset and start over when them hot rockets start peelin their skin off their bones and leave 'em washed up on the curb, dead."

"Tell me something I don't know," Ball said, interrupting L.

"You know shit! In this way of life, killers won't even respect you unless they respect what you do, and just because someone respect something about you, don't mean that they're gonna respect everything about you. A whole bunch of men get murdered by the cowards that respected and feared them.

"See, little brother, it's best to be loved than feared. When people fear you, they'll laugh at your jokes, even though they're not funny, and they'll even agree with you, even when you're dead wrong. It ain't because they like you or because they respect you; it's because they are too damned scared of you to be honest with you, which means they are deceiving you.

"They'll even do stupid shit, like kill people, to try to gain your friendship in hopes that you won't mess with them. Soon as those niggas get in an interrogation room with the Feds, they be the first niggas to start tellin. They be the same niggas that'll help your enemies kill you so they can be at ease."

"Hey," Ball said. "I got a couple of loyalists on my side."

"You got peoples?"

"Ya, I got peoples!"

47

"You think you got people and that's gonna be the first mistake you make out here. How you know I didn't lace that blunt you puffin' on with cocaine or PCP?"

Ball looked at the nearly finished blunt in his hand, as fear came over him.

"You can't trust nobody in these streets," L said, as he rolled up another blunt.

"Out here a man, woman or baby will fuck you over for a million different selfish reasons. All day long, I hear you young'uns talkin' about it's all good. Niggas getting' killed out here for cigarette butts. A broad will have AIDS and convince you not to use a condom so she can pass it on to you. So tell me what part of this shit is all good?

It's all bad out here cause at any second, things can go wrong," L said.

He looked at his little brother, who was still looking at the blunt in his hand.

"Stop geekin, I ain't on no coke or any of that other garbage, but can you honestly say that about the hundreds of jokers on your block, who you smoke weed with every day?

"Look, baby bro, it's only two things guaranteed to us out here in these streets and that's death and jail; whoever got it figured otherwise, ain't dealin with reality and they must got the prosecutor on speed dial.

"Ninety-nine percent of the stuff we do out here is illegal. Ninety-nine percent of the stuff we do is gonna put us in jail; the same stuff is enough to make a man rich or get him killed in his effort to become rich."

Ball waited for a minute to see if L was finished talking.

Then he said, "Ok, I get all of that, but it's only one way out of the hood for brothers like us, so what other choice do we have, especially when we gotta hold the torch our uncles, fathers and grandfathers passed down to us?"

"Everybody got a choice on how they wanna live their lives. Everybody that was holding that torch before me and you is in prison for the rest of their lives, or dead. So, the question is, are you willing to go through that?"

"Like you told me yourself, L, if a man stands for nothing, he'll fall for anything."

"Once again, you took what I said out of context. A man has to always hold his own, no matter the circumstances. The question you need to be askin yourself is this: Can you handle your own, and if you can't, then what?"

Ball shrugged his shoulders, then said,

"I know when I can trust people and when I can't."

L shook his head. "You just don't get it," he said. "It's only one way to trust people and that's to trust them to be exactly who or what they are. If a man is on crack, you can trust and believe that if you leave some

50

crack with him to watch, he's gonna smoke it up. If your man is always tellin you how sexy your girl's ass looks, you can trust and believe this, the first chance he gets to have sex with her, he's gonna take it.

"People are gonna be people and a lot of us don't even know ourselves as good as we think we know everybody else.

"You'll never really know what you'll do in certain situations until you go through those situations.

"A lot of niggas are bitter right now because they got snitched on by somebody they trusted. Them damned fools should be mad at themselves, first of all, because a person can't say what they don't know. If a joker is tellin on you, it's because of something you either showed him or told him."

"So you saying keep my mouth shut, right?"

"It's much more than just keepin your mouth shut. Some things go without saying. I know about your man, Lil Kurt gettin killed and I know who he got killed by and what it was over, and I don't even hang around 1000.

"Just like I can tell you who around the Gardens is gettin major money sellin weed, or heroin. The thing is, if I know, and that's not even my hood, don't you think the Feds already know?

"One thing about sellin drugs is this; you can't sell them to yourself. The Feds don't need to know who's sellin what anymore. All they need to know is who is buying what, and if they watch the buyers, eventually the buyers will lead them straight to the dealers."

The more and more L talked, the more and more Ball re-questioned his every move.

"How you know all of this?"

"Listen up, little brother, this here is hood life 101! I know you're gonna do your thing no matter what, so I'm gonna try to help you stay alive while you're doing it.

52

"Like now… We riding around the deadliest city in American and you gotcha eyes half-closed, all highed up off some weed. Not once did you look to see if we was being followed by the police, a couple stick-up kids, or a rival."

Ball's eyes quickly shot to his mirror on the passenger door next to him.

"Always watch your back, even when you don't think you have to. You might not be beefin, but that don't mean that I'm not."

A BP station came up on the right and L steered the car into it, pulling up to the nearest gas pump.

"You need anything out of here," he asked Ball.

His brother nodded.

"Nigga, well speak up; I ain't no god damned mind reader!"

Ball focused through the high that was making it

difficult to think.

"Um, a soda, cookies, chips, ice cream, candy…"

"You about as high as it gets," said L.

As L got out of the car and walked towards the store, Ball watched him attentively, intrigued by all he had said to him. For the first time in what seemed like forever, he was thinking about what it was he really wanted to do with his life.

A real legend of the game had taken enough interest in him to school him. That itself was an honor that many would never receive. He wouldn't be caught sleepin, he thought, keeping his eyes on both side windows and the rear view at the same time.

After paying for the things he had on his grocery list, L strode back to the car and handed Ball the bag full of snacks. Ball grabbed a soda and some sunflower seeds right away, while L pumped the gas he had pre-paid for.

He set the pump on automatic and began to scan the entire area surrounding the gas station.

Just then, a blue Lexus pulled up to the pump beside him and a voluptuous red bone, with hair down to her shoulders stepped out.

"Ay, shorty, come here," L called out to her. She turned to look at him.

"No! How about you be a gentleman and come to me," she retorted, putting her hands on her hips.

Without delay, L walked to her.

"You blessed, shorty," he said.

"Now what makes you say that?"

"Cause if you was looking at what I'm looking at, you'd be saying the same thing. Smooth, peach complexioned skin, pretty face, phat ass...mmmm!"

She blushed and L went on.

"You gonna let me in on the blessings?"

He pulled his cell phone out of his pocket and began pushing buttons.

"What? You ain't even gonna ask me my name?"

"Naw," L said. "Ima just call you Gorgeous for the rest of your life."

He handed her the phone and she keyed in her number. When she handed it back, L saw that she had set the display to read, "Gorgeous Ganiva," and he smiled.

"Alright, Gorgeous, I'm definitely gonna get at you very soon," L said, staring her down as he walked backward to the car.

"Ay, boy," she called after him. "What's your name?"

"They call me L," he said.

"L? What does it stand for?" He looked down towards his groin.

"Long, or long stroke, depending on how long you like it."

What he said made her smile. He removed the gas nozzle from the tank and replaced it back on the pump. *Damn*, he thought, *I can't wait to get between those juicy thighs.*

He screwed the gas cap back on then jumped into the car. After closing his door, he fired it up, put it in drive, and swerved out of the parking lot onto Good Hope Road.

Ball was laid back, enjoying his ice cream as he slumped down in his seat. *I wonder how good he responds to pressure,* he thought to himself.

"Ay, didn't you say something about having a beef with Little A-Rod and them young'uns he roll with around Barry Farms?"

"Oh yeah, little young'un and them some light work. They fired on us a few times but they couldn't handle how we came back so they just stay out of our reach from now on. If I ever catch any of them niggas in their hoods or out of bounds, they're as good as dead," Ball said.

"Is that so," L said, merging through traffic.

"Ya, that's pretty much how I see it. Catch em and mash they asses up like potatoes."

"Man, you be talkin that big man stuff like you a certified head hunter. I bet if them niggas catch you out of bounds you'll plead the Fifth to all that noise you talkin now.

"See, there you go again, doubting me. I told you that I'm a Staten and Kool Aid don't pump through my veins."

L glared to his left then grinned as he passed the Anacostia subway station. He then made a quick right up into Barry Farms projects.

"Hey," he said softly. "You see where you at?"

Ball was high as hell and his eyes were bloodshot red and barely open enough to see where he was. He slid back up in his seat and what he saw in front of him nearly took his breath away. His heart began to race and his palms were suddenly drenched with perspiration.

"Man," he screamed. "You lunchin all the way out. What the hell is we around here for?"

"What? You said you wanted to see them niggas, so here you are."

"I don't even know where these jokers be at around here, so we wasting our time."

"It don't matter where they be at," L said, snapping, with the humor gone from his voice. "A beef is a beef! If you can't catch the victims you beefin with, then keep shooting up everything around them and eventually you'll hit somebody they love or you might get lucky and hit them. By killing everything around them, you'll send them a clear message that says you are not to be messed with ever again in life.

"Since this their hood, everybody around here should pay for helping raise the little bastards!"

Ball stared at him, shocked. "Man, I..."

"Don't," L yelled. "That talk shit doesn't fly with me, little brother. You was talkin all that big boy shit just a while ago. Now it's time to shoot pool. This is where the boys separate themselves from the men."

Ball sat there, heart pounding, waiting for L to say that he was only joking, but he didn't. It felt like a nightmare and Ball realized that his mouth had finally put his butt in trouble. He looked down at the Ruger .45 that was still sitting in his lap and began to wish it hadn't been there.

In his mind and heart, he had always felt that if it came down to it, he could kill without hesitation, but now he was seriously doubting himself.

"I need to get straight first," he said at last, breathing in deeply.

"Yes, we gonna get straight, then we gonna come straight back around here. It's time you learn not to let your mouth get you killed."

Chapter 3

The bell rang to signal the end of the day. Instead of heading straight home though, nearly all the students hung outside on the school grounds; waiting to see who came through shining, like all the gangsters in the city usually did every year on the first day of school.

Anacostia Junior High looked like a fair ground. Everybody who was anybody hung outside on the corner of the school, looking to see how far advanced everybody else had become over the summer.

As tradition required, the city's thugs washed up their hoopties and drove down to the school thirty minutes before it let out. They stalked the young women who seemed to have grown up over the short summer months, as the women flaunted their bodies in the most revealing and provocative clothing they could find.

A hustler with a pocketful of drug money was something the ghetto girls who were poor had their eyes set on. To them, he was a come up, and to him, she was worth every cent of the money he felt he didn't work at all to acquire.

The corner boys went for the hood rats, while the hustlers, the real breadwinners, went for the top-flight women. As always, the attraction ran both ways. The young women were infatuated with the cars, money, houses, lifestyles, and jewelry that came with the rush of living on the edge.

The hustlers were simply geekin to have sex with as many of the women that would let them. As they went up and down the block, hanging from their car windows, calling out to the girls, go-go music blared from their stereo systems.

With all the hustlers' cars cruising up and down the street, the front of the school was looking like a car show. New Mercedes Benzes, Cadillacs on 24-inch Giovanni rims, Lexuses, and Porches debuted; even as the old school rides with new expensive paint jobs came through, jockeying for position in the exclusive entourage.

Brad walked from the school building, across the school ground and over towards where the buses sat waiting. Wow, he thought, noticing that the front of his school looked like the players' ball.

Like most of the younger boys who were freshmen at the school, Brad saw the girls from his school as the most beautiful women he had ever laid his eyes on. One day, he hoped to be intriguing enough to make them want him the way they wanted the other boys from his neighborhood.

He liked all the girls at his school, but one stood out to him much more than the others. Her name was Felisha. She was 16 and, hands down, the most beautiful and classiest girl in the school. Everybody in school and out of school wanted her but she didn't bother giving anyone the time of day.

Brad daydreamed of her being his as he watched her standing at the curb, looking so good that every car that went up the street stopped to holler at her.

One day she'll be mine, he thought to himself, reluctant about taking his eyes off her. As a young man growing up in the hood, Brad knew the difference between young, hot-butt girls and women; to him, Felisha was all woman, and then some.

She was five-feet, four-inches tall, with long, jet black, silky hair that extended down her back to the small of her waist. It stopped just short enough to reveal the plump, juicy looking derriere that protruded down into a pair of caramel-complexioned, thick thighs that looked as if they were concealing a very important treasure between them.

Her flawless skin was so delicate that it looked as if it could melt in one's mouth like the creamiest of marshmallows. Going the opposite way, her flat stomach ran up into a perfect pair of small, tender breasts.

Any man would say she had the body of a goddess but to Brad she had the body of the most beautiful woman on the face of the earth. Her lovely neck was the honorable pedestal blessed to hold the perfect masterpiece that was her face. With a smile that could melt the sun, her eyes were Caribbean blue, colder than water falling from a mountain after the snow up top melted. She had the loveliest dimples; Felisha was created nearly to perfection.

"Ay, ay, ay, girl, ay, shorty, lemme holler at you," so many young men cried out as they tried their best to get Feilsha's attention.

Like a stuck-up white girl, she turned her nose up and ignored them all, as Brad laughed to himself, *Keep it moving, losers; she'll never be caught dead with any of you low lifers.* He knew Felisha had too much class to desire the glitter and glamour the men flaunted in front of her.

Suddenly, everyone seemed to get quiet. Their attention was diverted to the far corner of the east side of the street.

All the other cars in front of the school seemed to fade from view as the beige on black Vanquish bent the corner on its custom-made, 20-inch, gold-plated,

Giovanni rims that looked like rolling diamonds. The car slithered along the block like the new "Batmobile," dominating the show.

Haters mugged and acted as if the bad muthafucker that was driving it wasn't on his top boss player shit. Still, no matter how hard one hated, they still had to give props to whoever owned such a masterpiece and dared to have the balls to drive it through Death's City.

As slowly as it could, the Vanquish crawled up the block, giving all spectators a chance to become awe-struck. When the car reached Felisha, it stopped and Brad's beating heart stopped with it. The passenger door opened and Moe, dressed down in a cream-colored, velour Coogi suit, stepped out. He pushed his seat forward and, without saying a word, Felisha walked over to the car and climbed inside.

Brad stared, heartbroken and Moe glanced up to see the wounded look on the boy's face. Brad's glare drew his attention and Moe called him over.

"Young'un, wassup,' Moe asked, as Brad

approached.

Brad was staring at Felisha as he came closer to the Vanquish. Moe tapped his shoulder.

"Hey!"

Brad glanced up at him, and then looked at Gutter, who sat behind the wheel with a mug on his face.

"Little nigga, I ain't the one that called your ass over here, so you can stop looking in my face like some lost, stray puppy."

Moe turned to Gutter and frowned. "Ease up, G."

When he turned back around to face Brad, he noticed him staring at Felisha. Suddenly, Moe understood.

"Look, young'un, she in the back of this car because she chooses to be. A woman is gonna do whatever she wants with whoever she wants to do it with, not matter what we think, cause at the end of the day, she's gonna be satisfied, no matter who she gots to hurt."

"Ya," Gutter said, turning in his seat to face the wounded Brad. "As long as you ain't gotta take the dick for her you shouldn't never be worried about who she given her pussy to."

"Chill, G," Moe warned again. He slid inside the car and closed the door behind him. He let his window down.

"Stay focused on things you got control over," he said to Brad. "Cause no man has total control over no woman. Now get over there to your bus before it leaves you."

The car moved away slowly.

"Why the hell you be talking to that little boy," Felisha asked Moe, as she uncrossed her legs allowing Moe to glance at the fruit sitting between them.

"Some people be asking me the same thing about

you," he said, smiling as he slid his hand between her legs. "Shorty on some other stuff, he ain't out here tryna be the next Tufline Shaw or the next Wayne Perry, he tryna be the next president, and for that reason and that reason alone, in my eyes he's a true legend in these streets."

"Man, fuck that little nigga and his whole family," said Gutter.

"Man, what the hell you got against them niggas G?"

"I know that nigga L had something to do with Pappy trying to murder me! Before L got shot up he was making a lot happen in the city. I had told Omar and Joe Joe that I was gonna snatch L's ass; and that same night, Pappy, who I had no beef with, caught me loafing and hit me up. I know L put that nigga on me!"

"You need to be beefin with your dumb ass self for tellin Omar and Joe Joe what you was plottin on. Them the niggas you need to be trying to get at!"

"Ya'll get them in due time but for now my mind is set on killing that pretty red nigga and his whole family."

*****

Flashback to L's assault

The entire city was shocked to read, on the front page of the *Washington Post,* that a shooting star had been shot down. "All-Pro basketball player who was expected to be drafted as the first-round pick in last night's NBA draft failed to show up at the draft."

The newspaper continued, "After checking the hospitals and jails, the city police did a sweep around the treacherous neighborhood of Lincoln Heights, where the star sometimes played ball and they were given a tip that the star, Mr. Kevin Staten had been shot multiple times. He was at an undisclosed location where he was being closely watched by the Feds, who wanted to question him about the assault; if he recovered from the assassination attempt on his life."

"The city today, along with the rest of the world, is in great mourning. All everyone can hope for is that the Legend survives, but from what has been given to us through confidential sources in the FBI, Kevin Staten has been wounded fatally and he may never return to the game of basketball again."

Up under the news article was a picture of the bloody spot on the ground where, it was rumored, he fell.

*****

Present day

As he climbed the steps into to the bus, Brad shook his head, trying to escape the vision of Felisha allowing herself to be used by Moe and Gutter.

"Hello, Mr. Neil," he said as he passed his bus driver.

"Hello, Brad," the old man said, smiling.

Brad was the only kid that rode his bus that had enough sense to show anyone respect. He reminded the old man

of better times in the Nation's Capital.

As Brad continued walking towards the back of the bus, he spoke to everyone, even though they didn't bother to speak back. As always, the ride to his stop would be short. The city did not allow the buses to take the kids into their neighborhoods. It was too dangerous, extremely dangerous, with all the beefs going on between the different streets.

The bus came to a stop in front of the Eastern Market Subway station. Along with 20 other kids who lived up and down Pennsylvania Avenue, Brad got off.

It would have been a faster walk if he had gotten off at Potomac Garden Station but he enjoyed the walk. He crossed the street and entered a corner store. As soon as he stepped in, an overwhelming smell of feces and urine stung his nose.

The old Oriental man, who everyone knew as Poppasan, sat behind the counter, protected by three-inch bullet proof glass. He wasn't worried about the many villains of the city, because even if they wanted to, they could not get to him. From behind his counter at the front of the store, Poppasan watched as a junkie staggered up and down his aisles. The man's body reeked of urine, old wine, cigarette smoke, and feces.

In just five minutes after the junkie entered, the smell had begun to permeate throughout the store. With his eyes nearly completely closed, the drug addict, who looked to be sleep-walking, wove his way through the store. Brad watched in amazement, wondering how the man managed to keep from running into anything.

"Ay, you muddafucker. You hurry up and buy. Me don't fall for that Michael Jackson "Thriller" junkie shit you trying to pull, okay," Poppasan yelled to the man.

"Fuck you, slanted eyed gook. I dare you to come from behind that glass and say that shit," the man retorted.

"Hurry up and get cho ass out, you piece of shit!"

"Fuck you, Johnny Appleseed; you and your little slanted-eyed buddies better stop eatin up all the cats and dogs in this neighborhood before I report ya'll asses to the animal protective services and the Humane Society."

"Fucka you! I eat yo ass?"

"No, fucka you, Charlie Chan; you ate my kids' pet rabbit!"

As the two men argued and exchanged insults, Brad slipped a candy bar into his sleeve. He had watched Ball do it many times without the slightest sign of remorse, but that wasn't the case with Brad. His palms were sweating bullets; he wanted to put the candy bar back, but for fear of getting caught, he did not do so. He grabbed a few other snacks and went to the freezers where he pulled out a 20-ounce Coke. As he turned around, his heart dropped.

The dope fiend was standing right behind him, looking down at him. *Had the guy seen me steal the candy bar*, he wondered to himself.

"Hey, shorty, spare some change so an old man can buy something to eat," the fiend said, smiling at Brad.

His teeth were yellow and had stuff on them that looked as if it was still alive.

"Okay, I'll give you some money, but you can't spend it on cigarettes or alcohol," Brad said.

"You got that, baby boy. I won't do no such thing," the fiend said, following Brad towards the counter.

Brad figured helping the man would make up for the candy bar in his sleeve. He turned and looked at the man. He could see a really young kid behind the filth on his face and unkempt beard. The fiend's hair was filthy. He didn't look a day over 25.

76

The visible scars on his face made it seem he had had a very rough life. The filthy clothes he wore looked like they once fit him perfectly, but were now drooping and sagging from his body as if they were five sizes too big. Each article of clothing, including his worn-out shoes, appeared to be stained with dirt, grease, rust, and everything else from where he had slept in abandoned buildings throughout the city.

Brad handed Poppasan a ten-dollar bill, then picked up the brown paper bag from the counter.

"Wait for your change," Poppasan said, as Brad walked toward the front door.

"Give it to him," Brad said, looking back at the man.

"You piece of trash junkie! You take candy from a baby. You should be ashamed of yourself!"

"Fuck you and the boat you snuck over here on, you slimy piece of shit. Now give me two packs of Newports and a forty-ounce with that change."

As Brad walked alongside Pennsylvania Avenue, he began to wonder if he should chance taking the alley that ran through the buildings, or stick to the main street. If he stayed on the main street, he would have to walk past the front of Building 1430. The boys his age from around 1430 had already jumped him once and he knew there was nothing to stop them from doing it again.

They would have never dared to jump any of his cousins or his brothers, but they considered him to be soft and they knew he would never retaliate against them. They would beat him again, given the chance.

In pondering how they had beat him the first time, Brad decided it best to take the cut that ran directly behind their building.

The alleys were the fastest way to travel; they cut straight through the buildings. The alleys were also the places where all the killers and low lifes of the city hung out and did their most private dirty work.

"Ay, whatcha bitch ass doing in that alley," yelled a boy looking out his window facing the alley.

Without turning to look up, Brad took off running through the cut and didn't stop until he was in front of his building. Brad wasn't willing to take the chance of being jumped again. He knew if he had told his brother Ball what the boys around 1430 had done to him, he could get them off his case for good; he just didn't want anyone getting hurt over him. The very thought of it didn't sit right on his mind and heart, so he kept it to himself, hoping that one day the boys around 1430 would finally leave him alone, for good.

For some reason that he could not understand on his own, the projects of Barry Farms Housing appeared more sinister than they had ever appeared to him before. The fading cream-colored brick buildings looked like a lost city that had no intentions of being found.

Barry Farms was the belly of the beast. It looked as if it harbored the souls of all the murdered men and women who had died in the city streets. Long empty fields ran between each of the buildings, separating one from the other. The fields, which had once served as back yards for the residents, were now manmade cuts that the killers, fiends and hustlers used to stash their drugs and guns.

Basically, if you weren't from the Farms, or you weren't the police doing a raid on the block, you had better not be caught creeping through the alleys. To Brad, the buildings looked like they were perfectly aligned with one another from a distance but looked very uneven, up close.

The Farms was a death trap that was very hard to get inside of, but even harder to escape, and not just to its residents; it was that way for many of its visitors. At the back of the Farms was a 15-foot gate that separated it from a small forest; which served the purpose of keeping anyone from entering or to keep them from leaving.

To its front, there ran a highway called Suitland Park. Across that eight-lane road there was a city subway train station. One would instantly be hit by a vehicle if trying to flee in a rush from the Farms from that direction.

To its right was a hill that was too steep to climb. Even if one did manage to climb the hill, they had another problem to face. Just over the hill was another rough neighborhood known as Park Chester.

Park Chester was home to a bunch of wild men who weren't too fond of people entering their block unless it was to purchase narcotics its hustlers sold.

The last side of the wicked box that made up Barry Farms was deserted. You had to cross a huge, abandoned train track from that side to enter the Farms. Further down the road, a bridge ran across and into the Potomac Gardens area, or the southwest side of town, depending on which turn one made.

Down from there was an empty wasteland known as Blue Plains. It ran beside a long strip of highway that would either lead a traveler into northern Virginia or Maryland.

Bottom line?
To open fire on anyone in the Farms meant making a hell of an escape.

To Ball, opening fire was the least of his worries. Staying alive long enough to open fire was the thought that was eating at him. From Sumner Street, where L's car was idling next to the curb, the Farms looked like a ghost town.

Ball knew that wasn't so. Its many villains, killers and dealers lay tucked away behind the safety of their project buildings, either watching everything from the alleys or the abandoned houses they used as drug houses.

Never would Barry Farms be empty and Ball knew it. The neighborhood just so happened to be the Chocolate City's biggest, exotic weed and boat strip at the time. It was also a trading post for the pirates throughout the city, who could just simply jump on and off the city trains as need be.

"Go ahead and get out," L said, blowing a cloud of weed smoke from his nose.

Without hesitating, Ball slid the handgun up under his shirt, concealing it in his waistband. Then he opened the door and stepped out of the car. Without even giving him warning, L put the vehicle in reverse and sped out of the neighborhood the way he had entered it.

Damn, this shit just got too real, Ball whispered to himself as he tried to keep the gun in his waistband from pulling his pants down to the ground. *This is a suicide mission and right now Ima cold blooded crash dummy*, he said to himself, as he walked up the narrow path that led back down to Sumner Street.

I can just walk right up out of here and fire off a few shots, once I get on Martin Luther King Avenue. I'll tell L I hit this joint up and he won't know. Then I'll run up Robinson Place, Ball thought to himself. He tried to find a way out of the suicide mission he had willfully walked into. Just before he was about to continue up the street, he saw a large group of boys in all black, hanging in the alley at the end of the street.

"Who the fuck is that," one of the voices called out.

Damn, Ball thought to himself. The voice belonged to Puss Head, a villain known throughout the city for gun play. He knew Ball well, due to the little beef both of their hoods were involved in.

Before Puss Head could see him, Ball crossed the street and headed up the stairs to the top of the hill. *Damn, damn, damn,* he said to himself. *There is no way out now.* If he turned back around, he would put himself deeper into the Farms. If he kept straight, there was no doubt about what would happen next.

Ball climbed the steps, hoping not to see any more familiar faces he recognized or who would recognize him. He cursed L for sending him on such a crash dummy mission.

"Who dat? Who dat," called out the men standing at the entrance of the buildings alongside the steep stairwell.

Ball continued to walk and did not answer them.

The top of the hill seemed so far away and from where Ball now stood, so did the bottom. As he climbed the stairs, he watched as the villains standing on both sides of the steps in front of the buildings watched him attentively.

"Slim, what's up? That boat over here," said a man standing in the grass in front of the building closest to him.

"I'm just tryna find that exotic OG Kush," Ball said, never breaking his stride.

"They got that at the next building," the man said, lowering the black ski mask from his face.

"Black, who dat," asked a man coming out of the building.

"Some nigga tryna find some exotic," Black said.

"Hey, Slim hold fast. I got that," the man who had just spoken said.

He walked to the steps of his building and leading to the main steps. Ball paused and reached into his pocket to retrieve his money. As the man, whose name was Big Face Melvin and was called MT, continued approaching Ball, his heart dropped. At the same time, both of them reached for their weapons and Ball got to his first. He raised the .45 caliber pistol and without hesitation squeezed the trigger. The first two shots met their mark, striking MT in the chest.

MT fired back but the impact from the gun caused the shell to go towards the ground. Ball pointed his weapon towards MT's face and fired. This time, the shots struck him in his face and head. He slumped to the ground.

Black, who had taken shelter behind the heavy metal door of the building, took fire at Ball as he sprinted full speed, heading towards the stairs that separated the buildings. The gangsters who stood ahead of him were still in so much shock that they didn't even respond to what was going on.

As MT lay dead, shot in his face and head, Ball opened fire on the men standing to his left before they got the chance to fire at him. Several of the men ducked and ran for cover, while only a few tried getting to their weapons that were stashed in various spots around the buildings. As they got their guns and fired back at him, Ball returned fire, tearing up the pavement around their feet as his bullets missed their marks.

The villains inside the building were now firing out and down towards Ball, but many of them were hitting their own homies as Ball ran past them. As he continued to run at full speed, he tried to remember how many shots he had fired, but it did no good because he had no knowledge of how many shots were in the gun at all.

Just as he bent the corner his eyes grew wide and he threw himself to the ground. The Mossberg pump shot gun blast barely missed him, firing three times almost simultaneously. The impact of the gun shook the whole building; the three blasts intended for Ball had struck two other men instead, splitting them in half.

He quickly jumped back to his feet and fired on the man with the shotgun, striking him in the chest and leg and taking him to the ground. Ball ran, jumped over him and continued running, not even daring to look back. As he ran, he continued to fire on those who fired at him. Seeing that his shots came close to hitting their marks, or had hit them, he began to relax.

Then he squeezed the trigger and nothing happened. He panicked. The 20-shot clip was empty. Without losing stride, he reloaded the weapon, trying his best to reach the top of the hill.

He came upon a man who was crouched down beside the building in the direction Ball was headed. Before the man could get off a shot of his own, Ball pointed his .45 and fired, sending the man flying up against the building then dropping to the ground.

Ball turned to look and what he saw behind him scared him. A bunch of small red dots were visible, shining in the darkness. There was no way in hell that he was getting out of this one alive, he thought. Half out of breath and tired, he ran full speed, still up the hill, trying to make it out of the Farms before a lucky bullet finally found its mark... him!

In an instant, the gunfire grew louder and louder; at the same time, they also began getting closer and closer. Ball knew, whatever they were firing, his luck was about to come to an end. Bullets were tearing up everything around him, convincing him even more that he would be the next thing to be hit.

Ball turned to look again and saw men retreating while others were chopped in half by gun fire at the same time. He frowned up his face and wondered what the hell was happening but he didn't dare stop running. Out of the corner of his eye, he noticed three of his assailants being torn apart by bullets. He could now tell the gunfire was coming from above him. *Damn, just my luck, I'm caught in a damned crossfire between the Farms niggas and the Park Chester niggas,* he reasoned.

He turned and looked up at the gate at the top of the hill, which was now only a few feet away from him. That's when he saw L, holding and spraying the A-Kick at any and everything that dared to stand or move. More confident now that he would survive, Ball ran in a straight line and reached the gate quicker, compared to all that zig-zagging he had been doing. He grabbed hold of the fence and began to climb, as L went back and forth, spraying the A-Kick.

As Ball reached the top of the gate and put his leg over it, a man stepped from behind the building closest to him and fired six shots. Two of those found their mark, sending Ball flying over to the other side of the fence, while L's shots found the man, splitting him and the brick building behind him in half.

All the wind was knocked out of him, but Ball managed to hop to his feet. He quickly limped over to L's car and jumped inside. He closed his eyes, finally, and he hoped that would help numb the pain.

L continued to spray shots from the A-Kick, tearing away at the buildings below. Once he was satisfied with the job he had done, he walked backwards towards the car. He kept his eyes open for anything or anybody that might jump out and would just be torn to pieces by the A-Kick.

Once inside the car, L noticed Ball holding his right hand with his left one.

"Let me see," L said, grabbing the hand.

After examining it carefully, then looking at the wound in his arm, L released Ball's hand.

"You're fine!"

"Shit! You sure I'm fine? Cause I damned sure don't feel fine."

"I said you're fine. They ain't do nothin but graze you."

"What about my leg," Ball asked, pulling up his left pant leg.

A long scar ran the length of his calf and stopped right below his knee.

"You're one lucky cat," L said, putting the car in reverse and backing up slowly from Park Chester.

"What the hell is that supposed to mean," Ball asked.

"It means you simply got grazed three times; that's what it means. How the hell you ain't dead, I don't know."

"Oh, so you sent me in there hoping I got killed," Bell snapped.

"Looks to me like I saved your ass, so you should be thanking me! Look, you dumb little punk, ain't nobody tell you to go through with that shit. All you had to do was say you wasn't cut out for that type of work. Don't go jumping into the ocean if your ass can't swim! You got that?!"

"Man, damn all that stuff; I'm your little brother and I almost just got my damned head blown off cause of you!"

"Here, drink this," L said, passing Ball a fifth of Remy Martin VSOP cognac.

Without hesitation, Ball took the bottle from L's hand, twisted the top off, and then began guzzling down the warm, dark, bitter liquor.

L fired up another perfectly rolled cigar and after puffing on it twice, handed it to Ball, who lowered the bottle from his mouth and said,

"Killing a man ain't such a hard thing to do."

"Ya, tell me that after tonight when the faces of the jokers you shot wake you up every hour on the hour, askin for mercy," L said.

"Do you think Grandad or my father and them started crying like you just did when they was killing people and almost being killed? If this the line of work you're gonna be into, you have to accept whatever comes with it, whether that's good or bad.

"Everybody wants to be the killer but don't nobody wanna get blood on their hands."

As he sat listening to L talk, something clicked inside him. He was a Staten and the Statens didn't cry about nothing. He thought to himself, *Ya, Ima killer just like the men that came before me and Ima be the best and most treacherous killer this damned city has ever had!*

The alcohol and weed smoke began to take their effect and Ball couldn't keep from smiling.

"What the hell is so funny?"

"You just created a monster," Ball said. "From this moment on, any and everybody can get it! I ain't takin no prisoners and I ain't gonna for nothing. Anybody that jumps out there with me is gettin blasted!"

"You just feelin yourself and you're feelin my weed a little too much," L said, snatching the cigar out of Ball's hand.

L turned on the radio and Ball dozed.

"Wake up, slim, we back around your way," L yelled.

Ball jerked awake. As the car exited the cut heading into the parking lot behind Building 1000. He scanned the entire projects complex.

Everything was normal, just like it always was. Like clockwork; sells came and left and the homies didn't miss a beat. Like zombies, everybody seemed to move in slow motion as they crossed the "valley of death" and looked for the antidote for whatever ailment they would eternally suffer.

Sexy ghetto girls, known to the hood as rats, because they were always chasing cheese, stood around in tight clothes that barely left any part of their frames unconcealed. With their voluptuous booties and the things hanging out, they made the filthy red brick of Building 1000 look more pleasing to the eye.

The scandalous beauties and the constant flow of illegal money made project living more bearable for everyone, especially those who were forever condemned to spend their lives in the ghetto for eternity. To them, the ghetto was heaven and they were willing to die to protect it and its reputation.

Coming from nothing usually meant not having a thing to worry about. In the ghetto, most people found themselves on the same level and that was the level of being poor. Some dreamed of getting out, while others couldn't even imagine life from outside the streets.

In this world, is where they belonged. In this world, they were somebody, because in this world, killers were glorified, drug dealers were worshipped, and a man's reputation, whether good or bad, made him immortal.

Some wanted better for themselves and their families but others knew better than to want better. They worked, played, killed and died right where they lived, as if the world outside of their projects didn't exist. Kings existed in the street, but the same ones that usually authorized them to be crowned also murdered them, sooner or later, for their treasures and positions.

Nobody was safe and no one was above being murdered. Success, the poor felt, was being able to say they survived through the day. If killing a person meant life for the ghetto boys and girls, then it was murder they were committing on a daily basis. Drugs were the factor that made it all worthwhile. They turned poor men into rich men and turned rich men into bums.

Most hustlers didn't expect to live long, due to their lifestyles, so they spent their money just as fast as they could make it.

"Go head in the house," L said, snapping Ball out of his deep thoughts.

Ball opened the car door and stepped out.

"Before you go in the house, go up pipe head Tico house and let his baby mother wash that blood off you and stitch you up."

Ball said he would as he slammed the car door.

"What's up, slim? What's up," Pac Man and Chapelle, two of Ball's homies said, as they slid from behind the black steel gate and crossed the parking lot towards him.

"I got shot," Ball said.

L rolled his window down and gave his baby brother a cold stare.

"I mean, I got grazed three times," Ball said, looking away from L.

"Man, everybody told us what happened to you and Esco. Didn't nobody say shit about you gettin shot."

"I didn't get shot during the situation me and Bar had. I got shot…"

From his window," L interrupted, yelling at Ball, "Man!"

"Man, Ima holler at ya'll," Ball said, heading towards Building 1000.

"Ya'll know I'm famous for running muthafuckas over with cars, so get the hell out the way so I can pull off," said L.

That made the boys move to the side. L turned his stereo up, fired up another cigar, then swerved out of the parking lot and headed back through the cut. Once L was gone, Ball turned back around and met Pac Man and Chappelle on the steps.

"You know Lil Jesse got aired out up at the Gardens just a few hours ago," Pac Man said.

"Naw, what happened," asked Ball.

"We beefin with near everybody in the city so it's hard to tell who hit Slim up, but rumor is, that it was an inside job. That nigga lucky he ain't dead, cause they hit him like seventeen times. Slim came home from down Wackenhut, fakin like he was the reincarnation of his cousin Apple Jack, and that's when all his problems got started," said Chappelle.

Ball said, "So ya'll just let niggas shoot the hood up and walk away like nothing ever happened?"

"You know I got my bust on," said Rico, another one of Ball's men.

"Me too," said Pac Man, pulling out the 10mm handgun he had tucked up under his shooter's hoodie. "I ain't put no work in for that Jesse though. I can't stand that petty ass nigga, but I did give them a run for their money so the hood could save face."

Ball shook his head then smiled,

"So, what's up? Ain't nobody hear nothing from Esco yet? Man, that nigga got out of the hospital the same day. The knife just hit all muscle so he good."

Ball started walking again, saying, "Well, good. Look, ma niggas, I got to get going before L comes flying back around the corner."

"Man, your brother crazy as hell," Pac Man said, saluting Ball as he went up the stairs.
Walking inside the building, Ball could hear gunshots off in the distance, which made him smile. He told himself, *The whole city was getting it on, but like the saying went in the ghetto streets, it didn't matter about who was doing what; all that mattered was who got who first!*

Chapter 4

"What's up, Ma," Escobar yelled down from his bedroom window, seeing his mother carrying an armful of groceries from the car to the house.

"Shawn, get cha tail down here and get these bags," she said, looking up at him and smiling.

"Here I come right now, Ma," he said, ducking back inside his room.

He snatched his All Daz hoodie from the bed and pulled it over his head. Then he reached inside the dirty clothes hamper and grabbed the Mac 380 assault pistol he had stashed there. After putting the gun and its extra clip in his hoodie pouch, he left the room and went downstairs.

"I'm on it right now, Man! I mean, Ma... Ma," he said smiling as he leaned down to kiss his mother's cheek.

He walked to the front door and opened it, then stepped

outside. After looking to make sure there was no immediate threat, he walked to the car. He looked around again, checking to see who might be eyeing him. When he was satisfied no one was lurking, he opened the trunk and snatched up the grocery bags.

Everybody was standing around, drinking and smoking weed while trying to sell their drugs. Wasn't nobody thinking about him, he thought. But he wasn't about to let false hopes or nothing else rock him to sleep.

Was the "prisoners," as he called them, really trippin off a fight that happened between a bunch of kids? People in Arthur Capers had bigger problems to worry about, like trying to pay their bills and staying out of jail. Still, Bar wasn't taking any chances after getting stabbed.

As he saw it, he didn't belong to Capers anyway. Building 1000 was where all his homies were. He wished his mother had never moved around 501. The place was a graveyard. Most of its gangsters were beefin with so many people they couldn't even leave their block. That's why Bar considered them to be prisoners.

"Ay ma! Ima put these groceries on the table then Ima ride my bike around to Ms. Linda's," he yelled up to his mother.

"Go ahead, Baby, just make sure you back in time for dinner because I'm cooking your favorite food," she said.

"Ok, Ma, I'll be back for sure," he said as he walked out the front door.

He grabbed his bike from in front of the house and carried it out of the fence and onto the street. He headed towards the Navy Yard, which was right up under the bridge.

Arthur Capers was unlike any other projects inside the Chocolate City; it was unique. It stretched from southwest to southeast, running the distance of both. One could not leave Virginia to go into DC or leave DC and head down 395 without passing Arthur Capers.

Nothing but the 6th Street Bridge divided it from the rich people who lived up on Capitol Hill. Capers was Capitol

Hill. It was the side of Capitol Hill the news reporters never allowed their cameras to focus on when they told the lovely story of the Capital of the United States.

America and its dread existed inside a nightmare. Its dream was the life the whites on Potomac Avenue lived; its nightmare was that of the blacks who lived throughout the rest of the city.

It was amazing how a person could take the wrong turn-off at Capitol Hill's dreamland and be in a world of killers, prostitutes, thieves and bandits within a matter of seconds.

It took Bar less than three minutes to reach the front of Building 1000 but he didn't stop there. He rode his bike down K Street until he reached 13th and K. There he made a right and continued until he was standing in front of Buildign1025, where Ms. Linda lived.

On the balcony right above his head, Ball, Lean and their cousin Omar knelt on the concrete rolling dice for fives and ones.

"Grab the dice. Grab the dice," Omar said as the dice nearly rolled off the balcony before Lean caught them.

"Well would you look at that," Lean said, watching Escobar tie his bike to the fence in front of the building.

Ball and Omar leaned over the balcony to get a better look and Ball's eyes locked with Esco's, and then they both started smiling.

"Come on up," Omar yelled down to him.

"Naw, stay where you at, we coming down," said Ball, disappearing inside from the balcony.

Ms. Linda was in the kitchen cooking when she heard the door open. "Who the hell is at the door," she asked.

"Come on, come on," Ball said, sliding out the door with Lean right behind him.

"Hey, where ya'll little muthafuckas think ya'll going," asked Ms. Linda, as Omar slid through the door and quickly disappeared down the steps.

All three of the boys ran around to the side of the building as Ms. Linda went out on the balcony.

"Derrick! I know you hear me you little fat fucker. If you don't get your faggot ass back into this house, there's gonna be hell to pay!"

Omar, Lean and Escobar were on the ground, rollin in laughter.

"Damn, Mad Max, she be cursin your ass out," Bar said.

"Man, fuck that bitch. That's why I stole the little bit of weed she had left," he said, holding up a Backwoods cigar he had already rolled.

"Here, fire this up, Bar," Ball said, passing the cigar over to his best friend.

106

"I ain't got no lite."

"Here, O, fire this joint up," Bar said, passing the blunt to Omar.

"No! No," Ball yelled, snatching the cigar out of O's hand just in time.

"You know that nigga don't smoke. He was about to tear the weed up, fool!"

"I told ya'll not to be making the mistake of passing me cigarettes and weed; if I get them, Ima tear them up."

Ball fired up the blunt then said, "And Ima tear your ass up, too, Cousin."

"So, what's up, Bar? You alright," Omar asked, looking at Bar.

"Ya, I'm straight."

"O, you straight. You ain't say that when that nigga put that knife in your red ass," said Ball, making Lean and Omar laugh.

"Man, we need to get back at them niggas for what they did," said O.

"Man, I just left from around there and them dudes was actin like they wasn't trippin," said Bar.

"Ya, they tryna rock your ass to sleep, that's all," said Lean.

"Man, I wouldn't give a damn if a dude was scared petrified of me. I wouldn't let my guard down, ever."

Every one of the boys nodded his head in agreement.

"Don't forget that it be his homies who be the ones that's gonna try to keep that beef going."

"Niggas be skirts! All it take is for a bunch of cowards with little bits and pieces of hearts to come together and then they'll have a full heart," said O.

"That's why you gotta kill them all, cause as long as one of them is still breathing, your life is at risk," said Ball. "But I gotcha back now and forever," he said smiling and hugging Bar around his neck.

"Aww," Ball yelled in pain as Bar hugged him back.

"Damn, you alright," Bar asked, concerned about his best friend.

"Ya, I'm good, I just got shot three times, that's all."

"Grazed, you mean grazed," Lean said, making Omar laugh.

"You got shot," Bar asked, a concerned look on his face.

"Ya, I got hit three times the other night. L took me on a crash dummy mission.

"Damn, L let you roll with him to go put in work," Bar asked.

"Ya, I be rollin wit that nigga all the time, cause unlike ya'll, he knows my work is official," Ball said, smiling.

"See, Bar, us Staten boys don't be slippin," Omar said, pulling the Calico from under his shirt.

"After getting stabbed, I ain't slippin no more either," Bar said, pulling the Mac 380 out of his hoodie pouch.

"Damn, that jont sweet," Omar said. "How many bodies does it have on it?"

"I don't know but I'm sure it has a few."

"Naw, nigga, he mean how many bodies did you put on it," Lean said, smirking.

"O, I ain't killed nothing yet; I'm still a virgin," Bar said, tucking the automatic pistol away.

"Don't worry about that, my man. We'll put some on there before this night is out," said Ball. "Cause having guns don't mean a damned thing if you ain't usin em."

Just then, little Brad bent the corner with his book bag hanging from his left shoulder.

"What's up, baby brother? Where you going," Ball asked as he hugged and kissed his little brother on the cheek.

"I'm going to the Library of Congress," Brad said, trying to lift his book bag over his right shoulder.

Ball grabbed the straps and lifted it to his little brother's shoulder.

"Do you need me to go with you," he asked, looking down at Brad.

"No, that's ok, but thank you, I'll be fine."

"Ok, but I can walk with you if you'd like."

111

"Man, why the hell you goin to the Library of Congress from this way, when all you gotta do is go up past 1430 and you'll be able to catch the W bus that'll get you there in no time."

Brad knew better than to tell his family why he didn't wanna go past Building 1430.

"I just wanna walk so I can get some fresh air," said Brad, looking down at the ground.

"You got too much heavy stuff in that bag, Brad. You should catch the bus like Omar said."

"Please, can I just walk, Derrick," Brad pleaded with his big brother.

"Ya, you go ahead and walk this time, but from now on you gonna have to start taking the bus up there, ok?"

"Ok," Brad said, hugging Derrick and then walking off.

"That's the only person I would tear this whole city down for," Ball said, looking at O.

"Tell me about it, Slim. If something happened to my little cousin, we all gonna tear this city down."

Ay, look, I gotta move; we can go on if ya'll tryna get some real money."

"What's the move" asked Escobar.

"I know some hustlers up the forty that got major chips to spare."

"So what you saying," Bell asked Lean.

"I'm saying we go rob all them niggas; that's what I'm saying."

"What forty? Six forty," asked Lean.

"Nigga, what other forty you know?"

"Man, we might have a problem tryna take that joint by storm," said Omar. "But I got an inside man if you super serious about it."

"You damned right I'm serious about it. We got three guns and four thorough niggas."

"Who got three guns? All we got is two," Omar said.

Ball pulled out the chrome .45 automatic from up under his Solbiato hoodie and said, "Like I said, we got three guns, nigga."

"Damn, why you ain't tell nobody you had that jont," asked Lean.

"As long as I know I got it, that's all that matters."

"Damn, what type of stuff you on, cousin? We let you know when we got our hammers on us," Lean said, frowning up his face.

"If niggas stayed hammered up, wouldn't nobody have to wonder who had a gun and who didn't. But enough with all of that. Let's make this happen."

"So how the hell we gonna get there? By train," Bar asked.

"Naw, nigga, we all gonna ride your bike," Ball said, being sarcastic.

"We gonna go up to the avenue and either steal a car, or catch somebody slippin and rob them for their car," Lean smiled, indicating to Ball he was game.

All three boys began walking down the street. When they were in front of 1430, three younger boys Ball knew from the neighborhood asked him what's up.

"What's up with you, little dirty muthafucka," Ball asked.

"We chillin, that's all," one of them said.

"Why the hell my little brother Brad don't like walking by this building? I know ya'll little jokers ain't fuckin with him, cause if ya'll are, and I find out about it, Ima bury this whole clip in your ass," Ball said, revealing the handle of his gun.

"Ya'll already know that us Staten boys don't mind killing kids," Lean said.

The three little boys just froze in place, not knowing what to say.

Omar busted out laughing, saying, "Them little niggas probably pissin in their pants.

"If I find out they messin with little bruh, they gonna be pissin blood," said Ball.

They made it to the end of the street then turned into the McDonalds parking lot.

"You see this nigga," Ball asked, looking at the driver of a blue Buick Le Sabre idling in the lot.

"Ya, he trippin," said Bar, looking at the man who was nodding off in his car.

"Come on, come on," Omar said as he walked over to the car.

At just about the same time, all four boys opened a different car door and hopped inside, startling the hell out of the driver. Lean, who had opened the driver's side door, smacked the man with the butt of his gun. Blood from the man's nose flew all over the windshield.

"Get cha punk ass out," Lean demanded.

"Ok, ok, young buck," the man said, fidgeting around in his seat.

"Get cha punk ass out, I said," Lean yelled, hitting the man again.

The man's hand slipped under the seat, down to the blue steel snub nose 357 hidden there. Bar spotted the gun but before he could say anything to Lean, shots rang out and everybody jumped. Ball, who was in the passenger seat had opened fire on the man, hitting him in the head and face twice. He jumped from the car and walked around to the driver's side door and yanked the man out of the car. He stood over the man, pointed his weapon in the man's face and fired seven shots.

"Now he dead," Ball said, walking around to the passenger side. "Get the hell in the car," he yelled to Lean, who stood outside the car and looked down at the man lying dead.

Lean hopped in the car and put it in reverse. After backing out of the parking spot, he hit the gas and accelerated into the traffic on Pennsylvania Avenue that was jam-packed with rush hour traffic heading back into the city from Maryland and Virginia.

"Man, what the hell is you doing, sittin here waiting on the police to come arrest us?"

"The light red! Where the hell Ima go," asked Lean.

"Here, slide over," Ball said, moving into the

118

driver's seat.

Ball whipped the wheel back and forth as he merged through traffic. He side-swiped a few cars but didn't stop until he reached Minnesota Avenue.

"That's how real G's drive," he said, flying down 37th Street.

*****

Flashback of L's Assault

Just as Gutter said he would, there stood L in the middle of the basketball court at Lincoln Heights. The entire hood was vacant, except for a few dope fiends who had no life outside the alleys where they got high.

Everybody else was glued to the TV, waiting to see their own countrymen get drafted into the NBA. This was a historic night for everybody, rich and poor, living in the Nation's Capital. One of their own was about to be drafted into the NBA. What Bang Bang couldn't figure out was why L, the city's basketball legend, would be chillin in the projects on the day of the biggest night of his life.

"This nigga tryna say farewell to the hood for good," said PJ, trying to un-jam the .50 caliber Gutter gave him to kill L.

"Man, this nigga Gutter gave us two broken ass guns. That Tech 9 keeps jamming up and this jont here won't even fire."

"Man, the hell with them guns," Bang said, as he stepped out of the cut at the bottom of 50th Street, knowing it was either now or never.

His palms were sweaty and his heart pounded in his chest. *Just last year, everything was all good between him and the Legend,* he thought to himself. L had been the only real gangster that showed any interest in boys like him. He didn't condone the way they chose to live but he understood it too well. The streets were about survival and L took enough interest in the inner-city youths to help them survive. *Damn you, G! Why'd you have to pull L into this*, Bang Bang said to himself, crossing to the other side of 50ᵗʰ Street.

Today and forever, he would be known as the nigga that killed a Legend. The boy he had once been was about to graduate into a man. From this point on, he would never again be taken lightly, or taken for granted by anyone. *Do this right and real G's will start paying you top dolla to kill muthafuckas for them,"* he could still hear Gutter saying.

He slowed down as L started to leave the basketball court. He walked into the building on the corner and Bang wanted to run after him. *I can't let this pass me by,* Bang told himself. Instead of disappearing into one of the apartments like Ball thought he would, L just stood and smoked a blunt in the hallway.

That must be his victory cigar, Ball said, almost laughing out loud. As he watched L smoking the cigar, he just stood there and waited for the right moment to strike. Once he was confident that L was all alone inside the building, he began making his move. Without hesitating, he lifted his shirt and grabbed the small .22

caliber German Ruger automatic pistol from his waist. The pistol was very light and very deadly; it was equipped to shoot twenty-one rounds.

L barely noticed Bang when he entered the building, until he looked into his eyes. Fear fell over L but he was determined not to show it. In the streets, fear alone was enough to get a man killed.

"You tried to kill me, you rotten sucka," Bang said, pointing the pistol at L's chest.

With a cigar in one hand and a basketball in the other, L was at a disadvantage and he knew it. He could tell from the way Bang was twitching that he was highed-up on something much stronger than weed. From the way his hand was shaking, L could also see that Bang was scared. A scared man would kill a person quicker than a skilled killer.

Contemplating his next move, L put the cigar back in his mouth and inhaled deeply; he kept his eyes on Bang's every move. *This is a scared little boy who doesn't wanna do this,* he thought to himself.

For both of them, it came down to this exact moment.

Without giving it a second thought, L popped the ball and lunged at Bang. The ball hit Bang in the face and L took off running out of the building. All he heard, as he ran, were the shots fired from the small caliber pistol.

L made it to the corner of the building and felt his legs give out. The next thing he saw was the great sky above. On his back and unable to move, he could only stare up and watch as the scared and angry Bang, still holding the gun, approached him.

"Die, muthafucka! Die," Bang yelled as he placed the burning hot barrel of the pistol on the tip of L's nose. The skin simmered beneath it.

"All legends must die in order for them to live forever," L said, staring into Bang's eyes.

Bang looked down at L then squeezed the trigger.
Click, click, click, click, click, the gun was empty. L laughed and blood came from his mouth.

"I'll see you again," he said, grabbing Bang's leg.

Shots rang out from behind Bang as Foxy and Maniac, two of L's cousins, ran towards him and Bang, firing their weapons. Bang pulled away from L and ran before the two boys could get him.

From a window in an abandoned building, Bang watched the crowd of people form around L. He could hear sirens in the distance and could see the ambulance lights shining off the tops of buildings.

What was the beginning of a long-standing feud was about to begin. It didn't matter whether L died or not; either way, it meant eternal war. Bang knew, the way Gutter figured it, the Statens would not retaliate for L's shooting because they no longer had honor among themselves. Their petty differences had done what no one had ever been able to do, and that was divide the once-powerful family into man factions.

From his window, he watched the ambulance drive up and onto the curb, stopping next to L's body.

Paramedics quickly lifted him onto a stretcher and put him in the back of the ambulance. Even from so far away, Bang could still see and hear people crying for L. What had seemed just like yesterday, when everything was fine, was now far behind. The hood would forever be divided. The killers had already begun to choose their sides. There was no longer any loyalty at all; every scared nigga who got their hands on a gun was trying to prove something.

The streets had seen the last of L, and Bang would eventually end up down at Lorton, where the notorious killers from the same Staten family were doing life.

Chapter 5

"Man, we might get our asses handed to us messin with these Forty Brick niggas," said Omar.

"Nigga, if you scared, change your last name and move to Georgia," Ball snapped.

"You know I ain't scared, cousin, but I ain't never been stupid either."

"Stop bitin your nails. I told you I got an inside man," Lean said.

Northwest and Southeast DC were as different as night and day. Uptown women had more class than Southside women, and Southside women were more ghetto than Uptown women. Southside broads would set you up, have you robbed and killed for no reason at all; while Uptown women were more loyal and they valued true companionship.

Uptown hustlers had more finesse than Southside hustlers. Southside niggas would just take what they wanted from whoever they wanted it from; while Uptown niggas used enough talk game to convince you that you wanted to give them what they wanted from you. Southside niggas were shiesty. They robbed their connects, killed their homies, and shot up their drug strips, over a five-dollar beef. No out-of-towner was safe on the Southside. The hustlers Uptown had more connects because they allowed the Hispanics, Jamaicans, Dominicans and any other race to hustle around their way.

Ball pulled into the gas station across from Morton Street and the four boys got out. He turned around and looked at his three men and said,

"Ya'll niggas better be ready for war."

"We more than ready," said Bar.

"Ok, look, me and Bar are gonna move slowly behind ya'll. Lean, you know some of them niggas, so you go up in there and do your thing. If anything goes wrong, we'll be right there to handle it."

"We probably should have drove up in this jont," Bar said, and they crossed the street.

"Naw, that wouldn't work. Every alley up in the Forty got center blocks up in them so we would not be able to drive all the way up in the Forty."

"You know we about to have to shoot our way up out of here if anything goes wrong," Lean said, looking at Omar.

"We good. Everybody got a gun now, so we all gonna be bustin this time around," said O.

Ball asked, "How far do we have to go up into this dirty muthafucka before we reach the spot where they gettin the most money?"

"It's like four buildings up on the right-hand side," said Lean.

"This shit still don't feel right. When has going into another niggas hood to rob all of them ever felt good," Ball asked, making all the boys laugh.

"I know the key niggas up in here, so they'll think I'm really tryna buy some coke," said Lean. "But if anything goes wrong, I won't be coming back up here again, unless it's to release some steel."

"Tell me about it," said Escobar.

"Look, when this nigga pull the work out, throw me up against the wall O, to make it look like you robbed me, as well."

"Oh, I'll do more than throw you up against the wall, I plan on pistol whipping you, too."

"Man, stop playing," Lean said, as the three other boys burst into laughter.

"Man, if ya'll niggas scared, I'll go up in that joint and lay this whole block down by myself," Ball said.

129

"Man, chill with all that scared talk, Ball. You ain't the only thorough nigga in this family. We all here cause we wanna be, so don't forget it," said Omar.

"We got this," Lean said, grabbing Omar's arm. The Forty was packed with what seemed to be more than a thousand niggas who just stood around in the darkness of their projects.

"What's up? What's up," the hustlers began to chant as they tried to get their drugs sold before the night was out.

"We good, slim, we good," said Omar, as he and Lean continued to walk ahead of Ball and Bar.

"Man, fuck ya'll Southside niggas," yelled one of the men in the crowd of men at the end of the first alley.

"What," Ball yelled, reaching for his gun.

"Chill," Bar said as he caught Ball's arm.

"I'll fry these civilized niggas like turkey bacon on a George Foreman grill," Ball said, mugging.

"We ain't here for that, man, and you know that."

"Well, I remember what the sucka look like and if shots get to flying, he'll be the first-person Ima shoot," said Ball.

As the hustlers sat on crates getting their hair corn-rowed by sexy women, Ball said, "These niggas uptown way too comfortable. Ima have to change all that."

He licked his lips as he eyed one of the women up and down. Lean and Omar finally reached the middle building where a crowd of guys stood around a craps game.

"What the fuck ya'll need and who the hell is that," a voice from the crowd yelled towards them.

"I'm here to holler at Lil Zeno or Musa," Lean said, stepping up to the man who was holding a sawed-off Mossberg shot gun at the entrance of the alley.

"Ay, Zeno, these niggas over here looking for you," said the man.

A curly headed light-skinned pretty boy with Dolce and Gabana shades covering his eyes, looked up from the crowd and towards where Lean and Omar stood.

"I'm out," he said, picking up his money from the ground.

He stepped off from the crowd and told the man at the gate to allow Lean and Omar to pass.

"What's up, slim," Zeno said, shaking Omar's hand then Lean's hand.

"Ain't shit, champ. We just tryna get some work."

"How much," Zeno asked.

132

"I need a quarter key of that soft, white virgin love. Notice I said 'virgin,' cause the last time I hollered at you that broad was damaged goods. Somebody had raped the hell out of baby girl."

"Nigga, you must got me mixed up with one of your other connects. All my broads' virgins, except for that hood rat."

"Naw, we ain't lookin for that hood rat; her hair all over her head and her nails all cracked up."

"She sposed to look like that," Zeno said, as he, Omar and Lean headed towards the building.

"Who the hell ya'll here for," the big man at the gate said, looking at Ball and Bar.

"Ay, that's my man and them," Lean said.

"Well, they can post up beside the building cause I can't have all ya'll niggas up in the building like that."

133

"That's cool" said Lean, nodding his head towards Ball and Bar.

They posted up on the side of the building outside of the cut. Lean and Omar followed Zeno into the building and down the hall. Once they reached the back of the first floor, they stopped.

"Hold up right here," Zeno said, walking to a wall where there were locked metal mailboxes.
He reached down in his pants and retrieved a set of keys, then opened the first box on the last row. He reached into the box and pulled out two bricks of heroin, and then he put them back inside of the box and locked it.

"What the hell was that," Lean asked.

Zeno opened another mail box and pulled out a zip lock bag full of what looked like powder coke. He retrieved a scale from the same box then knelt on the ground and began weighing the powder.

"Ah, Z, what the hell was that other stuff you had at first," asked Lean.

"That's that Here-on."

"What," asked Omar.

"Heroin, stupid," Lean said. "They call it here-on cause those who try it are doomed by it from here on till life ends.

"Look, this like about four grams over because of the bag weight. I ain't no shiesty Southside nigga, so I ain't gonna be tryna sell you no bullshit or charge you for bag weight," Zeno said, smiling up at both Omar and Lean.

"Yea, us Southside niggas be on crude time," Omar said, pulling the gun from his waistband and pointing it at Zeno. "Ima take all that shit you flamboyant clown!"

"Man, what the hell is you doing," Lean said, trying his best to sound concerned.

"Nigga, get cha ass up against the wall too, before I turn you and this jerk here into beef snacks for the rats."

"You will never even make it out of this building; that's a promise," Zeno said.

"Oh yea," Omar said, smacking Zeno with the pistol, knocking him to the ground in pain.

Omar reached down and began frisking Zeno with his free hand, still holding the gun on him with his other hand. Zeno, who was bleeding from his face, began squirming around on the floor, making Omar step on his back.

"Where the hell you think you going," Omar said, removing the money from Zeno's pockets.

He took the Beretta hand gun from the small of Zeno's back and placed it in his own waistband.

"Give me those keys," Omar demanded, kicking Zeno in his ribs and making him yell. "Nigga, shut up before I end your career right now," he said, trying to take the keys to the mail boxes from Zeno's right hand.

With all his might, Zeno clutched the keys trying to keep Omar from removing them.

"Oh, you wanna play that shit," said Omar.

He pulled out a switchblade and began cutting away at Zeno's fingers, covering his mouth to muffle the screams. He took the keys from Zeno's mutilated hand. Trying to save his own life, Zeno kicked up with all his might, striking Omar in the chest so he stumbled back up against the wall.

Omar dropped his gun. Like a wounded wild animal, Zeno fought to get his own gun free from Omar's waistband.

As they struggled with each other, they slipped on the puddle of blood from Zeno's wounds. Both tumbled to the ground and Zeno fell on top of Omar. Before he could get the best of him, Lean ran over and grabbed the knife that Omar had let go of to keep Zeno from taking back his gun. Lean grabbed Zeno's face and ran the sharp knife against his neck, nearly decapitating him. He let go and Zeno's lifeless body fell to the floor. In a panic, Omar got to his feet, breathing hysterically. He bent down and grabbed the key ring, looking over at Zeno's motionless body.

"Damn, O, I ain't wanna kill that nigga," Lean said. "That was my man."

"Blood is always thicker than water," Omar said, walking to the mail boxes and leaving Lean to stare down at Zeno's body, now circled by a pool of his own blood.

"Here, take this stuff," Omar said, grabbing the two bricks of heroin and handing them over his shoulder to Lean.

He went to the next box and what he saw made his heart drop. He reached inside and pulled out a bag full of money.

"Damn, Lean, this gotta be about forty, fifty g's or at least a whole step."

A step was a thousand thousands, which represented moving up in the street world.

The puddle of blood around Zeno's body began to form a river and run towards the entrance of the building.

"Come on, O, we gotta get the hell out of here."

"Man, it's more stuff up in here," O said, frowning up his face.

"The hell with the rest of that shit, O, pigs get fat but hogs get slaughtered."

Omar turned to look at his cousin then grabbed the bag of coke off the floor and stuffed it in his shirt.

"Let's go," he said. Quickly, they made it down the hall and out of the building without stopping. They ran down the steps and sprinted over towards the cut.

"Ay, ay, where ya'll going? Where the hell is Zeno," yelled the man with the Mossberg at the gate.

"He said the Feds coming; he heard it on the scanner so he told us to roll out," said Lean.

"Naw, ya'll little niggas hold up right here," the man said.

He pulled out his cell phone and began punching in some numbers. Omar looked at Lean and Lean pulled his weapon from beneath his hoodie. He fired on the man, hitting him in the temple. The man's brains flew from his head, his body jerked then dropped to the ground. Ball, Bar and Lean pulled out their weapons and opened fire on everyone standing around outside. They began running while men ducked behind the buildings and cars as they returned fire.

The sound of gunfire came from every direction as the four boys ran at full speed from the Forty. They headed towards the car they had stolen, but changed their course when they saw men running towards them from that direction. Unable to move now, without being shot, they were forced to take cover in the gas station behind the gas pumps.

"If one of them bullets hit one of these gas pumps, we dead," said Bar, who sat ducked behind Ball.

"Tell me about it," Ball said, firing on a man running straight at them.

"We gotta get the hell out of here," Omar yelled.

Ball looked around and suddenly saw their chance to move. The jump-out swerved up on the block and hopped out, making the men take off running the other way.

"Come on, ya'll," Ball said, standing up to run.

All three boys took off running hard and didn't stop. They ran for nearly twenty minutes before they stopped on Florida Avenue. After catching their breaths, the boys began to laugh.

"That was fun," said Omar.

"Tell me about it," said Bar.

"Ya'll tryna go back up there," Ball said, looking at them.

The statement would have been funny if they knew Ball was playing, but like always, Ball was dead serious.

"Let's see what we got," Ball said, looking at Lean.

"Come on, let's go in the cut real quick," Omar said.

Once inside the alley, Lean pulled out the two keys of heroin.

"Damn, that's a lot of coke," Ball said.

"That's not coke, cousin, that's Here-On."

"What the hell's Here-On," Ball asked.

"Something that'll have you strung out from here on out," Escobar said, laughing.

"So how much is it worth, Esco," Ball asked.

"Shit, in the street, that's like a mill ticket but you can sell that shit wholesale for at least like two hundred grand."

"Two hundred grand? Nigga is you serious," Lean asked.

"Hell ya, I'm serious. Heroin is big business," said Bar.

"We not gonna be able to get that much money for some stolen drugs," said Ball.

"Nigga, you crazy. That shit can be stolen, lost or found and it's still worth over a million dollars on the street," Bar said.

"Man, if it wasn't for the police, our asses would have been dead," said Ball.

Each of the boys began to laugh.

"Niggas ain't scared to run straight at them bullets or catch a body, but don't nobody wanna go to jail."

"Did you see how fast them niggas ran off when the jump outs showed up," said Omar.

Again, the boys began to laugh.

"Forget all of that. This here about fifty stacks," Omar said, pulling the bag of money from his pants. "And this here is at least a key of cocaine."

He retrieved the bag of white powder from his hoodie sleeve.

"How in the hell you know that's a whole chicken," Ball asked.

"Because that's what the nigga Zeno told me before I killed him," O said.

"Ya'll killed him," Bar asked.

"Yes, we had to, cause the nigga got the jump on O and almost crushed his skull."

"Ya right," said O. "I told that nigga get down or lay down and when he refused to lay down, I laid him down, simple and plain. On the Southside, we don't tell no nigga to give us nothing, cause we can just simply take it off their dead body if they refuse."

"Ay, ain't that the city bus that just went past," asked Escobar.

"Aw spit, let's go, ya'll," said Omar, breaking at full speed out of the alley.

"Hey, hey, stop," the boys all yelled, trying to get the driver's attention as they ran after the bus.

They chased down the bus for nearly a block and a half and it finally came to a stop, allowing them to get on. The bus was crowded, so all four boys had to grab a pole and stand. As the bus moved through the city, they all watched as the killers and hustlers on the blocks they passed did their thing.

"This city ain't just ours," said Ball, looking over at Omar.

Each boy knew that catching the bus was a bad move but they had no other way to make it back on the Southside so late at night. The only people who caught the bus was old people, wine-o's and kids, so they weren't worried about any drama kicking off on the bus. A few buses had been shot up throughout the city when a hoodlum caught one of the dudes, they were beefin with riding on it.

The entire city had beefs and those who got caught out of bounds always paid the ultimate price. After twelve consecutive stops, the bus was headed down Minnesota Avenue and the boys were glad to finally be back on the Southside.

They got off at Pennsylvania and Minnesota and crossed the bridge, a walk that only took two minutes. Once across the bridge, they went through the cut behind the same McDonalds where they had stolen the car. Home was only a few feet away now, and in no time, they would be there.

Southside, to the boys and many others, was a lovely sight. Though treacherous, dark and very poor, the ghetto was a work of art that had been crafted by poverty, struggle, timeless cold nights, bloodshed, and bullets. This art was a masterpiece. There was nothing else in the world like the project slums, and not even by intention, could a man make such a place exist.

Within every corner, instilled in every brick that made up every building, was a sign of history telling of struggle that went back for decades and carrying with it the voices of those whose lives had been lost to it forever.

Not something easy to deal with was the life of the poor and those in the world of the less fortune. Their struggle meant triumph and their stories were those that made Hollywood blockbusters. Nobody wanted to live out the life of the poor but their lives held together the backbone of that which was America.

After passing the McDonalds, the boys came to 1430 Project housing, a cluster of run-down buildings that sat at the end of the Potomac Garden neighborhood.

Fourteen-thirty was divided from the rest of the Gardens by a street that ran no longer than a block. Each side of 1430 was separated by an alley that ran straight through the middle of it. Like all the Gardens buildings, 1430 was surrounded by a huge, black steel fence that trapped its residents in, and kept the rest of the world outside its borders. In other words, to simply explain 1430 was to say that it was a deathtrap. No way in and no way out.

As the boys walked past, they watched its villains lying across cars and hanging off the rail that was up top of the 8th Street Bridge.

Knowing the legacy of the Staten men that set the stage way before L, Omar, Lean or Ball existed, the gangsters around 1430 respected Ball and his cousins. As they passed through, the men nodded their heads at them in acknowledgement. Although it was part of the Gardens, 1430 was its own hood and nobody would say otherwise. No matter how close together the streets were, those on them stood divided; and all it took was for the wind to blow the wrong way to kick off a full-scale war in minutes.

Ball and them entered the black steel gate that surrounded Building 1025, on 13th and K Street and headed up the stairs to the house. Soon as Ball opened the door, Ms. Linda, who was sitting at the table with Butterfly and two of her brothers, jumped to her feet saying,

"You little muthafuckas, where the fuck ya'll been?"

She was tipsy drunk off the Hennessey she was drinking and high on powder coke.

"Leave them boys alone," Butterfly said.

"You shut up, Butter, before I cut into your ass, too," Ms. Linda said, almost falling as she rose from her chair.

"Aw, Linda, it's our play. You either gonna play cards or Ima take my money and leave," said Buck.

"Ya'll little muthafuckas been into some shit," Ms. Linda slurred, pointing her fingers at them. "Ya, ya'll been in some shit but ain't none of ya'll been in no shit until you get into some shit with me.

She fell backwards into her chair.

"She drunk as hell," Ball said, walking off.

"Ya, I'm drunk enough to kick your fat ass and all you punk muthafuckas, too," she said, spitting on Buck.

"Damn, Linda, you tryna give me a shower?"

Lean, Bar and Omar all shook their heads then walked off, disappearing down the hallway and into the bedroom. The kids were spread out all over the bed, so they found a spot on the floor wherever there was room to lie down.

Lean and Omar pulled out all the stuff they had taken from Zeno and laid it on the floor in front of them.

"Let's count this money," said Lean, pouring all the currency onto the floor.

Each boy grabbed a handful of money and began counting it.

"Ay, Ball, call Butta in here," said Escobar.

"Nigga, Butta don't want your young ugly butt. How many times do I gotta tell you that," Ball told him.

"Nigga, call her in here so I can ask her to help us get rid of the coke and heroin," O said.

Ball opened the door and crawled down the hall, whispering and looking back at the boys,

"Ay, ya'll put that ink up."

But they ignored him and continued counting the money.

"Psssp, pssp," Ball called out, trying to get Butter's attention.

When she didn't hear him, he began waving his hand and finally caught her eye. She got up from the table, saying, "I gotta use the bathroom. Ya'll play the next hand without me."

She walked down the hall to where Ball was. He grabbed her hand and led her into the room.

"Damn, where the hell ya'll get all of this money," she asked, bending over to grab some of it. She grabbed a handful of money from the stack of hundreds near Bar; he watched her butt, geekin off how sexy her body was. She turned and smiled at him while putting the money into her Chanel handbag.

"Look at this sucka for love ass nigga," said Lean. "He about to let her rob us for what we robbed somebody for.

"Who ya'll robbed," she asked, looking at her brother, Derrick.

"Some niggas from Uptown. Look, you can help us sell this," he said, grabbing the two keys of heroin and the key of coke from the floor and handing it to her.

"Boy, is this what I think it is," she asked, looking at the three kilos in her hands.

"Ya, that's that Here-On," said Lean, laughing.

"Do ya'll have any idea what this stuff is worth?"

"Ya, we got an idea, Butta; we don't live on a dope strip for nothing," Ball said, faking like he knew something about selling heroin.

"I can sell this tomorrow morning," Butta said. "My friend up the Gardens be sellin a lot of blow. This stuff look like coffee so it might be uncut. If that's the case, I can sell each brick for over a hundred thousand dollars," she said, still looking at the drugs.

"Man, look, just sell that shit for two hundred grand. We'll take a step and a half, which is…"

"Shut up, boy. I know what a step is," she said, cutting Omar off.

"So what do ya'll want me to do with the rest of the money," she asked, batting her eyes at Escobar.

Before anybody else could say anything, Esco looked at her thighs, then said,

"You can keep the rest."

"Hell naw," said Omar. "You can keep like a half a step but make sure everybody in the family, especially your mother, gets some of the money."

"Ya make sure Ma gets some money and then maybe her grumpy butt will chill out for a while," said Ball.

"Ok, I'll do that but what about this coke," she said, looking down at it.

"Here, let me see that," Ball said, taking the bag from her hand.

He reached inside it and broke a large chunk off the right corner. Then he grabbed a pillowcase from a pillow that was under Brad's head and put the rest of the cocaine inside it. He handed the pillowcase to her and she dropped the two kilos of heroin into it.

"I'll take care of everything and have ya'll money by tomorrow night," she said. Then she looked at the chunk of coke Ball was holding and asked, "What the hell you about to do with that coke?"

"Well, Ima take some of it with me so we can rent a car tomorrow from one of the shoestrings (another name for pipe heads) and Ima put the rest in Ma's room, under her wig, so she can have a nice, early Christmas."

"Boy, you stupid," she said, smiling as all the boys began to laugh.

The boys stayed up all night counting the money. Around 6am, Omar, who was half-asleep, looked at the other three boys and asked,

"How much you got?"

"I got thirty stacks over here between me and

Bar," said Ball.

"Well, I got like twelve g's and O got about seventy-five hundred."

"Shit, we good," Ball said, as he got to his feet and stretched his arms. "We about to go to the Pentagon City Mall and blow all this shit!"

"Man, I'm about to get some sleep first," Omar said, pulling the hoodie over his face.

"Ya'll don't sleep too long, because you know my mother gonna be hounding us in about an hour to get out of here and go to school."

Chapter 6

Tebetha burst through the door, yelling, "Ma said get up!"

She frowned her face up, then said, "Pee-yew, ya'll stink in here!"

Lean grabbed one of the kids' shoes off the floor and threw it at her, striking her in the leg.

"Aw boy, you dummy."

"Get up, ya'll. Brad, ya'll need to get up," she said, kicking Omar as she walked out of the room. She slammed the door behind her.

"Ay, Brad, get up," Omar said.

Brad stretched his arms and jumped out of bed, and then he quickly began getting dressed.

"Ay, Brad, you wanna skip school today," Ball asked, looking from under his North Face coat he had used as a blanket.

"No," Brad said, shaking his head and making Escobar laugh. "I don't wanna be in trouble."

Brad looked over at his brother. Lean stood up and began stretching his arms, then said,

"That's right little cousin, don't let nobody get you in no trouble, cause we going to jail," Lean said, laughing.

"Naw, nigga, you going to jail," said Ball, as he got to his feet.

"Ay ya'll, Dashawn, Delnautice and Little Bruce, ya'll need to get up; this ain't' no sleeping beauty contest," Omar said.

"You, too," Ball said, kicking Escobar.

"I'm up," Ball said, getting to his feet. "Look what I got," he said as he pulled a handful of money from his pocket."

All four of the little boys who were peeking from under the covers jumped to their feet and ran over to him.

"That's a shame. You even got kids who know the power of a dollar," said Lean, looking at his little brothers and cousins.

They each took turns taking the money from Ball's hand. Once he had finished passing out the money, Ball turned to Brad and handed him three hundred dollars in fives.

"Here, don't let them spend they money on nothing today. You make sure ya'll go eat good and have fun, but for now ya'll need to get dressed and get going to school," he said. "Come on ya'll, we gotta roll."

He walked out the door with Lean and them on his heels. Soon as the four boys got out of the apartment into the hallway, Ball pulled out a blunt and fired it up.

"Damn, you keep some weed, don't you," Omar said.

"It ain't our fault you don't smoke," Ball said, passing the blunt to Bar.

"Ay, ain't that the nigga Moe standing there? And wasn't that Thee who just held the door to the back of his car open?"

"What," Ball mugged and asked.

He, Lean and Omar looked through the holes in the wall of the building that gave them a clear view of the front of the building. Without saying another word, all three boys took off down the steps with Esco following them.

Ball grabbed the handle of the cream 745 Benz and yanked the door open so hard it smacked the trashcan and left a dent in it.

"Get cha little hot ass out of this nigga's car," Ball said, grabbing Tetheba by her arm and yanking her out of the car.

"Stop, Derrick, you're hurting me," she said, making him let go of her.

"You bitch ass nigga, stay the fuck away from my sister," he yelled, stepping up in Moe's face.

Gutter, who was in the driver's seat, jumped out of the car with his gun in his hand.

"One wrong move and off goes your head," Lean said.

He pointed his gun at Gutter before he could pull his at Ball. Omar and Escobar raised their guns as well, which made Ball smile.

"You can't tell me who to be around or what to do," Tebetha said.

She raised her voice as she walked up behind Ball. With all his might, he hit her with the closed back of his hand, sending her flying to the ground. She burst into tears.

Ball spit on the hood of Moe's car then said, "Ya'll niggas keep faking and Ima make ya'll famous."

"Legends are always worth more dead than they are alive," said Omar.

Lean and Escobar laughed at that.

"Now slide out before ya'll niggas get slid," Ball said, lifting his shirt so Gutter and Moe could see the butts of the two guns he had on his hips.

"Trust me, if I gotta pull mines out, Ima make bloody marys out of you chumps."

With his jaw clenched and his pride hurt, Moe looked at Gutter and said to get in the car. He climbed into the passenger seat himself. Gutter looked over the four little niggas and laughed, then went on the other side of the car and got in. In no time, the creamy eggshell white Mercedes disappeared off K Street.

Bar turned and looked down at Tebetha who was still on the ground and crying. Her hair had grass in it and her top lip was bleeding. Her silver and black Mossimo blouse was torn and her beaver-skin Velladorchia shoes were scratched.

"Damn, Ball, you fucked her up," Omar said.

He lifted Tebetha to her feet. Brad and the other boys who had come out of nowhere just stared at Tebetha. She looked scared and frazzled. Brad wondered why his brother had hit his sister, instead of Moe or Gutter. He had always thought that Moe and Gutter were untouchable, but from that day on, he looked at them both in a different light.

"Your little sneaky hot-ass better be glad I got something to do, or I'd put my foot in your ass all day," Ball said, getting up into Tebetha's face. "If this is what you sellin yourself short for, then here you go."

He dropped a stack of hundred-dollar bills at her feet.

"Come on, ya'll, let's go before I kill this little," he said, walking off.

As he slid through the hole in the back gate, he turned to Brad and said, "Ya'll go to school."

All four of the boys made it through the hole in the gate then took the alleyway down to 1000 Building.

"What's up, Chapelle," Lean asked, shaking his hand.

"Ain't shit, my nigga, just livin this hood life to the fullest, laid back and in my style."

"What's up with ya'll," asked Charles, another one of their homies who was standing by an OG from around 1000, known as Cutt.

"We about to hit Pentagon City Mall so we need a ride," Ball said. "Ain't none of you seen Pipe head Roy hot faggot ass?"

"Ya, he around the corner trying to sell his kids' shoes," said Cutt.

"Damn, Ima go catch that nigga before he roll out," Ball said.

He walked off from the crowd of boys who stood all over the black gate in front of 1000 Building. They were so thick that one looking on from down the street wouldn't have been able to tell that a gate was even there. More of their homies stood on the basketball court out back, in the parking lot, and in the parking lot on the other side of the front of the building.

Close to 500 villains were hanging all over 1000, and 90 percent of them was skipping school. Nobody wanted to be caught dead in school. School was a deathtrap. School had a set schedule for everyone that attended so if you were beefin, your enemies knew exactly when they could catch you slippin and exactly where you would be so they could.

"Ay, ya'll niggas know it only take fifteen minutes to get out Virginia to the Pentagon Mall, but it takes fifteen years to get back," said Cutt.

"Ya, ya'll niggas crazy to be going out Virginia, especially while ya'll skippin school. The Feds be on over time out there, so ya'll going straight to jail."

Lean, Bar and Omar looked at each other, then ran off after Ball. When they reached the cut where Ball and Pipe head Roy stood, they were nearly out of breath.

"Look, nigga, don't ever question me, Roy, or I'll shoot you in your face," Ball said, hopping in the driver's seat of Roy's car. "I'm just sayin, 'Baby Boy.'"

Roy came back, "Your homies around here sellin walnuts and peppermints they done chewed the red off of. Ya'll be fucking a nigga pipe up. I had to hire a mechanic to fix my stuff last time so I'm just tryna be sure this is real, that's all."

All the while he talked; he was sticking the crumbs Ball gave him into his mouth. Then he began smacking his lips.

"Yea, yea, nephew, this here got my whole mouth numb as hell. You working with a monster unless this some of that BC headache powder mixed with Anbesol that your man Chapelle and Monster be making," he said.

"Man Roy, stop playing with me. That's pure powder coke right there. You don't even have to coke the back off that. Ya'll come on," Ball said, putting the car in drive.

All the boys jumped in the car.

"Ay, nephew, I gotta pick my wife up in an hour. Ya'll gonna be back by then, right," Roy asked as he licked the coke off his lips.

"Nigga, you ain't even got no wife. We'll be back when we get back," Ball said, speeding out of the alley and onto K Street.

"Ay, Ball, we ain't going out to the Pentagon City Mall, so let's go up to Georgetown," Lean said.

Frowning up his face, Ball asked, "Why the hell not?"

"Because if we go to Virginia on vacation, we gonna leave on probation," Bar said. "You know how the police be around that Pentagon and anywhere else out Virginia. Plus, we skippin school, so we gonna stick out like a nigga in a KKK rally."

Making a right past the Navy yard, Ball said, "Ya, ya'll right.

"Let's just go chill up Georgetown," suggested Bar.

Ball made another right and said,

"We can do that. I ain't about to do nothing until I go past Gainesville to holler at JT."

"Ya, Jamaican Toney does have that OG Kush," said Lean.

"Here, Lean, put this in," Omar said, handing

him a CD.

"Damn, I'm surprised this ragged piece of junk still even got a CD player. I'm surprised Roy didn't sell it like he would sell his ass for a hit of crack," Ball said.

"He probably didn't know what it was," said Omar, as he put in the CD.

A nice street beat began blaring from the speakers, making Ball ask, "Who dat?"

"That's Little Damo, who used to stay right next to your mother," Lean told him.

Bar said, "Yeah, he been messin with the Dirty Cide Records, nigga."

The boys began nodding their heads as Damo's voice came through the speakers.

Let me introduce you niggas to the city I come from
We got more beef than a cow.

You can come if you want some

But you might get cha ass robbed if we don't
know *where you come from.*

Throw your squad up.

Nigga, throw your mob up.

Squaaaaaaad UP!

As Damo continued to rap, the boys continued to nod their heads.

"Lean, cut the music down. Ball, pull into the Big K right quick so I can get some blunts."

"For what? You ain't got no weed to smoke," Bar said.

"Nigga, you don't know what the hell I got," Lean said, pulling out a zip lock full of weed. "I took this out of Zeno's pocket."

He hopped from the car as Ball came to a stop on Naylor Road.

170

"Get me a beer," Omar yelled, trying to get Lean's attention.

"Man, don't worry about that," Ball said, waving Lean off.

"Why the hell you do that," asked Omar.

"We about to go to Fifty-One liquor store right after this," said Ball.

He turned his head to look at a brown-skinned female who was heading across MLK.

Jumping from the car, Ball called out, "Ay, shorty, hold up."

The female stopped and waited for him on the corner and when he reached her, he smiled.

She asked, "Why you smiling so hard, boy?"

She stuck her butt out to give him a better look at how sexy she really was.

"You got everybody on the block smiling," Ball said, looking over at the men standing along the street and staring at the girl in front of him. Her name was Sabrina.

She blushed then asked, "What's your name?"

"They call me Madball," he said, pulling out his cell phone. "And you can call me or I can call you. It's your call," he said as he handed her his phone.

Ball looked down at her thighs and asked, "So, Sabrina, you got a boyfriend?"

"See, you got me, now you tryna lose me," she said, looking away from him.

"Damn! What'd I say," he asked, looking into her fiery red eyes.

"You shouldn't be worried about another man. If I gave you my number it's because I'm feelin you, so don't remind me of the nigga I might be trying to cheat on."

172

"Okay baby, my bad," he said, smiling. "You need a ride to wherever it is you're going?"

He hoped she'd say yea but she said, "Naw I'm good. I don't know you well enough to be trustin you to know my whereabouts yet."

"That's cool, shorty. I ain't pressed for you to be in my presence."

"Ya, right," she said, turning so he could see everything that she was working with. She batted her eyes at him and said, "I gotta go.

"Ok, I'll just hit you up later," Ball said.

"You do that," she said and crossed the street.

"Damn, who the hell was that," Lean asked as he hopped back into the car with Ball following right behind him.

"Some freak," said Ball as he pulled out of the parking lot and headed up Naylor Road.

"That's your new girl, Ball," Escobar asked.

"How the hell she gonna be my girl when we just met?"

"I guess I was just tryna find out if you had intentions of making her your girl."

"Naw, nigga, that ain't his girl," Lean said.

"That's all of our girl, haw Ball," Omar said, smiling. "Ya, we all gonna get that sweet pussy, haw, Ball?"

"It ain't no fun if my cousins can't have none," Ball said, looking at Bar through the rearview mirror.

"Man, ya'll niggas some cold-blooded hypocrites," Bar said.

He reached over the seat and into Lean's lap where he grabbed a backwood.

Ball asked, "How the hell you figure we some hypocrites?"

"Ya'll niggas was just about to kill two niggas over Theba but now ya'll right here, talking about doing the same stuff to somebody else's sister."

Ball said, "It's different."

"Hell, ya, that's way different," Omar said.

"How is it different," Bar asked.

"See, you don't have no sister so you don't understand," said Ball. "Look at all the girls you be messin with, Esco. If you seen a nigga tryna do your pretty ass mother the way you be doing them girls, would it bother you?"

"Hell, yea. I would kill a nigga about my mother but she ain't out in the streets making herself fair game."

Ball said, "From what you know, she ain't. As fine as your mother is, not once have you seen her with a man. Every fine woman we see we be hollerin at, so what the hell you think dudes do when they see your mama, look the other way and say she a holy roller so don't try to get her coochie?"

All the boys started laughing but not Escobar.

"Man, just drop it before you get cha feelings hurt," said Omar, "cause real talk, if I got the chance to holler at cha mother, she gonna be my girl and you gonna be my son."

Bar punched Omar in his arm, which made him say,

"Aw, nigga, now I gotta get my hit back on your moms."

Ball turned off Naylor and onto Gainesville Street, continuing down until he came to the middle of the block.

"Damn, it's a thousand niggas and a thousand police out here," said Omar.

"Forget them niggas and forget them police," Ball said as he hopped out of the car. In a low voice he said, "Damn! Look at all these fucking housing authority police."

They were passing a crowd of gangsters that were dressed in all black and taking up the entire sidewalk.

"Slim, I got that loud pack right here," said a dark-skinned man wearing a ski mask over his face.

He approached Ball with his palm open. In it, were several yellow bags of weed.

"I'm good man," Ball said, continuing toward the last building on the block that was in a dead end.

"Young'un, over here," several of the men said, trying to get him to purchase their weed.

"I'm good, champ. I'm about to go holla at Toney," Ball said, pulling his black hoodie over his head.

Once he reached the steps of the last abandoned-looking building, he began to climb the steps, watching the corner out of the corners of his eyes, both ways. He reached for the door handle but it wasn't there, so he stuck his fingers in the hole where it used to be and pulled on the heavy metal door. It looked as if it had been fired on by an A-Kick and several other weapons. It squeaked loudly as he pulled it open.

Ball stepped into the dark hallway and moved toward the second apartment door. He listened for any sign of danger. When he reached the second door to his left, he banged on it three times, *bam-bam-bam,* and waited. After a minute or so, the door knob came off, revealing a hole where it had been.

A very deep voice told him, "Stick yah money through de hole, dreds."

Ball pulled a knot of money from his pocket.

"This here is money for two pounds and I ain't sticking it through no goddamned hole! I'm here to see

Jamaican Toney anyways, so tell the Don, Lil Derrick, Butterfly's lil brother out here to see him."

The doorknob was put back in place; after a few minutes the door opened and two very dark-skinned men stepped out. One had long dreds and was holding an A-Kick in his right hand. The other man was dressed in all blue with no dreds.

"So wha yah want," asked the shorter man of the two, with the dreds.

"I need a pound of OG Kush, Toney. My sister Butterfly told me to come holla at you." Toney's once-twisted, mugging face changed into a smile upon hearing Butterfly's name. Damned near every gangster in the city wanted Ball's sisters and he knew that. On the strength of that, he had them eating out of the palm of his hand.

"She be close round?"

He didn't really understand what was said.

Ball asked, "What?"

"Shorty girl outside or something, boy? Haw?"

"Naw man, she gonna come holla at you though; I promise you that, Dred. Now do me this favor so I can roll out, because the fucking police is deep as shit outside."

The two men began to laugh.

"Them not dee police, Dred, dem housing authority."

"Same shit; both of them can lock my ass up. So let's get down to business so I can roll."

"Get him what he want," Toney said, waving off his bodyguard.

Ball then handed him the money. Toney quickly counted it, and then put it into his pocket.

"Me don't' take well to threats, dred. Me kill wit

the best of dem in this city, all the way to Kingston."

"That's not a threat, Dred, I'm just saying a favor for a favor. You do this for me and I'll promise you that my brothers and cousins won't be trying to get at you for hollerin at Butta."

"Respect then, rude boy. I understand you now," JT said, cracking a smile. A favor for a favor, right?" Looking into Ball's eyes, he said, "Put you money away. This one's on me but make sure Sexy Fly girl contact me later today. Tell her Ima take she to eat at my restaurant, then take she shopping."

Just then, another door opened and a man carrying a book bag handed it to Ball. Then he disappeared just as quickly as he had appeared.

"How the hell he knew we was right here? And how he knew to bring me the weed," Ball asked.

JT opened his coat then lifted his shirt, revealing a small wire.

"Boy, my dred listen to me every time I speak and they got eyes on me every time I move. I'm the most powerful shoota in the States and that means I'm too important to be killed or kidnapped without anybody knowing about it," he said, smiling.

"You one bad muthafucka, Toney," Ball said.

"Va-iree now," Toney said, turning to walk off.

Ball exited the apartment building and walked back to the car. He hopped inside quickly.

"I told you that nigga wasn't gonna serve you shit," Lean said.

"Here," Ball said, tossing the book bag to Lean.

Opening it, Lean said, "Goddam, you a bad muthafucka."

Ball put the car in reverse and backed off Gainesville then swung onto Naylor. He drove up towards the MLK Memorial Library and continued until he got to Hope

Village Halfway House. He could hear shots in the distance; that caused all the boys to turn and look behind them.

Ball said, "That's coming from down there off Gainesville."

"Damn, we made it up out of there just in time," Lean said.

"Those weed strips are a deathtrap. Everybody in the city be coming there to buy weed, so a nigga is bound to run into somebody they beefin with," said Bar.

They drove across Alabama Avenue and continued down the hill. When they reached Fifty-One liquor store parking lot, Omar and Lean hopped out.

"Ay, get some Alize and Cristal," said Bar.
Ball turned around in his seat to look at him.

"Man, ain't nobody tryna be drinkin that female liquor. And stop trying to roll our blunts, cause evidently, from the look of the stuff, you couldn't roll a bike down the street. I know you ain't joning, you crooked eye nigga turtle."

"You look like the pink version of Donkey Kong on crack," Bar said, laughing.

Just then, a dark blue Land Rover pulled up beside them.

Ball said, "Damn, you see all of them bad ass females inside that jont?"

"Ya I see them," said Bar.

"Holla at em then, nigga, you know you a ladies man."

"O, I done went from Donkey Kong to Superfly in record time," Bar said, stepping out of the car.

"Ladies, what's up?"

He leaned his head inside the driver's window. "Damn, you sexy as hell," the driver said, smiling at him and licking her lips.

Bar asked, "Can I lick those lips like that?"

The pretty-faced girl in the passenger seat said, "You can lick all these lips like that."
All her girlfriends busted out laughing.

"Slow down, sexy, before you make me climb in this truck and suck the honey off of your skin," Ball said, smiling. "Look, my men gettin some alcohol and we tryna linkup with ya'll now or after we come from Georgetown, gettin fresh and make this a party you won't soon forget."

The woman in the back behind the driver said, "Ow girl, his little sexy ass know how to use his tongue in more than one way."

The pretty passenger was blushing and said, "Ya, we gonna see how good he knows how to use it."

"Ya'll crazy, but I love crazy women. So ya'll chillin with us later or what?"

"Hell yea, we can chill,' said the driver. "Is that

your friends right there coming out of the liquor store?"

"Ya that's my men," Bar said.

All the women looked out the windows at Lean and Omar.

"Aw girl, they cute too and they got two bags full of liquor. We definitely rollin with ya'll, sexy boy," the passenger said.

"What's up with your man who's driving? He looks evil as hell, like he ain't had pussy since pussy had him," said the driver. "Ya he looks scary, girl. He might have people shooting at us."

"Naw, it's like you said. He ain't had no pussy since pussy had him," Bar said, smiling.

"Okay then. We like gangsters but he look like a stone-cold killer."

"He a stone-cold teddy bear; you'll see," said Bar.

186

"Look, here goes my business card. You can reach me on that," said the driver, holding out her card.

"Take my number too," said the passenger, smiling.

"What is it?"

"202-889-0074, and that's Roeshell."

Bar keyed her number into his phone then said, "Ima be hittin ya'll as soon as I get from up Georgetown."

"Ya, ya'll can come chill at my house out in Bowie, Maryland," said the driver, whose name was Natasha.

"Bet that's what's up. We'll holla at ya'll later," Bar said.

He walked back to the car where the boys waited. Roeshell got out of the Rover and went into the liquor store. Bar watched her the whole way, amazed with how phat her butt was.

"Damn, young'un, you just booked a super model. That broad top flight. Man, did you see her butt," Lean asked.

"I appreciate you noticing my skills," Bar said, smiling, getting back into the car.

"Man, I hope you told her buddies that you had friends who was tryna be friends," said Omar, who was still gawking out the window at the other women who stayed in the Land Rover. "Guess what, though," Omar said, smiling.

"What," Lean asked.

"Shorty that got out of the car ain't even the best looking one. Look at baby in the back," Omar said, grabbing Ball's shoulder.

Ball looked across the seat at Escobar. "So, they rollin with us or what?"

"Yes, they rollin if they can drink that thug passion with us," he said.

"Nigga, you know I had to get that. You know females on that passion hard. The hell with what Ball talkin about," said Lean. "Man, the hell with wining and dinin these women. I just go up to the Gardens and get em an O cup.

That made the boys laugh. Omar ordered, "Ah, Ball, pull up over there beside JR's van so I can see if he got Kingdawud's CD."

Ball put the car in drive and pulled over to the huge brown van parked in the middle of the lot, next to a large stand. Omar jumped out of the car and walked up to a huge man standing with his back to the parking lot.

"Yo, JR! Do you got any of Kingdawud's CDs?"

JR turned around and said, "What's up young'un?"

"Ain't shit," said O. "Look, I'm tryna get Kingdawud's CDs if you got em."

"Naw, slim, I sold out of them jonts as soon as I hit the block."

"Damn, that's bad."

"I got them other Dirty Cide artists, though, up in here."

"Who you got?"

"I got LIFE, or L.I.F.E," as he's known to the streets. I got Master Farad, Sallah, Shams, Whiteboy, and a few other beats."

"Let me get all of them jonts."

Omar handed JR a $100 bill. JR took the CDs from his van and placed them in a black plastic bag. Then he grabbed a bottle each of Jannatul Firdaus, and Jannatul Mawa from his table and put them in the bag.

"That's my new Muslim fragrances I'm given you, free of charge," he said, handing the bag to O.

"Thanks, JR," Omar said as he turned to walk away.

"You got it, young'un. Ya'll try to stay out of trouble."

"Bet," said O, hopping back into the car.

"We got some tunes and some oil," said Omar. He took Damo's CD out and pushed Sallah's CD in the player. The beat began cranking through the speakers and Omar cut the volume up, as Ball pulled out of the parking lot and drove down Suitland Parkway.

Sallah's voice ran out over the beat and the boys nodded their heads as they drank liquor and smoked blunt after blunt.

"All my niggas say,
'Fuck em, fu-fu-fu-fu fuck em, fu-fu-fu-fu fuck em, ya all my niggas say.

191

I be pissed off as I gets raw from some shit you
done started
Extended clip full of hard shit,
Ya, I'm rollin, regardless how you all faced
down
From the waist down, all shit the fuck up,
Ears in they eyes now, like circus clowns
Bitch, shut the fuck.

Sallah rapped and the boys rolled blunts on their way to Georgetown. They was high as hell, drunk, strapped and black without a worry in the world, looking to do damage to anyone that got in their way as they rode through the Nation's Capital, which was the Murder Capital of America.

Chapter 7

"Damn, look at all them fine ass snow bunnies," Lean said as the car turned left onto Wisconsin Avenue.

"When you start seeing them pretty pink toes inside of the Chocolate City, you know you in Georgetown," said Bar, gawking out the window at the lovely looking European women wearing skinny clothes and parading up and down the street.

"Damn, she bad as hell," Omar said, trying to get out of the car.

"Let me out," Ball said, opening his door.

"Naw, nigga, we about to park right up there in the parking lot next to the Georgetown Café, so chill."

"Alright, now we can hop out," he said.

Before he could even finish his sentence, the boys were already out of the car.

"This where you gonna find out if your mac game is some garbage or not," said Lean. "You can tell a hoodrat anything, but these Georgetown graduates and Howard University females ain't just going for anything. Some rich broads and lawyers down here too."

"Ya, you right," Ball said. "These classy broads be on some other shit."

The streets were jam-packed with people and all the shops were full but that didn't stop the boys from navigating through the thick crowd on Wisconsin.

"What's up? Ya'll tryna go hit the Solbiato shop up," asked Omar.

"Ya, let's go hit it up," said Lean, making his way through the crowd of people.

"Man, I ain't about to step foot in that high ass shop. Sob be tryna rob a nigga with no gun or no nuts," Ball said. "A headband damned near cost three hundred and some change."

"And," said Lean.

"And I ain't about to let a nigga rob me with or without a gun. That's the only shop that you can't just walk inside of; they gotta buzz you in like you a freakin VIP or something," said Bar.

"Well, me and O about to go hit the Sob up real hard, then we gonna hit the other stores; ya'll rollin or what," Lean said, looking Ball and Bar in their faces.

"Naw, cousin ya'll go ahead."

"Ima go hit the Coogi store up, then Ima go to Gucci."

"Me too," said Bar.

"We'll catch ya'll later then," Omar and Lean said, beginning to move through the crowd.

"Come on, slim," Ball said, trying to make it across the street.

Bar began trying to talk to every woman he saw and was rejected by them all.

"We told you. These some different type of girls around here. They used to these NBA niggas and lawyers our color."

"Ima get one of em, watch," Bar said, nearly getting hit by a car.

Ball shook his head and said, "Don't let the same thing that brung you into this world take you out of it, you horny fool."

They made it across the street to the other side then began pushing their way through the huge crowd of people moving up and down the sidewalk.

"Damn, her ass phat," Esco said, turning to look, as a pretty oval-faced woman with long legs and silky hair crossed the street. "All these bitches trick," he said, walking behind Ball as he walked toward the Coogi shop.

"Hey, baby," Esco said, winking at another woman that smiled as she walked past them.

They entered the Coogi shop and Esco went straight to the wall in the back that held all the shoes.

"I like all this shit," Ball said, looking at a mannequin wearing a gray velour Coogi zip up jump suit.

"Ay, man, you gonna help us or what," asked Ball, mugging on a man of Arabic descent who was crossing the floor toward them.

"How much cash you tryna spend," the man said, looking down at Ball's sneakers.

"First off, it don't matter how much cash Ima spend, cause you definitely about to give me a deal cause I'm about to spend at least twenty stacks up in this muthafucka," Ball said. "I want two of those velour suits in every color for me and my man over there," he said, nodding his head towards Bar. "Give him whatever he wants and give us some champagne."

Ball pulled a knot of money from his right pocket then another from his left pocket.

"Awe, we don't do champagne," said the man.

"Well, hell, ya'll better do beer or something for all this money we spending."

The man smiled. As he walked off he said, "I'll be right back."

Bar walked to Ball with ten pairs of pants, ten shirts and five pairs of shoes.

"That's all you gettin," Ball asked him.

"Ya, this a lot of stuff," he replied,

"Alright, go ahead and take it over to the counter so the sister can bag it up," Ball said, looking back at the Gucci jacket the mannequin wore.

The Arab man came back with two huge bags and handed them to Ball.

"And here you go, too," he said, passing Ball a bottle of Dom Perignon.

"See, buddy, I told you I'd take care of you," Ball said, smiling. "So how much is this stuff gonna cost me?"

The man said a little over ten thousand dollars.

"And that stuff he got up, too, and we'll be sittin over here, drinking this champagne with the mannequins," Ball said, handing the man both knots of money.

"That's exactly twenty thousand, so go ahead and throw us some watches in the bag and a few pair of socks, okay man?"

"My name is Sammy," the man said, taking the old rubber band from around the money and holding up one of the hundred-dollar bills to see if it was real.

"My money real, Sammy," Ball said, popping the top on the Dom P as Bar came back with a bag in each hand.

"Your name ain't no damned Sammy either," Ball said, watching the man move toward the counter.

"Where the hell you get Dom P from," Bar asked.

He and Ball took seats on one of the steps leading up to the area where the mannequins from the front windows stood. Like they were on the block around 1000, they passed the bottle of Dom P back and forth, taking gulps until the bottle was empty.

"That stuff was real good," said Bar.

"Ya, for how much they be chargin for it, it better be good." Sammy walked back to them, holding a small bag and two black velvet cases.

"These watches cost over ten thousand dollars apiece, my friend, but Ima give them to you for five and we'll be even," he said, handing the boxes to Ball.

He took one box and handed the other to Bar. They both opened their box and stared, marveling at the masterpieces in their hands.

"Now this is what I call a watch," Ball said, putting the Gucci watch on his right wrist, as Bar did the same.

"We straight now," Sammy asked, looking down at Ball as he handed him the other small black bag.

"Naw, what's your real name," asked Ball.

"It's Samir," the man said.

Ball smiled then said, "Why you didn't just say that?"

"Well, it's because a lot of people don't know I'm Arab and I prefer to keep it that way."

"Do a lot of people know you're Muslim," asked Ball.

"No," Samir said, shaking his head. "After 9/11, a lot of people began trying to kill my people, so we just lay low and act as if we are American or Spanish."

"That's some real coward shit," said Ball. "My father is Muslim and he in jail. He told me that man is not to fear no other man, but instead is to fear Allah, because whatever God wants to happen to you will happen, no matter what."

"That's true," said Samir. "Your father is a good man to teach you the truth but until my faith is on the level that his is on, I will continue to hide my Islam."

"Damn, that's crazy," said Ball, standing to his feet.

"Damn, look at baby right there," Bar said, staring at a young Muslim sister with green eyes who had just come out of the back of the store. She had on a pair of tight jeans that revealed the curves of her body.

"Man, she probably got some of the best pussy in the world," said Bar.

"Man, shut up, you idiot," Ball said, grabbing hold of his arm.

"What," asked Bar, as he and Ball headed towards the exit of the store.

Once outside, Ball began fiercely cussing out Bar.

"Damn, my nigga, it ain't even that serious," Bar said.

"Ay, slim, all women are not the same," Ball said, mugging on Bar as he grabbed his arm, forcing him to face him. "You don't approach every woman the same way you be trying to handle rats out the sewer. A woman is like a rose, if you pull her wrong, you're gonna get stuck by her thorns."

"Damn, you trippin, cause I said what I said, about the Muslim chick back in the store. How the hell you gonna demand for me to respect a woman that doesn't even respect herself or what she believes in?"

"I was just simply saying what a lot of men who

see her dressed like that be already thinking…"

"That's your problem right there. You think you can just say anything to anybody and it ain't happenin. A nigga will kill you over a woman and that's a fact."

"Well, it's been working for me so far, so Ima continue to do it," said Bar.

"You think it's been working. Broad don't even like that stupid stuff you be saying to them; they just like how curly your hair is and that you red, so they be overlooking that stupid childish stuff that you be saying to them."

"Man, whatever, nigga! If it wasn't for me, you would be gettin no pussy ever… Broads ain't on that fake ass killer image you be trying to portray. It's time for that stuff, but whenever you're with a woman definitely ain't the time for it."

"Nigga, fuck you! I'm the reason niggas ain't robbed and killed your soft ass. You ain't got no power out here on these streets and I do. My name known on over one hundred different blocks in this city. Killers fear me, so damn what a pussy think. While you in the bed sleepin, I'm out in the streets puttin in work, so nigga, don't ever tell me about you helping me get pussy, cause to me you ain't nothing but a pussy!"

"Damn, slim, you just said some real foul stuff."

"Ya, and I got the nuts and the guns to back it all up."

"You talking to me like you gonna kill me or something," said Bar.

"Shit, I might. Anybody jump out there with me Ima bury their ass and that's point blank, period. You got that little pretty ass nigga?"

Bar was shocked by what he heard coming out of Ball's mouth. He shook his head and then said,

"Ima take that shit you said to be a joke."

"See that's your problem. You taking me as a

joke, but the joke right here will leave you dead. The last nigga that took me for a joke is in Harmony Cemetery right now."

Ball's words hurt Bar deeply and, without saying another word, he stepped off the curb and began walking away.

"Roll out then, you hoe ass nigga," Ball said, turning to walk away.

When he reached the car, Lean and Omar were standing next to it, stripping out of their old clothes and getting dressed in some of the new ones they had just bought.

"Damn, ya'll just be out here doing the indecent exposure thing, haw," Ball said, hopping inside the car. "Lean, you drive," he said, and stretched out across the back seat.

Lean put on his Dolce and Gabana shades to hide his eyes; O put on his Solbiato shades at the same time. They both jumped in the car.

"Where Bar at," Lean asked, looking in his rear-view mirror at Ball, who was pretending to be asleep.

"Ay, nigga, where the hell Esco at," Omar said, smacking Ball's foot.

"I guess his hoe ass gonna walk home."

"What? What the hell you talkin about he gonna walk home. I know my man ain't about to walk nowhere, especially all the way back around the way."

Lean turned around, faced Ball and asked,

"What the hell would have possessed him to wanna walk home?"

"Man, he was talking that shit so I had to check his hoe ass, that's all."

"Man, nigga you trippin," Lean said, putting the car in drive.

"What the hell did you say to him, Derrick?"

asked Omar.

"I told that nigga I'll kill his ass, that's what I told him."

"What?"

Both boys turned around to look in the back seat at the same time.

"Man, look man, I ain't going for nothing and I ain't taking shit off nobody no more, from this day forward. A nigga try me and Ima wipe the streets clean with their ass," Ball said.

"You on some other shit, slim. So what. I guess you gonna kill on one of us next, haw man?"

"Shit, he ain't gonna kill me," said Omar. "Nigga, you ain't the only one that fire that iron, and you definitely ain't the only one in this car that got bodies up under his belt."

"Ya, whatever the fuck then, O I see you just like

any of these other niggas," Ball said.

"Well, see me then, nigga," Omar said, unbuckling his seat belt and turning around in his seat to face Ball.

"Man, ya'll niggas chill before the police end up locking us up," Lean yelled. "This why all the men in our family locked up or dead. Cruddy ass niggas like ya'll gonna be the reason other niggas gonna always take advantage of a Staten. We ain't shit without each other."

Ball said, "I don't need nobody."

He was still looking at Omar, who looked as if any minute he was gonna strike Ball across the face.

"Man, pass me that bag up front with the liquor in," Ball said, looking at Lean.

"Naw, nigga, get it yourself, since you don't need nobody. I'm about to go find my little man before he get locked up down here for something," Lean said, turning onto Wisconsin Avenue. "Ya'll niggas look on both sides of the street to see if ya'll see him."

Omar and Ball, though mad at each other, kept a close eye out for any sign of Escobar. They went up and down M Street, looking for him but to no avail.

"Man, this nigga gone," said O. "He probably caught the train on Farragut. If he did walk home, which I doubt, he definitely ain't gonna be walking up and down the main streets. He in the cut somewhere, so we ain't about to spot him anyway."

"Ay, Lean, pull over right here at the Genesis so I can see if they got any of Kingdawud's CDs up in their store."

Lean pulled the car over to the side of M Street. Omar hopped out and headed into the Genesis.

"Ay, ya'll ain't got none of Kingdawud's CDs," Omar asked, looking down at the glass case that was up under the cashier's counter."

"Yes, we have all of his new music," the man said, unlocking the case.

He reached inside and grabbed *Pieces of a Gangster,* the triple disc; *Blood of a Jinn,* the double disc; and *Sheikh of War,* Kingdawud's only single disc.

"Do you want all of these," the man asked, looking at Omar.

"Ya, and any other ones you got as well."

"Well, come back in an hour and I'll have his other four CDs."

"Damn, how the hell you be having all his CDs, when nobody else in the city has them?"

"He's Muslim. That's my brother so he makes sure his nephews drop me off fresh stuff weekly."

"That's what's up," Omar said, smiling.

"So, do you know what a Jinn is? asked the

211

man, putting the CDs in a small plastic bag.

"Naw, what is it," Omar asked.

"It's a being that Allah has created from fire. It's just like man but it's unseeable to our eyes. The Jinn dwell on earth here with us. Just like mankind they have been given a free will to choose whatever it is they wanna do. Unlike angels that are created from the light, the Jinn was created from a smokeless flame of fire and mankind was created from mud. The devil, Ibis, as Allah has named him, is also a Jinn."

"Naw, the devil was an angel," Omar said.

"And what is your proof to prove that which you just said?"

"It's in the Bible somewhere," said O.

"He was no such thing. Angels have no right to choose. They simply do as Allah has commanded of them to do and no more. They have no free will. Also, you know that Ibis was a Jinn because he was created from smokeless flame of fire and not of light, like the angels."

"So what's your proof," asked Omar.

"Sahih Bukhari, Abu Dawud and the Quran itself."

"Man, I don't know what the hell you just said."

Omar snatched the bag of CDs off the counter and said, "I didn't know a lot of the stuff you just taught me, so I gotta say that you are smart."

"I don't intend to be considered smart. As a Muslim, I just wished to share with you something you may have had no knowledge of, and that's part of our way of life."

"I appreciate that."

Omar left the store. He hopped back in the car and said, "I bet ya'll didn't know that the devil was created from fire and he's a Jinn, not an angel."

"Man, my father already told me that; it's in the Sahih Bukhari," said Ball.

"Ya, whatever that is."

"Ay, Lean, what did you do with them two hundred fifty-dollar cigars I told you to steal out of the cigar shop?"

Lean reached down into his sock and brought out two greyish-colored cigars that were in a glass tube. He handed them to O and he began opening one.

"Those cost how much," asked Ball.

"Two hundred fifty dollars," said O.

"It must come with the weed already in it; gotta be able to roll itself," joked Ball.

O handed Lean the *Blood of Jinn* CD and he pushed it into the CD player.

Kingdawud's Blood of a Jinn (song) Ghetto Style

They put my homies in history, like things from Sicily

When I die, I guarantee you the ghetto gon be missin me

From head to toe kissin me, wishin me to be buried in peace.

Not in hell at least. My memories will never cease

A legend in the belly of the beast. Kept sacred like Japanese

Laid back in my style, calm, collective and wild

Living this dirty life, Baby, but I'm still so proud.

My dogs crawl. At the sound of haters speaking my name.

Then set their bodies to flames.

All for the king of the game.

The last one had to leave when I came.

(hook, R&B)

Styleee taken em back to that ghetto styleeeeeeeee

That ghetto styleeeeeeeee

That ghetto styleeeeeeeee

Verse 2

Hustler in vacant spots. Rollen dice in parking lots.

Releasen shots at my rivals. Strapped for my survival.

Reliven parts of the Bible

Always ducken the five O
My hands dirty but my wrist glow
Gettin cold yet still I'm piss poe.
Drunk off of that hurricane.
Hennessey and Cisco,
"This no game." What would I play for?

As they listened to Kingdawud telling their story, a story barely spoken of by the media or acknowledged by white America, the boys nodded their heads, kept their eyes on their door mirrors, had their hands up on their guns and put weed smoke into the air.

Chapter 8

Escobar exited the train station at First and Independent and walked down Pennsylvania Avenue, towards the more treacherous side of Capitol Hill. From where he stood, his side of the street didn't exist and was invisible.

The beautiful condos, store fronts and historic buildings across from the Navy base almost gave him a false sense of security, until he saw the 5th Street bridge. Just beyond that bridge lay a world full of rapists, killers, drug dealers and violence that would not be extinguished by any of the politicians who sat in the shops just a few feet away, trying to make laws to govern the world's affairs and its American interests within it.

Esco could feel the hairs on the back of his neck standing at attention as he walked up under the bridge and began crossing the street. Now the world that was once invisible, all of a sudden came to life again.

"Reality," he said out loud to himself, as he looked down at the shopping bags he carried.

Before he could look up, a dented up brown station wagon flew around the corner and crashed into him, sending the bags and his body flying ten feet into the air. In what seemed to take only a few seconds, his body came crashing to the ground with a bone-crushing sound. From his back, Bar stared, confused at what had just happened to him. The fact that he was unable to move or to breathe allowed the reality of the situation to come through clearly. As he began to catch his breath, he turned to see two men emerging from the station wagon, both holding Micro Uzi sub machine guns. Esco tried to move, but his body would not budge and his arms would not work, no matter how badly he wanted them to.

This can't be happening, he said to himself, trying to picture the faces of the two men who were now standing right over him.

"This is a mistake. Ya'll got the wrong guy," he said in a whisper, barely able to speak as blood flowed from his mouth.

Without speaking or thinking twice about what they had come to do, the two men opened fire, spraying Escobar's body with bullets. The burning hot steel peeled the skin from his head and face, and nearly severed his right hand at the wrist. He lay there on the ground, in a puddle of his blood that ran down from the curb where his twisted body had landed, to the street below the bridge, where the two men stood, still waging their assault.

From where she sat at the bus stop on Pennsylvania Avenue, Tebetha could hear the multiple gunshots.

"Oh, my god," she said, turning to look in the direction the shots came from.

She covered her mouth with her right hand. Standing, she said, "Oh, my God, somebody is probably dead!"

Just then, a silver Porsche Cayenne pulled up in front of the bus stop and its passenger side window went down. There sat Moe, smiling. Tebetha smiled back at him and walked to the car. Moe opened his door and stepped out. He lifted the seat to allow her to get inside.

"So, where we going," she asked, looking at Moe through his door mirror.

"Ima take you to my mansion out Maryland," he said, turning around in his seat to see the expression on her face.

She was at a loss for words.

How many women, who had come from where she did, had ever seen or been inside a mansion or had the pleasure to say she knew a person who owned one, she thought to herself.

She knew her friends would definitely envy her, once she told them about it.

"We only going there for a little while, right, because I do have a curfew," she said, crossing her legs, while both Moe and Gutter tried to see her panties. They were concealed by the thick, flawless, caramel thighs she had and the Red Moschino skirt she was wearing.

"Here, drink this," Moe said, passing her a bottle of Moet and Chandon.

She took the bottle and said, "Thank you, but this is too much for me."

"Naw, it's cool. I got my own," Moe said, raising another bottle in his right hand. "So feel free to drink the whole bottle and don't be shy."

Tebetha put the bottle to her lips and began sipping the champagne. She lowered the bottle and said, "This tastes good."

Her pink lipstick-painted lips looked as juicy as her tender cheeks. Not missing a single detail, Moe fired up a cigar and asked,

221

"Do you smoke?"

"No, not really, but I won't mind smoking with you, if you like."

"Good. I hate little girls who only talk like women but act like kids," Moe said, passing her a cigar and a lighter.

She looked at the huge cigar and said," "What's in this thing?"

"Only the best," he said, staring at her thighs in the rear view.

Moe began to feel himself getting hard. She had a body unlike any woman he had ever seen before. She put the cigar in her mouth and fired it up, inhaling the smoke.

"This has a nice taste," she said.

She laughed as she exhaled the smoke from her mouth.

"What's so funny," Moe asked, looking at Gutter, who was driving.

"I don't know. I feel really good, but higher than I expected to be," Tebetha said, putting the bottle up to her lips.

Gutter and Moe both stared at her through the rear view. Their plan was working brilliantly and they thought she would soon be unconscious. All she had to do was finish the bottle and she wouldn't even remember what hit her, if she was lucky enough to ever wake up again.

Tebetha could feel the drink and smoke nauseating her so she put down the bottle and placed the cigar into the ashtray next to her.

"You okay," Moe asked, looking back at her.

"Ya, I'm cool. I'm a little dizzy, but I'm cool," she said, closing her eyes.

"Why you ain't finish your blunt or the champagne? That stuff cost me a couple hundred dollars, so please don't let any of it go to waste," Moe said.

He was still staring at her legs. She kept her eyes shut, not responding to what he said. Moe looked at Gutter and began unzipping his pants. He climbed over into the backseat on top of her and began kissing her as he pushed up her skirt.

"Stop," she said in a faint voice.

But he didn't.

"Stop," she said again, trying to grab her skirt to keep him from lifting it, but she was too late and he was too strong.

"Please! What are you doing, Moe? Stop it," she screamed.

He grabbed her panties and began pulling them down but she was able to hold them, preventing him from taking them completely off.

"Please stop," she said, crying. "I don't want you to do this. Please stop, Moe."

He tore off her panties and forced her hands to her sides.

"Moe, please don't do this. Moe, please," she pleaded, but to no avail.

To silence her screams, Gutter turned up the music full blast and Kingdawud's voice told the story of how the two men truly felt at that very moment.

> Pimp Who
> (Verse #1)
> Pimp who? Trick I pimped you to this game I'm true.
> Now you stuck like glue.
> Like Owwwwww. Flossen on these hookers in everything brand new. (hook)
> When I see hoes I close in.
> With a whole trunk full of Trojans.
> Love pussy when it's wet as the ocean, with a body that's softer than lotion.

With a pretty face and a sweet taste, cause a brother like King to catch a case.

Thanks for the grace.

I be all up in her hole like the ace, making more space, condoms never go to waste.

I can tell that I'm good from the look on her face,

Now she looking to chase, wearing panties with the lace.

It cost to be the boss.

Hurry up and take your clothes off.

I don't be hand-cuffin this hoe.

Hoes I toss like a dirty cloth picture that loss.

As the music played, Moe continued forcing himself on Tebetha. Once he finally had her naked, he raped her, as Gutter watched with excitement. She continued trying her best to fight him but he just kept over-powering her as he stroked away, in and out of her, pleasuring himself with each stroke.

Gutter pulled near a wooded area near Tantallon Square in Fort Washington, Maryland then parked. Tebetha cried in the backseat, naked, as Moe came inside of her.

226

Once he finished relieving himself and was satisfied, he climbed off her and began pulling up his pants.

In an attempt to save her own life, Tebetha grabbed the bottle of Moet beside her and struck Moe across the head. As she began climbing out of the car, Gutter reached out to grab her. She hopped out of the car and ran at full speed. Gutter snatched his gun from up under his seat and got out of the car after her.

He couldn't see her, once she entered the woods, so he opened fire in the direction she had run until Moe grabbed his arm.

"The police is gonna be all over us!"

"Damn," Gutter said, kicking the ground. "Damn, we in a world of trouble if we don't find that bitch and kill her dead!"

Chapter 9

Ms. Linda and her company sat at the table, getting drunk, smoking cigars, and waging bets on Bid Whist. All of a sudden somebody began knocking at the door, over the loud music; but to no avail, because she could not have heard if anyone answered, Linda yelled,

"Who the hell is it?"

"I got it, Ma," said Buttafly.

She got up from her seat at the table and went to the door but when she looked through the peephole, she saw nothing but darkness.

"Getcha damned hand from in front of the peephole, fool," she said, yanking the door open.

Lean stood in the doorway. He looked down at his sister with a blunt in his mouth. He walked past her to the table and kissed his mother on the cheek.

"Hey, baby," she said, looking up at him as he passed her the blunt.

"Ma, where the hell is Derrick, Omar, and Leanardo?"

"They should be back there in that room."

He started toward the room but when he reached it, he found the door locked.

"Man, open this damned door," he said, bumping his shoulder into it.

"That's L. Go ahead and open up.

Ball unlocked the door allowing L to enter. He looked around at the boys.

"Why ya'll got the door blocked? "Ya'll up in here smoking weed?"

"I know damned well ain't nobody back there smoking no weed without letting me hit it," Ms. Linda said, hopping to her feet.

"Damn, you bout to get a nigga late," Lean said, passing L the blunt he had in his hand.

Ms. Linda walked in and began looking around. "Who the hell back here smoking," she asked, looking at Omar.

"Me, Ma," L said, passing her the blunt in his hand, as Ball shook his head.

"Ay, Ma, call Butta in here, please," L said, looking at Ball.

"Butta, come here," Ms. Linda screamed.

Butta came rushing down the hall and into the room. With a concerned look on her face, she asked,

"Ma, what's wrong?"

"Nothing, girl, your brother asked me to call you," Ms. Linda said, passing the blunt to Butta.

230

"Ay, look, this right here some disturbing news, so don't nobody go kicking and screaming when I say it," L said.

He looked around the room at everyone, then put his arm around his mother's shoulders and grabbed Butta's hand.

"Tebetha got raped," he said, looking his mother in the eye.

Everyone in the room stood motionless, as if the air had been sucked out of them. Tears began to run down Ms. Linda's cheeks.

"So where is she," Butta asked, hugging her mother tightly.

"She in Sibley Hospital, uptown, off New Mexico Avenue. Butta, ya'll need to go up there right away," he said.

As Butta turned to leave, he pulled at her hand. She turned around.

"Look, I got something else to tell ya'll," he said, lowering his head.

"O my God, my baby alive ain't she Kevin?"

"Ya, she alive, Ma, but Little Shawn got killed…"

"Little Shawn who," Ball asked, as Lean, Omar and Butta all began to cry.

"Your friend, Little Shawn, with the good hair," L said, reaching for his brother.

"Fuck naw, that nigga ain't dead. You trippin," Ball said, pulling away from L.

Ms. Linda was wailing and screaming and Buttafly would have been, as well, had she not been trying to remain strong for her mother's sake. Everybody in the room was crying, except L.

"Look, I know who did this. My private investigator already got back with me and we gotta go handle this," he said.

Without saying a word, the boys grabbed their guns from under pillows, dressers, and coats. Ms. Linda was still too busy crying and screaming her sorrow. She too knew what had to be done.

"Ya'll go kill every last one of the bastards," she said, looking at her boys.

"Come on ya'll," L said.

He walked out of the room, with Ball and the other boys right behind him. They left the house, went out of the building, and didn't stop until they were in the alley that ran behind 1430 Projects. L unlocked the doors on his Cadillac Escalade truck and all four of them piled inside. Still in shock, confused and hurt, all the boys sat silent.

"This is the point where boys are forced to be men," L said, firing up the blunt sitting in his ashtray. "If we let this shit ride, all of us might as well pull our pants down and let the whole city hump us in our butts."

"This cannot slide for one second; retaliation is a must."

"This wasn't no random act of violence, no! This was a nigga sending a strong, strong message."

"They hit our peoples back to back to let us know how easy it was to do it."

"Now we gonna hit them harder than they ever been hit before."

"Everything these niggas ever seen or smiled at must be destroyed."

"Tonight, we won't worry about consequences… going to jail or being killed doesn't matter at this point."

L opened his coat revealing the Calico he had hanging from his shoulder and said, "Some niggas don't respect nothing but this hot steel in their chest and heads. For this act of transgression against us, we'll spare no one. Kids, old women, babies… they all gonna die."

As he pulled away from the curb, L put the blunt in his mouth then turned up the music and Kingdawud said in his own words, exactly how they were all feeling.

All Alone (hook)

All alone in this world, all alone

Vicious brothers, like Toney Fortune and Al Capone.

So tired of being all alone that in their sleep they moan

All alone in this world, all alone.

(Verse 1)

How can my homies respond to my cries when they gone?

Elected and left as the don

My other homies in prison, I wish that I could pay their bonds!

But they beneath the prisons, wishin they would have got murdered instead of doing life and still livin.

Still shiverin from the cold.

Reminiscin on those that died young as they get old

How long will it take til they fold?

As the song played on, the blunts burned and the Escalade moved through the city, carrying four soon-to-be Grim Reapers who had no mercy in their hearts for anyone or anything.

"Here, hit this," said Lean, passing the blunt he had just finished rolling over to L.

L put the blunt in his lips and fired it up. "This some good weed. Where did ya'll get it," he asked, inhaling deeply.

"We took it off this nigga we robbed and killed," said Lean, firing up the second cigar he had just finished twisting.

"This that mid-grade from around 640 that Iron Sheikh and them Mahdi boys be selling," said L. "I hope ya'll little niggas know that Musa and them got a bounty on ya'll head for robben that spot."

"Don't nobody got nothing on my head," Omar said.

"Niggas don't even know us," said Ball, who appeared to still be out of it.

"We had an inside man and he dead, so can't nobody tell nobody else who we was," said Lean, letting his seat back and with a smirk on his face.

"Ya'll little niggas be doing some dumb stuff," said L. "I don't even respect niggas whose hustle is fobbing. That's some weak-minded lazy nigga stuff."

"Ya, whatever," said Ball.

"We ain't trying to get a nigga to respect us, we trying to get a nigga to pay us off," Omar said, laughing. "How would you feel if you sat out on the block all day, duckin bullets, trying to keep from going to jail, watching fiends with a microscope all day, just to have a lazy nigga with a gun come up to you and say, 'Thanks nigga for doing all the work, now I'll take it from here?'"

"Wouldn't none of ya'll like that," L said, mugging on Omar and Lean through his rearview mirror.

"Man, that shit is all part of the game," said
Lean.

"Nigga what game? What game are you referring
to," L asked.

"The drug game," Lean said, taking the cigar he
was smoking away from his lips. "If shit is a game then
explain to me how the fuck Little Shawn just lost his life
for real, or how Tebetha is really laying up in a hospital
bed right now as we speak and might be pregnant or
have AIDS. What the fuck is the joke about that? How
the fuck is that something to play with," he said, placing
the cigar back in his lips.

"This street life ain't no game but you still can't
know the nigga who make his money off catchin niggas
slippin," said Omar. "Everybody out here is involved in
some messed up stuff. Ain't nothing nobody doing out
here in these streets considered honorable. Niggas killin
little kids, sellin drugs to they own flesh and blood,

tricken little girls out of their purity, rappin, robbin, stealin, cheatin, snitchin... Man, everybody out here on some cruddy shit."

L made a right off Good Hope Road and kept straight down Alabama Avenue until he reached Savannah Terrace.

"If it's all part of the streets and a nigga got to respect it, then why should we be mad that somebody just raped Tebetha or that a nigga just killed Shawn? From what I'm understanding, ya'll saying that ya'll cool wit the shit because it's a part of the game, so we should just let it go out of respect for a nigga's hustle."

"Man, ain't nobody said no shit like that, Staten! All we saying is, ain't no honor in none of this shit no more, at least not in our generation, and niggas gonna pick and choose who to respect and when to respect them."

"If a nigga had real respect for the people they should have it for, Theba would have never gotten raped," said Lean."

239

"Right now, everything is fair game, even the police. As far as I'm concerned, before I let them lock me up, Ima kill they ass or make them kill me wherever I stand," said O.

The Escalade pulled into Garfield Terrace and stopped. All the boys got out and went upstairs into L's apartment and they made themselves at home. L and Bar went straight to the backroom, while Lean went into the kitchen and Omar flopped down on the couch and turned on the TV.

"Damn, this my movie" O said, looking at *Scarface*.

"What's that O," Lean asked as he left the kitchen with a plate of cold chicken.

"*Scarface*," Omar said, snatching a piece of chicken off the plate.

L walked out of the room holding a black gym bag in each hand. He walked to the end of the couch and sat down, then placed both bags at his feet. He unzipped the bag closest to him, reached inside, and pulled out an M-4 A1 assault carbine; the military's version of the M-16.

"Damn that muthafucka beautiful," said Lean.

"Yes, that's like the gun Scarface had in this movie," Omar said.

"This ain't no movie," L said, raising the barrel of the gun to the ceiling. "And that coward ass nigga Scarface wasn't no real gangster."

"Hold, L, how you gonna say some shit like that about my man Face? That nigga was as gangster as they get, haw, O?"

"He was a filthy piece of shit," L said, pulling two Browning assault rifles with drumroll fifty round clips from his bag.

"Damn, L, what's that," asked Ball.

"This your man BAR," L said, passing one of the Brownings to his little brother. "It's a Browning assault

assault rifle, better known as a BAR."

"That's what's up," Ball said, smiling as he felt the weight of the weapon in his hands.

"Pause up, L, back to Scarface. How you gonna disrespect my man like that," Lean asked.

"Alright, let me put it like this. Let's say you went over to Africa and helped a nigga who ain't have shit come into the country, but when he got here, you ain't just leave him to fend on his own, but you helped him make millions and got him a green card so he could stay here and enjoy his life," Lean said. "Now let's say that same nigga started trying to fuck your wife or your main girl behind your back and was tellin her, fuck you, cause you would be old news soon. Would you respect him?"

"Hell, naw. I'd kill his bitch ass," Omar said.

"No bullshit," said Lean.

"Okay, let's say Little Escobar, who ya'll know got a bunch of girls, falls in love with Tebetha and marries her. Would you kill him," L said, looking at Ball.

"Hell, naw, I would be happy for them, my man and my sister. Who would make a better couple," Ball said.

"Alright, what about this? Let's say I'm your drug connect. I been dealin with other niggas on your block longer than you, but I cut them off to deal with you, but I start giving you a better price than them. If I asked you to do something for me, would you do it?"

"Hell, ya, without question," said Omar.

"Hell, who you want killed," L said, smiling.

"Ok, let's say I tell you to kill some kids. Would you do it?"

"Shit, why not? I'm already sellin drugs to damn near every city in America. And we all know that 90%

243

of deaths in the streets, especially those where kids get killed by stray bullets; and are a result of the sale of drugs that I'm putting in the streets."

"I'm glad you said that," L said. "Everything ya'll just said ya'll wouldn't do, that piece of shit ass nigga Scarface did. He tried to have sex with his man's girl the moment he laid eyes on her. He killed his right-hand man for marrying his sister, and he turned his back on Sosa when he needed him, even when Sosa was having Federal charges dismissed against him."

"That nigga sellin drugs to every city in America, which is the leading death of our ghetto youths and he got the nerve to say he can't kill no kid. He been killin kids ever since he landed in the country."

"Damn, I ain't never seen the shit that way," said Lean.

"Me neither," said Ball.

"Here man, ya'll take these weapons," L said, passing Lean and Omar FN-fal assault rifles.

244

"WE gonna kill everybody we see," L said, looking at the boys.

Chapter 10

Tebetha lay in pain in the hospital bed. With tears in her eyes, she wondered to herself why anyone would have wanted to hurt her. Why had she been raped and almost killed by a man she had adored when she was a little girl growing up? How could someone who seemed to be out of a dream be such a monster out of a nightmare that she could not stop envisioning. She had always believed that nobody deserved to lose their life or go to jail, but the anger she felt made her wish both fates upon Moe and Gutter.

She burst into tears as she thought about how he had ravished her over and over again. She had taken more than twelve showers since the assault, but she still did not feel clean, inside or out.

Just as she turned to try and rest, Buttafly and her mother entered the room, causing her to cry even more. The two women came to the bed and hugged her, and they began to cry, themselves.

"Baby, I promise to find out who did this and have them killed," Ms. Linda said.

"Who did it," Butta asked, looking into her baby sister's eyes.

"Moe and Gutter," Tebetha said, shaking.

"Come on baby, we taking you home," Ms. Linda said, taking hold of Tebetha's arm.

She and Butta helped Tebetha up from the bed. She slid on her shoes, and then all three women walked towards the door.

"Excuse me, Ms. Staten, this will only take a moment of your time," said a detective.

He introduced himself as Mr. Ybarra. He pulled his badge from his hip and flashed it before their eyes. All three of the women stood, looking at the man.

"Ok, Ms. Staten," he said, looking at Tebetha. "We have been given the results from the semen the

247

doctors found inside of you and the DNA traces back to a man by the name of Moenay Shaw, AKA Moe Money."

Ybarra went on, "We have been investigating this man for some time, waiting on him to do something stupid like this, so that we could put the axe to his neck. Now he has done just that. We are confident that, with your help, we can put him and his cousin Rasheed Evans away forever."

Ms. Linda asked, "Help? What do you mean by help?"

"Help meaning testifying, Ms. Staten," Ybarra said.

"Hell no, my baby ain't about to become no snitch for you or nobody else. You say you know whose sperm was in her, so go arrest the muthafucka."

She began to walk away, holding Tebetha's hand. Agent Ybarra just watched as the three women walked out of the hospital.

Moe paced back and forth, sipping liquor from the Hennessy bottle in his hand. He contemplated the worst.

"Shit, shit, shit," he said out loud, making Gutter enter the room and meet him out on the balcony.

"You ok," Gutter asked, holding the Franchi SPAS 12-gauge combat shotgun in his right hand.

"Fuck naw, I ain't alright. Do I fucking look alright to you?"

He passed Gutter and walked back inside the house.

"This shit is gonna ruin me," he said, putting the bottle back up to his mouth.

Gutter watched him guzzle down the cognac as if it was a bottle of water.

"We should have killed that bitch just like we had planned to do. We should have shot her and cut her into little pieces and let the animals eat her remains," Moe said, turning to Gutter.

Moe's phone rang and he grabbed it from the dresser beside him. He was silent as he listened to what was being said.

"No," he yelled then, and threw the phone against the wall.

"What is it," Gutter asked, raising his weapon to his shoulder.

"This bitch is ruining me."

Moe dropped to his knees and put the bottle back to his mouth. He guzzled the cognac until the bottle was nearly empty, then stood up, wiping his mouth with the back of his hand.

"They just hit the spot around Trinidad and another around 106 and Park. That's over six million in drugs and another million in money."

"Did they kill anybody?"

Moe looked up at Gutter then lowered his head

again, saying, "Everyone in the building is dead."

Moe knew it was only a matter of time before the Staten boys would be coming for him. They had destroyed, in less than an hour, what had taken him over a decade to build. He looked at Gutter, somehow feeling that it was all his fault. Had he killed L himself, instead of sending JP and Bang Bang to do it, he would no longer be a problem for them.

And it was Gutter who suggested raping and killing Tebetha for her brothers' disrespect. Had the man who had protected him for so many years not proved to be more of a liability than an asset?

Chapter 11

Lean, L, Omar and Ball swept through the city, robbing and burning all of Moe's dope houses and killing everyone inside. Finally, the boys reached the spot they had been dying to hit all night.

The black Yukon pulled up to the side of 501. Omar and Ball jumped out and without warning, opened fire on everyone standing around. The two BARs opened up, sending multiple rounds in the direction of the men standing out on the block in front of building 501.

Men fired back, but the BARS were too much for them to handle. The two boys sprayed the street, clearing a straight path to 501. They ascended the steps and entered the building, crushing all life forms in their path of havoc. After clearing the hallway from top to bottom, the boys shot the door of Apartment 601 and then kicked it in.

As they entered, they were met with resistance from those inside. Back and forth, bullets flew as those inside opened up with their A-Kick 47s. The two men, Cho Low and Smallwood, who had killed Escobar, ducked behind a couch in the living room and fired shots at the two boys.

Both Ball and Omar had to retreat and take cover in the kitchen to keep from being sawed in half by the firepower.

"Shit," Ball said, ducking behind the wall.

"Here," Omar said, removing the strap of the Rocket Propelled Grenade launcher from around his shoulder.

He passed it to Ball and he set the RPG to "fire," then stuck it out of the kitchen. It fired toward the couch. An explosion shook the entire apartment, knocking both Ball and Omar to the floor. They sat back, listening, but heard no more gunshots coming from inside the house. Ball peeped his head around the corner and saw a fire that was burning the whole place.

"Them niggas toast," Omar said, running from

the kitchen and out of the apartment.

He and Ball reached the entrance but had to duck back in to keep from being shot. Villains were outside, thick as peanut butter and firing towards the building.

"Ain't no way in hell we about to get out of this shit alive," O said, looking through the crack of the thick steel door that guarded them.

Just then, they heard the screeching of car tires. What sounded like a high-powered machine gun opened fire, sucking the air out of the street.

"That's Lean and L," Omar said, pushing the door open.

He and Ball let the BARs rip as they ran to the vehicle and jumped in. L slid down in the car, almost falling because the power of the .20-millimeter Gatling gun he was firing was too powerful for him to wield.

"Here, take this," L said.

He passed the Gatling to Lean and slid over into the driver's seat. He stepped on the gas and they flew down the street, out of Capers behind Ball. The two cars raced over the bridge down Suitland Parkway but Ball told Omar to turn in to the Farms and he did.

"Shit," L said, following them.

He knew the Farms was not a part of the plan. Ball hung from the window and fired the BAR at everyone in sight as they took off running for cover. When they got to the end of Sumner Street, Omar stopped the car and Ball hopped out. He ran towards the cut. He opened fire with the BAR as the killers of the Farms opened fire, as well.

Ball stood firing the BAR in a sweeping motion, trying to kill as many people as he possibly could. He could see the fire and hear the popping of pistols in the dark but he did not flinch for a second.

Once his clip ran out, he turned to run. He sprinted towards the car but was nearly chopped in half, making him duck. Just then, L came flying down the street as Omar opened fire on the cut with the Gatling. He tore half the wall off the building and nearly killed Ball at the same time.

The killers took off running for their lives. They knew they were no match at all for the powerful weapon being fired at them.

As Ball stood up to run, he caught a bullet in the leg that sent him back to the ground. Omar, who was out of the car and standing at the top of the cut, opened up with his BAR, chopping down the man who had shot Ball in half, right along with the metal gate next to the man.

Ball got to his feet and ran to the end of the cut. O gave him another clip and he reloaded his gun. He rang back into the cut, firing.

"Come on! Come on," Omar screamed, trying to get Ball's attention.

Just then, a stray bullet struck the car window next to him, sending hot glass fragments flying in his face. He screamed in excruciating pain. Hearing the screams, Ball turned. He continued firing his weapon as he backed out of the alley. He grabbed hold of O, threw him in the truck, and then they swerved off.

As they exited Barry Farms onto MLK Avenue, two cars jumped behind them and the men inside started firing at them. They flew up the avenue, trying to shake their tail. Then, out of nowhere, Lean and L stepped from behind two parked cars on different sides of the street. They opened fire on the two vehicles trailing Ball and O.

The first vehicle flipped over, struck a building, and blew up on impact. The second vehicle just stopped in the middle of the street, with all four of its passengers and one driver, dead.

Both the boys' vehicles headed up Wheeler Road and then made a sharp left, heading to the front of Valley Green Projects. Ball drove over the curb and down over the creek into the field. He stopped his car and got out. He came around and helped Omar out.

In the Escalade, L pulled up beside them. He and Lean hopped out. L grabbed a gas can from the trunk, while Lean gathered all their weapons. L worked his way around the vehicles, pouring gas all over both of them. He stuffed a rag into the gas tank of the Escalade. He looked at Ball and them and said, "Ya'll go ahead and start walking."

They all did as he said and he lit the rag. He ran through the field towards where the boys stood waiting.

"Come on," L said, climbing the hill into 10th Place.

As they reached the steps, the Cadillac exploded, igniting the other truck; it blew up a few seconds later.

"That was some real Hollywood shit," Lean said, making the boys laugh.

"I can't believe you just blew up a sixty thousand-dollar Cadillac truck," Lean said.

L looked at him then said, "A million Caddies ain't worth my freedom."

The boys made it to 10th Place, while the killers who

stood in the dark cuts watched their every move. Most of the villains in the 10th Place Projects knew L and they also knew that nobody was crazy enough to run up in their hood, trying to start a war.

Catching them outside their hood was anyone's best chance of killing one of them and getting away with it. There was possible escape from the neighborhood, but killers like Motor, Kim, and so many others, made it a mistake for one to enter their block and open fire.

L reached the building with the three boys following him closely. They were all tired and pretty banged up, so even Ball had no intention of kicking off any more drama. Once they reached the floor where L's baby mama's apartment was, they stopped. They watched as L removed a key from up under the silver numbers hanging over the door, indicating which apartment it was. He put the key in the lock and turned, and then he pushed open the door.

"Come on," he said, holding the door open for all three boys.

He stepped in behind them, closed the door and locked it. As usual, Lean went straight to the kitchen and opened the refrigerator. Ball and Omar went into the living room and flopped on the floor. L walked down the hall to the bathroom.

As Lean walked into the living room with a box of beef and broccoli Chinese food, L came out of the bathroom, holding a bottle of Hennessy, a first aid kit, and a bottle of peroxide. He went to Omar and knelt down over top of him. He began pouring the peroxide on a rag and wiped blood away from Omar's face.

"It's not that bad," he said.

He opened the first aid kit and removed tweezers, then he began pulling the small shards of glass out of Omar's face. Omar flinched with each pull.

"Here, drink some of this," L said, passing him the bottle of Hennessy.

As O guzzled the liquor, L continued doctoring on him. He began cutting Ball's pants leg open with scissors.

Then with a small knife he cut an X into the spot where Ball had been shot. He pushed the tweezers into Ball's leg and he screamed in pain.

"Nigga shut up before you wake my daughter and her mother," L said.

He covered Ball's mouth with his hand and removed the bullet from his leg. Then he began sewing the wound closed while Ball and Omar drank from the bottle of Hennessy.

"Here," Lean said, passing L the blunt he had just fired up.

Without hitting it himself, L passed the blunt to Ball.

"Man, let me hit that," Omar said, reaching his hand out to Ball.

"You serious," Ball said, looking at O like he was going crazy.

"Damned right," Omar said.

He took the cigar from Ball's hand and put it between his lips. As everybody watched in shock, Omar began taking long puffs.

"Pain will make a man do some strange shit," L said, making everyone laugh.

L looked at Lean and said, "Ay, Lean, go put that piece of wood up under the doorknob."

Lean got to his feet and went to the door. He placed the two-by-four up under the doorknob as L had instructed him to do. He walked back into the living room and sat on the couch.

"I can't believe you smoke weed now," Lean said, looking at Omar while he resumed stuffing his face with the Chinese food.

"I can't believe you ate Denise's food without asking her first," L said as he took the cigar from Omar's hand.

"This shit good too," he said, smiling.

Out of nowhere the box of Chinese food went flying to the floor. Everyone stopped what they were doing and looked up. There stood Denise, in a halter top that revealed her stomach and her firm brown nipples, which were standing at attention. The small boy shorts she wore hugged her so tight that if one knew what he was looking for, he would have been able to see her clitoris.

She walked to the other side of the couch, giving each one of the boys a view of her voluptuous fat butt. She bent over, revealing to them that she wasn't wearing any under wear. She took the cigar from L and put it between her own lips. She turned to face Lean and said, "You trifling. Don't just be helping yourself to what's mine, you little punk ass niggas."

"All you had to do was say something," Lean said.

He tried to save face as he stared down at her vagina that was trying to bust loose of her boy shorts that wrapped her butt perfectly.

"Who the hell you talking to," she asked, pointing her finger in his face, making L and them start to laugh.

"I wish I would eat behind you, when you out there eating them little girls who don't even know how to wash their little coochie bootys."

"I don't be eating no booty," Lean said, rolling his eyes at her.

"As ugly as you is, you better be eating some booty cause I know you not going up in, not looking like 'slimy the creep' and all."

Everybody busted out laughing while Lean sat on the couch looking stupid, with embarrassment on his face.

"That's enough," L said, getting up from the floor.

"Nigga shut up and come pleasure me," she said, grabbing the bottle of Hennessy from Ball and strutting off to the back room.

"Damn, you lucky as hell," Omar said as he watched Denise disappear down the hallway.

"Nigga share, you got ten other baby mothers," Lean said, as L left the living room and followed her down the hall.

"Twelve," L said, entering the room and closing the door behind him.

He looked at the bed and saw Denise lying on top of the covers with her legs spread wide, playing with her clitoris. She pulled back the hood of her clit, allowing him to dive right into bed. He began tasting her as she moaned, palming his head and wrapping her thighs tightly around his neck. As he sucked away at her, she moaned and said yes, digging her nails into his shoulders. That only caused him to suck and lick even more aggressively.

"I'm cumming," she said, squeezing his neck tighter. Her thighs began to shake. As she orgasmed, he palmed her butt and pulled her closer to him.

"O my god, my god, my god," she said, still gripping his head tighter.

He unbuckled his pants and pulled them down to his heels then slid between her warm thighs. The heat from her body and her scent together were almost enough to make him climax. She grabbed his shaft and massaged the outer walls of her vagina with it. He kissed her passionately.

She knew Ball and them could hear her screams, or would soon be able to, if they hadn't already. She pushed "play" on the CD player on her night stand. As L entered her, moaning with satisfaction from her warm, wet, tenderness, she began to scream at the top of her voice,

"This your pussy!"

Just then the music began to play and Kingdawud said it all, as he had always done.

Give it to her Good
(hook) I give it to her so good she wouldn't dare

share

Wetting up her underwear

Sorry, Slim, you can't compare, cause what I'm given is rare YAAAAAAA!???

What I'm given is rare.

Baby, Ima have you climaxin behind the blow of an Anglo Saxon, making love while relaxin.

He's given you money sprucing you up

I'm just trying to loosen you, make you never want the next man

Making love by the beach on the sand

Yes, it's amazing what I'll do with my hands

Layin up, both cumming, bustin nuts, I long stroke then slow it down, riding through your guts.

Takin your breath away like asthma, you barely can breathe

When I'm finished, you'll be holding me, saying please don't leave

He's nothing compared to me

Just call me and there I'll be

You doing tricks all over the bed, wet up all the sheets

As the music played on, the two of them made love, pleasuring each other in every possible way until the clock struck 4am. L kissed Denise, who was sleeping on her back, and got out of bed. He quickly got dressed and went back to the living room where all the boys lay, sound asleep. He grabbed Lean's shoulder with one hand and covered his mouth with the other. Lean opened his eyes.

"Come on," L said in a whisper. He nodded his head toward the door, gave Lean a box of cigars and an ounce of strawberry Afghani skunk and said,

"Here, roll this."

L walked out of the living room and disappeared into his daughter's room. He walked to her bed and kissed her on the cheek. He pulled the covers around her then left the room and joined Lean, who was standing at the door.

Lean handed L one of the cigars he had rolled and then turned and faced the door. As L unlocked it, Omar woke up and looked at them.

"Where ya'll about to go," he asked, wiping his eyes.

"Nowhere, go back to sleep," L said as he opened the door. "When we wake ya'll up we'll be back with breakfast."

He and Lean left the apartment and were leaving the building when, at the exit, they saw people standing around everywhere.

"These niggas booted the fuck out," Lean said, following L through the corridor.

L laughed and said, "Who in this schizophrenic ass city ain't?"

They continued to the street and kept walking until they came to a black Crown Victoria with tinted windows. L unlocked the doors and he and Lean jumped inside. L started the car and pulled away from the curb, and then he headed down the street.

"Why the hell you driving a police car," Lean

asked, pushing in the lighter.

"I got this shit from my father. He was famous for creeping down on a nigga in disguise. If I roll up on your block with this car and hit the sirens, what's the first thing you gonna do if you dirty?"

"Run," Lean said.

"Yeah, most niggas do the same thing, but some are too lazy to run so they just start throwing their guns and drugs. As soon as they do, I raise up and air they whole block out. They can't fire back cause they are no longer strapped."

"That's smart," Lean said as he pulled out the lighter and set fire to his cigar.

"That ain't smart, that's genius. Real killers are mad men."

After taking several drags from the cigar, Lean passed it to L. The car was into Maryland in less than ten minutes. The streets, the houses and the scenery even looked different. Wasn't no mistaking the fact that they were no longer in the Chocolate City.

"I been doing this here shit for a long time, little cousin," L said, looking out his window.

"How many men do you think you've killed," Lean asked, taking the cigar from L's hand.

L turned and looked him in the eye and said, "None."

"None," Lean said, sounding surprised. "Damn, wait till I tell Derrick this. He's always bragging about how vicious you are out here in these streets. Hell, he had me fooled and the whole damned city thinks you about that head-hunting game."

"So how many bodies do you got," L asked, taking the cigar back from Lean.

"I got about ten by now, for sure." L looked at Lean then shook his head.

"Look, my dad once wrote me a letter and told me that his prophet, or the prophet named Muhammad, had said the strong man is not the one who overcomes the other man with his fist, but the strong man is he who can control his own anger in a fit of rage. What I get from that is this: You can't control others until you are first able to control yourself by handling your pride. Now, what's the reason you need to know how many people I killed?"

Lean shrugged his shoulders as if to say he didn't know.

"You ever go to jail; I guarantee you that you won't see too many guys who can't talk there. A nigga can't tell what he don't know. For a long time, I watched your father and my father and our other uncles tear this city apart with an iron fist. None of us actually can say we seen them kill anyone besides myself. They was feared for their legend, which proceeded them.

"Your father once said this to me when I asked him the same question you just asked me. He said he had got into an argument with a guy and the guy ended up getting killed later that same day. A few weeks later,

272

a man threw a drink in his face and cursed him out in front of everyone. Later on that week, that man was also found dead.

"Things went on like that for a while and nobody had ever seen him kill anyone but they knew the truth.

"You see, I'm not about to give nobody enough information to send me to jail for the rest of my life. There is no statute of limitations on murder.

"Do yourself a favor. The next time somebody asks you how many people you killed, get as far away from them as you can, cause they just might be recording that conversation," L said as they passed a sign that said, "Welcome to Accokeek, Maryland."

L took a back road through the woods and came upon a gated community. He rolled down his window and smiled at the security guard in the booth.

"What's your password and access number," the officer asked.

Without stumbling L ripped off both. The guard opened the gate and allowed him to pass the security point at the entrance of Humble Manors.

"Who the hell lives around here," Lean asked as he started in amazement at the huge mansions they passed on their way deeper into the Manor.

"You'll see," L said, keeping straight.

He pulled up next to a huge house with a for sale sign in the front yard, parked and got out, with Lean following him. L opened the trunk and took out two bags, one a black duffle bag and the other a light purple nylon bag that he handled with care.

"Here, take this," he said, handing Lean the duffel bag. "Come on."

They walked to the driveway of the house, then walked through the front yard and around the back of the house. They jumped a fence and began walking along a pond that sat directly behind the house facing them.

Two black shadows stood in the dark on the opposite side of the pond and they startled Lean, who reached for his gun.

"Hold up," L said, pushing his hand down. "They're with us," he said, walking towards the men.

On reaching them, L shook their hands then said, "Let's do this."

The four men crossed to the side of a huge mansion that had two Neapolitan Mastiffs guarding its back yard. A security camera swept the entire compound. L reached down and grabbed the duffle bag Lean was holding and unzipped it. He pulled out a rope with a hook at one end, a package of steaks, and some wire cutters. He tossed the steaks over the fence to the dogs that ate them quickly and died even more quickly.

"What the hell was that," Lean asked.

"Poison."

L began clipping the tiny wires at the bottom of the fence.

"Take that rope and toss it over the gate, up to that roof," he said, continuing to cut the wires.

Lean tossed the rope over to the roof of the house and it landed right next to the satellite dish.

"Here, take these and finish cutting those wires," L said, passing Lean the wire cutters.

He stood up and took hold of the rope. He pulled at the rope and a huge black cord came down with it. L pulled the wire over where the men stood, and then told Lean to cut it.

"Why we doing all this," Lean asked as he clipped the cable.

"Those wires I just cut along the fence are sending electrical currents through the fence powerful enough to fry anybody that touches it. The other wires you just cut were sensors. They would have given our exact location, had we tripped them. And this," L said, grabbing the cable Lean had just cut, "is the camera. Now we can go over this fence and infiltrate this house without them even knowing we're here."

Lean smiled as L and the two huge men climbed over the gate and entered the massive yard. L passed the two dead Neapolitan Mastiffs and headed up the steps. The two other men worked their way around the side of the house. L stood up on the patio deck, pulling himself up to the roof. He then reached back down, taking the bag from Lean. He lifted him up to the roof, as well.

"Watch your step," L said, as Lean slipped on one of the stone tiles that decorated the roof.

L worked his way across the roof to the chimney. He carefully took off the nylon bag he had tied around his belt and lifted it up over the opening of the chimney. Carefully, he untied the bag and placed it down in the hole, and then he began to shake it, releasing whatever was inside. He tied the nylon bag over the chimney, making sure what he had poured down the hole did not come back up.

"What the hell was that," Lean asked.

"Whipper snakes," said L.

"What the hell is a whipper snake," Lean asked, frowning up his face.

"Whipper snakes are snakes that will chase you down and kill you. They'll beat you with their tails until you are dead; their venom is deadly."

L listened as the people down in the house yelled and screamed as they ran for their lives. He could hear things being knocked over, and then he heard gun shots from inside the house.

L waited another five minutes then removed two black canisters from his bag. They were filled with poisonous gas. Before Lean could ask, L said,

"This will kill the snakes." He listened but heard no more noise. He then removed the nylon bag from the chimney. He pulled the pins on the gas grenades and dropped them down the chimney.

"Here, put this on," he told Lean, handing him a gas mask.

He pressed the chirp button on the side of his phone to signal to the other two men that it was now alright to enter the house. He and Lean climbed off the roof and entered the house.

They saw people lying dead, with snakebites to their faces and their arms. One of the men, who appeared to be a bodyguard, was lying in a puddle of blood. The whipper snake had eatin his face, all the way into his skull. L stepped over the dead man's body and walked down the stairs towards the basement. There, he was stopped by an enormous door made of metal of some kind with a combination lock fitted to it.

L pulled a small piece of C-4 Semtex explosive from his pocket. He placed the C-4 near the door's lock and placed a pin in it.

"Back up," he said. He and Lean backed up the steps a little ways, L pushed the button of the remote charger in his hand and the door to the basement blew off its hinges and fell to the floor. Once the dust and debris settled, L walked into the basement. He scanned the room with his flashlight until he found the light switch. He flipped it on. Both he and Lean were in awe at what they saw. The basement was full of hydro-plants.

"Yes, Lean said."

He ran to the first plant he saw, began picking its sticky buds, and dropped them into his pocket. L turned to his left and walked to an old bookshelf. He called out to Lean, who had occupied himself stuffing weed into his coat; he had taken it off to use as a bag. He set it down carefully and started going towards L.

"Hold up," L said, putting his hand out to stop Lean, then pointing to the floor, forcing Lean to look.

"That's a live tripwire, so step over it or you'll blow us both to pieces."

Lean stopped over the thin copper wire running the

length of the floor, one end to the other. He grabbed hold of the other side of the bookshelf and began pushing it as L pulled it towards him. As the bookshelf gave way they could see a hole in the wall.

"Keep pushing," L said, pulling with all his strength.

Finally, the bookshelf slid completely out of the way, revealing the huge hole in the wall. It appeared to lead into another part of the basement. L pointed his flashlight in the hole. What was on the other side sparkled like gold. There were bags of money, food stamps, antiques, and more. He stepped into the space and began grabbing bags and passing them out to Lean.

"Start taking that stuff to the car."

L moved to the corner of the room. He knelt down in front of an old plug socket and began unscrewing it. He reached into the hole where the plug had been and grabbed something and pulled it out. In his hand was a black velvet cloth tied with golden string. He untied the String and opened the cloth. What he saw made his heart sink; he nearly dropped the bag.

"Wow," he said, pouring the 36 flawless diamonds into his palm.

He had never in his life seen a raw diamond. The feeling overpowered him. He poured the stones back into the bag and retied the golden string around it. Then he placed the bag in his pocket and began putting the rest of the bags out of the hole in the wall. As he put them out, Lean came and carried them off. Lean took a book bag and began filling it with buds off the many plants. Once that bag was full, he filled another one.

"Come on, man, we ain't got time for no dumb shit like this," L said as he walked up the steps.

"Ya cousin I hear you and I would kill up this whole world for you but I ain't about to leave all this weed behind. You got what you wanted, now Ima get what I want."

Lean returned to picking buds and stuffing them into the bag in his hand. L laughed and just shook his head.

"Ok, one more bag," he said, going back down the steps to help Lean.

Once they finished filling the bag, Lean threw it over his shoulder. They went upstairs to the first floor.

"So how did you know all of that stuff was down there," Lean asked and they continued walking down the hallway and checking each room.

"I always treat a lady like a whore and a whore like a lady. When you do that, the whore, who has always been dogged by all the men she has ever dealt with, will love you because you treat her the way she never expected to be treated.

"On the other hand, when you treat a lady like a whore, she'll be on you so hard because she'll wanna know why you ain't trippin off her or tryna sweat her as all the other men she was with have done."

When they reached the last door on their right, L pushed it open and the scene reminded him of something out of a horrible triple rated movie. The two large men had

Moe tied to a chair in the corner, making him watch as they brutally ravaged and raped his twenty-year old daughter and his sixty-seven-year-old mother. Moe cried, unable to help them.

L walked to Moe and yanked the duct tape from his mouth so that he could hear him cry and scream in horror.

"Do you see this shit that you brought upon your family? I told your dumb ass that if you fuck with me or anybody that I love, I would literally fuck you and everybody in your little ass world."

L removed the golden chain from Moe's neck and put it around his own. He stripped him of the bracelet, pinky ring and charm bracelet he wore around his ankle, placing each item in his pocket.

"Fuck them, come fuck this nigga," L said, looking at the two men.

He raised his pistol and fired twice, striking each of the women in the head, killing them instantly.

"No! No! No," Moe said, crying and drooling from his mouth.

The two men continued molesting the dead women until L told them,

"I said that's enough!"

One of the men got up from the old lady's body. He strolled to the chair where Moe was tied and flipped it over. Moe's face was on the ground and his ass was in the air. As Moe cried and pleaded, the man tore away his pants and began raping him.

"This some shit I ain't gonna be able to watch," Lean said, leaving the room.

When he was down the hall and into the bathroom to throw up, he saw Gutter, lying dead with a whipper snake also dead around his neck. The snake had torn away most of Gutter's face, but Lean knew it was Gutter from his tattoos. He heard two gunshots, and ran out of the bathroom, back down the hall to the room he had just left. He saw the two men lying dead.

"What the hell you kill them for," Lean asked, looking at L.

"Retarded ass niggas don't know how to follow simple instructions," L said, walking to Moe.

Moe whimpered and cried in defeat.

"His man Gutter dead in the bathroom with a big ass snake around his neck," Lean said.

L smiled and said, "You hear that, you worthless piece of shit? Like I told you, I will destroy everything that you ever laid your eyes upon." Don't ever fuck with a Staten," he said, kicking Moe in his butt.

He walked to the bag the men had carried into the house and retrieved a can of gasoline. He began pouring it over the bodies of the two women lying naked and dead on the bed. He poured the gas all over the floor, leading a trail to Moe, and he doused him thoroughly, emptying the can on him.

L retrieved a blunt from his pocket and lit it. After

taking a few drags, he tossed it down on the floor, igniting the gasoline. Moe screamed in terror and excruciating pain as he was burned alive. Lean and L escaped the house and were long gone when it had finally burned to the ground.

Chapter 12

Ball turned over, stretched his arms, and opened his eyes. He stood up and looked down at Omar.

"Nigga, wake your ass up," he said, kicking Omar.

He woke up immediately, looked around the apartment and the hallway, then asked Ball,

"Where the hell is L and Lean? Man, they said they was going to get some breakfast," O said as he got to his feet and stretched his arms to the sides.

"You stupid ass nigga, what time was that," Ball said, frowning up his face and mugging on O.

"That was like a couple hours ago," Omar said as he wiped the sleep from his eyes.

"Man, they went to put that work in without us," Ball said as he walked to the door.

"What," Omar asked, still half-asleep.

"Man, just bring your slow retarded ass on," Ball said.

He unlocked the door and walked into the hallway. Omar stepped into the hall and said,

"So how the hell we gonna get back around the way?"

"Well it won't be in the vehicles we drove over here in, because they sitting in the middle of the field, char broiled to hell. We gonna have to jack a nigga around here for their car, that's all."

They went down the steps and out of the building. As they walked up the street, they watched the kids on their way to school, on buses or by foot. They saw a man warming up his car a few feet ahead. They walked to him and pulled their guns.

"Nigga, you know what this is? Your keys or your life."

Ball smacked the man with his gun and dropped him to the ground, bleeding.

"Man, what the fuck you do that for," O asked.

He and Ball jumped into the car and sped off down the street.

"Nigga don't you ever fucking question me again," Ball said, staring at him with a cold pair of eyes. "You got that?"

Ball saw a gas station and pulled into its parking lot. "Go get some blunts and a fifth of Absolut," he told Omar.

"Man, are you fucking crazy?" Omar said, raising his voice. "You just jacked a nigga for his car a block over. Now you gonna stop at a gas station right down the damned street?"

Ball looked at him and remained silent awhile. Then he nodded his head and said, "Ya, now jump the fuck out!"

Omar hopped out of the car and went into the store. He walked to the cashier's counter.

"Ay, look, I need a fifth of Absolut and a box of cigars."

"How old are you?"

"Here's my fucking ID," O said, slamming a hundred-dollar bill down on the counter.

"O, ya, I do see the resemblance," the Chinese man said, smiling.

"Yeah, what the fuck ever, Papasan. Just hurry up with my shit."

Papasan filled a brown bag with two boxes of cigars and two fifths of Absolut. He passed the bag to Omar. As he turned and walked away, two junkies approached the cashier. One of them pulled out a shotgun.

"This is a stick up!"

Papasan looked at Omar, who said, "Don't look at me, nigga. They robbing your ass."

"Naw young'un, we robbing you too," the man with the shotgun said, pointing the sawed off at Omar.

"Shit!"

Ball saw the robbery going down and slid out of the car with the BAR beside his leg. He didn't mind the two men robbing the store but he was gonna be damned if they pulled a gun on his flesh and blood, and lived to talk about it.

He reached the entrance. Without even opening the door, he took aim and fired, knocking out the front window and chopping the man holding the shotgun in half. The second man ran into the aisles and tried to hide behind a shelf. Ball walked in and ran the man down.

"Please young'un, you don't have to do this," the man said, pleading for his life.

"You was with this scumbag and now you're an

eye witness to a murder, so I gotta kill you."

Ball opened fire on the man and crushed him with over fifteen shots. Omar turned and ran outside. He jumped into the car as Ball reached the counter. The elderly Chinese man just stood there, shaking, knowing he would be the next to get killed.

Ball grabbed two lighters off the counter and stuck them into his pocket. He looked Papasan in the eyes and said, "From now on, whenever I come in this store, I want everything free. You got that?"

Papasan nodded his head to say yes and then let out a sigh of relief, knowing he was not about to be killed after all.

Ball left the store just as Omar put a bottle of Absolut to his lips and guzzled the liquor down. Ball hopped in, put the car in reverse, and they flew out of the parking lot and into the street.

"Damn, slow down," Ball said, watching Omar down nearly half the bottle without coming up for air.

"Shit! Shit! Shit," Omar screamed at the top of his lungs.

"What the fuck is wrong with you," Ball asked, looking at him again.

"Man, every time I'm around you, somebody gets killed!"

"So?"

"So? What the fuck do you mean," O said, raising his voice even louder.

"Man, you actin like a bitch. You better be thankful that you with the muthafucka doing the killin, instead of with the muthafuckas who being killed."

"How the hell am I supposed to chill when muthafuckas get kilt every day, right next to my Timberland boots?"

"Because you ain't the muthafucker gettin kilt, that's how! You drink too fucking much anyway."

Ball snatched the Absolut from Omar's hand and lap, saying,

"You used to be certified, but now you acting like a fucking wine-o who's scared of his own damned shadow. If you scared, go the fuck to church or get a dog!"

Ball made a sharp left turn past the roofless projects of Linda Pollin, less than a block up from Walls Place Southeast and across the street from the notorious Valley Green. Omar looked at Ball and said,

"Man, I used to think you was crazy because every time everybody else is at breakfast, you be lunchin, but now I know that you ain't crazy at all. You a fucking fool. You a young man who's gonna get himself and everybody else around him either locked up for the rest of their lives or killed. Now give me back my fucking drink."

He pulled the fifth of Absolut from the bag that was in Ball's lap.

"Yeah, go ahead and get drunk. That's what niggas do when they can no longer handle the reality of this vicious street life. They start getting drunk, sniffin powder coke and then they start smoking crack. I know what to expect from these streets."

"O yeah, and what's that?"

"Ima either get rich, get killed, or go to jail for the rest of my life but I ain't trying to candy coat that shit or stay drunk to numb my consciousness to it either."

Ball shook his head and continued, "Ya'll niggas hustle all day and then spend all night blowing your hustle money on weed and liquor, just to help ya'll cope with the outcome of the day. Backwards ass niggas."

"Man, you need to slow the hell down before you end up crashing us," O said as Ball sped around the corner and headed out of DC into Maryland.

"Fuck you, and fuck the police, so now who gonna stop me?"

Just as he said what he said, an unmarked police car hit its lights and pulled out behind them.

"Shit! Shit," said Omar, turning around in his seat to look at the cops.

"See all that shit you was talkin, now they about to pull us over and lock our asses up!"

"Shit! Ain't nobody about to lock me up." Ball slowly pulled to the side of the road. He sat watching as the policeman got out of his car and headed toward them.

"Man, you should have tried to at least run him. Now we going to jail!"

"Shut your scared ass up, nigga. If you was that scared, you should have jumped out and ran!"

"Nigga, do you realize we got a gun in here that you just used to kill a man with?"

Ball completely ignored Omar, who was scared to death.

He continued to watch the officer coming closer to the car. As he did, Ball began reaching for the weapon he had slid up under his seat.

"Man, what the hell are you about to do?"

Omar's eyes got bigger when he saw the weapon in Ball's lap. Without hesitation, Ball grabbed the handle of his door and pushed the door wide open. He stuck the weapon out of the car and pointed it towards the officer. The cop tried to pull his weapon from his holster. Ball, who had a mean mug on his face, squeezed the trigger and opened fire on the officer; bullets tore the officer's vest completely off his chest and lifted him off his feet. The officer was immediately down on the ground, in a puddle of his own blood. Ball walked to his body; he lay face down. Ball stood over top of him and fired one single shot that cracked the officer's head wide open like a watermelon.

"Damn, it's true, the bullets are so hot that they make niggas' brains boil."

"Nigga come the fuck on," Omar said as he slid

into the driver's seat and hit a U-turn in the middle of the street. He headed to the dead officer and Ball. Ball jumped in the car and they were off.

"Man, you just killed a police! A fucking officer of the law! Do you know what kind for trouble we are in?"

Ball said, "Nigga, if Ima go to jail for 20 years, it ain't gonna be for a UUV or a pistol possession alone. Now get us the fuck out of here." Omar swerved through traffic like a madman. He hit every neighborhood he came to, and flew through every cut he found. After twenty minutes of driving, he had gotten ghost.

When L found out about Ball killing the policeman, he made him go down to Fayetteville North Carolina until things died down. Ball spent his time on Murchison Road, killing even more people. With so many woods around Murchison Road, it was very easy for him to get away with every shooting he was involved in. Unlike DC, Fayetteville moved more slowly. The drama that he was used to wasn't poppin off daily, so Ball spent his time having sex with every pretty-faced woman who would let him between her legs. If he wasn't chasin money, which there wasn't a lot of, he was chasin his dick. He was collecting every gun the local crackheads, or the Beamers, as the hustlers on "the Murch" called them, would steal from the local pawn shops and sell to him. He had gotten cool with a GI who was selling him army weapons in exchange for drugs.

Chapter 13

18 Months Later

Ball had grown tired of the country. Word got back to him that L had put a hit out on the two witnesses who had seen him kill the police officer. That news made Ball feel that it was safe to go back to the city, even though L had told him not to.

Ball hopped off the greyhound bus at the Peter Pan bus station on K Street Northwest. He had a duffle bag full of guns and assault rifles. He left the bus station and flagged down a man who looked like a dope fiend posing as a cab driver. Ball knew, since it was Christmas Eve, no one would think that the huge bag hanging from the strap on his shoulder looked suspicious. He opened the back door of the cab and got inside, slamming the door behind him.

"So, what's up youngster? Where you headed," the dusty-faced, nappy-headed dope fiend asked. He started his cab and pulled out of the bus station parking lot.

"Take me around the Gardens, old timer."

Ball laid all the way down across the seat to keep himself from being seen by anyone. It took the cab less than eight minutes to get around Potomac Gardens.

"Stop right here," Ball said. He reached into the pocket of his black jeans and pulled out a knot of money. He peeled a hundred-dollar bill from it and passed it over the seat to the fiend driving.

"Either you can have this or I can give you a working fifty."

"Yeah, give me the working fifty," the man said, passing the bill back to Ball.

Ball reached into his other pocket and pulled out a folded ziplock bag that contained small baggies of what appeared to be crack cocaine. He opened the bag and grabbed one of the baggies, passing it over the seat to the man.

"You might wanna be careful around here with

all that money and coke," the old timer said.

Ball opened the door, but once he stepped out of the cab, he stuck his head back inside and said, "I'm Mad Ball. I'm a Staten and I got enough fire power on me to kill everybody around here three times in a row."

He slammed the door and made his way through the tiny, invisible hole in the black gate of the fence that ran around the entire projects. He continued walking through two alleys and when he reached the lower floors' balconies he began to climb. He climbed from one balcony to the next until he was on the fifth-floor balcony of his Aunt Ree's house. He knew she would probably not even be home. He opened the sliding glass door and went inside; the apartment was dark and quiet.

Ball knew that his Aunt Ree probably had gotten her heat and lights cut off and was probably staying with her friend Charly. He walked to the hall closet and opened the door. He tried his best to look around, once his eyes adapted to the dark. He grabbed a crate from the corner of the closet and stood on it. From there, he pushed open the hatch to the attic inside the closet. He placed the huge bag of guns up inside. When he replaced the hatch door and stepped down from the crate, he crossed to the front door. He unlocked it, opened it, and stepped out of the apartment. He relocked the front door and like a little kid, with a smile on his face, he happily raced down the steps.

As he walked through the building, the gangsters and females who stood out in the hallway just stared at him, as if they were seeing a ghost. He smiled, happy to be home. He came out of the building and saw a crowd of gangsters standing. They had on hoodies and ski masks that concealed their identities. When they saw him, they all stopped what they were doing and began speaking to him all at once.

"Damn, nigga, what's up," Little Keedie said, hugging him.

"Ain't shit," Ball said as he gave it up and hugged nearly every one of the men from the crowd.

"Where the hell is Lil Dirty Reds," Ball asked, looking over at Kaisha, who had grown into a beautiful

"Where the hell is Lil Dirty Reds," Ball asked, looking over at Kaisha, who had grown into a beautiful woman since the last time he saw her.

"He down at the ONE with your cousins Omar and Lean," Brasco said.

"Well I'm headed down to the ONE," Ball said.

He licked his lips at Kaisha who had leaned over in such a way that he got a good view of her voluptuous ass that had undoubtedly become the sexiest thing on her body.

He went over the fence and slid through another one of the nearly invisible holes on the other side of the projects. He passed through another crowd of men and women standing out on K Street Southeast, and then continued until he reached the black steel gates of the fence around 1000 Building. To keep from being seen he walked up towards the gas station and then cut through the alley between the two buildings directly across from 1000 Building.

As he passed the dumpster in the alley, he heard what

appeared to be someone moving around inside it. Without hesitating, he pulled the Heckler and Koch fully automatic Glock 90 assault rifle from under his leather coat and pointed it at the opening of the dumpster. He stood in silence, waiting for whoever was in the dumpster to come out. No less than ten seconds passed before he did.

"Nigga, what the hell you doing in the trashcan," he asked, startling Dirty Reds, who smiled when he saw Ball's face.

"Man, damn, I thought you was dead," Dirty Reds said. He pulled himself up and out of the dumpster, then dropped to the ground and hugged Ball.

"Damn, you smell dead," Ball told him, frowning up his face. "I know your dumb ass ain't still putting bodies in the damned dumpster."

"Well, that's better than leaving them lying dead where they fall," Reds said, smiling.

"Wasn't you supposed to be on the run," Ball

asked.

"I was just about to ask you that same question," Dirty Reds said.

He put his arm around Ball's waist and Ball said, smiling, "I am on the run."

He and Reds made it through the alley. "I'm on the run, too," Reds said.

"How the hell you gonna be on the run for murder in the same neighborhood where you killed two niggas, when the police are all over this bitch looking for you?"

"Hey, as long as I'm armed and dangerous, they gonna keep on looking past me, even when they see me."

"I know that's right," Ball said, laughing. "Hell, the police don't get paid enough money to get their dicks shot off."

"Man, my nigga! Your cousins got damned near every block from 18th and Deathrow to 17th and Compton sewed up. They even got them head hunters swole. Tank and black ass Rod rolling wit them."

"Yeah, you must be smoking that dust real heavy now." Ball said, chuckling out loud.

"Naw, young'un, real shit. Them Bama ass niggaz really gettin it. Slim, they are the inkwells source of ink." Ball couldn't believe his ears. He knew Dirty Reds wouldn't lie to him but he couldn't believe him for some reason.

"So where the hell are they," he asked.

Without saying a word, Dirty Reds pointed up towards the fifth floor of 1000 Building. Ball, who still was very excited to be home, looked up at the huge window in the middle of the fifth-floor hallway. The window had wire mesh over it so it was hard to see into it from outside. Whoever was inside the fifth-floor hallway looking down could see everything and everyone in the corridor of 1000 and as far up as the first building of Potomac Gardens.

"Nigga, what's up," Lean said, throwing his hand in the air.

He seemed to have appeared out of nowhere at the entrance of 1000 Building. Happy to see his cousin, Ball smiled as he walked to the entrance. He could see the Tourbillon Regulator watch on Lean's right wrist and he knew it had cost $274,000. He also knew what Dirty Reds had told him was true. Somehow, his cousins had come up and they were getting money all over the city.

Ball and Lean approached one another and embraced when they met. They held each other tightly for a moment, before either said a single word.

"I see you gained some weight down South," Lean joked.

Ball opened his coat and revealed the four hand guns that sat on his waist and the two assault rifles that hung from separate straps on his arms. He smiled, then said,

"Yeah, I guess you can say I gained a lot of weight."

Grabbing the Regulator, he said to Lean, "I see you finally stopped window shopping."

"Aw this ain't nothing," Lean said, smiling.

"Like hell it ain't nothing; that watch cost over a quarter million dollars and ain't no way that you about to tell me a pipe head sold it to you."

"Slim, you the one doing all the shining," Lean said. He grabbed the six-inch long platinum and diamond encrusted Tazmanian Devil medallion hanging from the diamond and platinum Cubin chain around Ball's neck.

"This here is block nigga jewels but that watch is every bit of Fortune 500 CEO type of shit," Ball said, looking down at the gold Rolex on his own right wrist.

"Come on," Lean said. "Let's go see Omar."

He put his arm around Ball and he, Ball, and Redhead Dirty Reds entered the building and headed towards the elevators. The doors were open. A man Ball had never seen before stood in the elevator holding an AK47.

"Who the hell is this nigga," Ball asked, grabbing hold of the HK that hung free from the strap on his shoulder.

"Man, chill, cousin," Lean said, entering the elevator car. "This Superstar; he work for me so he a part of the team."

Ball stepped in the elevator and moved to the back so he could keep his eyes on Superstar; he didn't trust him. Superstar pushed the button and the elevator doors closed, then the car rose to the fifth floor and stopped.

As the doors opened, Ball looked at Redhead and said, "That elevator used to be a pissy death trap that we used to only trick pipers in. Now ya'll riding it like it won't kill you."

Both Lean and Redhead busted out laughing getting off

the elevator. The three men turned left and headed down to the end of the hallway.

"Man, it took me more than a thousand dollars to get a dope fiend from around 751 to fix the elevator and clean all that piss out of it, but now it's good," Lean said.

"Yeah, right, and I still don't trust it," Ball said. When they reached the end of the hall, they made a right and walked around a corner where there was a single apartment door. Lean knocked twice and the door was immediately opened by another man Ball had never seen; he also had an assault rifle in hand.

Without saying a word, the three men entered the apartment and headed to the back. They passed the kitchen where naked women stood cooking up cocaine base. Ball stared at the women who all had very attractive bodies.

"Damn, you run a whore house and selling crack at the same time?"

Lean chuckled and said, "Naw, we don't trust anybody, so before the women are allowed to leave, we even check their vaginas and butt holes."

"And they go for that," Ball said, looking at Lean with a sign of disgust on his face.

"If they don't, some other anything ass broad will do. So yeah, the money they making is worth it to them and to us."

Lean tapped on the door in front of him and it was opened by another man holding an assault rifle. This time, the man was someone that Ball knew. He looked the man in the eyes but didn't say a word. Then he turned his attention to Omar, who stood in the middle of the room with his back to them. He was watching as seven boys, who appeared to be no more than ten, ran stacks of money through money machines while four teenaged girls bundled the money with rubber bands and placed it into nylon gym bags.

"O," Lean called out, causing Omar to turn.

The super serious look on his face disappeared when he saw Ball standing behind Lean. O went to Ball and the two embraced each other.

"Damn, cousin, you look good," Omar said, looking over Ball's attire.

"You look good, too," Ball said, smiling. He looked towards the kids still counting out money and said, "Man, ya'll niggas doing it real big."

"Yeah, we doing our thing but most of this shit you see is going to your brother."

"Who?"

"Yeah," Lean said, lowering his all black Versace glasses from his eyes.

"That night that they left us in L's baby mother's house, they had went to Moe's house and hit them real good. L has been eating off of that shit for the last eighteen months."

"So, where ya'll's take," asked Ball as he looked around the room.

Lean looked at Redhead and said, "We'll catch up with you later, Reds; and, o yeah, find somewhere besides the dumpsters around 1430, Kentucky Courts, the One, and the Gardens to put them stinking ass corpses."

"I just told the nigga that," Ball said, shaking his head.

Reds left the room and disappeared around the corner. The three of them then entered another part of the apartment, which had a window facing out over the whole 1000 projects.

"We gettin like five off each brick, but we moving close to two hundred bricks a day."

"So how much are ya'll sellin the bricks for?" Omar looked at Lean and then him at Ball.

"We sell each brick for $25000 and L expects us

315

to pay for all the security and all other expenses of the operation by ourselves."

"I see my big brother still is cruddy as hell. Ya'll made a freaking deal with the devil himself. I hope ya'll know that nigga won't hesitate to kill either of you if his money doesn't come out right, even if he is your big cousin."

"Man, what the hell are we supposed to do," Omar asked, raising his voice.

"I'll figure something out, but for now, try to just get him paid off and out of ya'll pockets as soon as possible."

"Does L even know that you back in the city," Lean asked. "I mean, he did tell you to stay out of the city until he told you to come back."

"Fuck L, he don't control me. Ain't no boss of this family; we all leaders."

"Well before we let you in on what we got

going on you are still gonna have to run this shit through L.

"Man, ya'll niggas still scared of L? I can't believe my fucking ears," Ball said, shaking his head. "I like how ya'll trying to be all loyal and shit but ya'll getting screwed in the process. If Ima risk my life for some money it's gonna be all mine, not L's or anybody else's. Ya'll got too many niggas eating off ya'll plate as well. Damn all this security. When you know the killers like I do, you can control the stick-up kids and the other shiesty individuals."

Ball continued, "Look, we Statens; we do our own killing. We gotta start acting like the men who brought us into existence. Charles Staten wasn't no sideshow Bob ass type of guy. If ya'll want, I'll show ya'll how to get rich, cause right now ya'll taking all the risk but ain't really getting shit out of the deal worth your while."

"It's a dragon with wings," Lean said, smiling.

"What the hell is a dragon with wings, some type

type of slang ya'll babes done come up with while I was gone?"

"Naw, it's a dragon with wings," Lean said, opening the curtain that had been draped over the window, allowing for the sunlight to shine into the room.

Ball walked to the window and looked out. He asked, "What exactly am I supposed to be looking for?"

"Look over there," O said, pointing to the church parking lot that was off Pennsylvania Avenue across from the Potomac Gardens train station.

Ball scanned the parking lot which was full of cars. Then his eyes stopped.

"Damn, that's two Maseratis parked over in that lot."

"That's you, dragon with wings," O said, smiling.

Ball rushed out of the apartment through the window and began climbing down the fire escape. He reached the first floor and jumped down the rest of the way. Once his feet hit the ground, he began running full speed up K Street. As he ran, the pipe heads and dope fiends who were out on the block continued to go about their business. They were selling their kids' Christmas gifts the day before they were supposed to give them to the kids. It was as if no one was running past them at all.

Halfway out of breath, Ball reached the parking lot but didn't stop until he was standing between the money green and the black Maseratis. He pushed the button on the black plastic key and the door lock of the black Maserati clicked. He smiled as he grabbed the handle, hopped inside the car, and closed the door behind him.

He heard a phone ringing, which caused him to open the center console next to his right arm. Inside was a stack of hundred-dollar bills that amounted to fifty thousand dollars, a cell phone, and a quarter ounce of blueberry Afghani skunk weed. Ball grabbed the phone. He looked down at the screen which read, "unrestricted." He pushed the green "send" button, placed the phone to his ear and said hello.

"Ay, don't go nowhere with that car," Lean said. "Come back and get the keys to the green one."

"Why?"

"Man, just don't take that car, that's why."

"It's too late. I'm gone," Ball said, starting the car and placing it in drive.

He drove out of the parking lot as Lean and Omar watched in horror.

"No bullshit cousin, don't take that car," Omar said on the phone to Ball.

"Tell me why," Ball said as he turned onto Pennsylvania Avenue."

"Man, look, I just remember that there's twenty-five bricks of cocaine in the trunk. I meant to drop it off at one of our other spots, but when I seen you I was so excited that I forgot to mention it to Lean," Omar said.

"Relax nigga, I'll be alright," Ball said. He ended the call and drove past the Library of Congress, smiling to himself. Things had just got more interesting. He picked up the phone and called Tiffany, who lived in Cleveland, Ohio. After five rings, Tiffany picked up her home phone.

"It's me," Ball said.

"Hey baby, I've been missing you," Tiffany said. From the sound of her voice, Ball could tell that she was smiling at that moment.

"Look, I'm about to come to Ohio in a flying dragon, so be ready to go out in, like, six hours," he said.

"Six hours? Boy, it takes at least thirteen hours to get from Washington, DC to Ohio."

"Not in what I'm driving. Look, Tiff, I know that

we have been best friends for at least nine years now, but it might be time to take our relationship to a new level."

"Boy, shut up. In my mind we have never been friends. I'm your wife and that's what I've always been. The only problem is that you don't know how to propose."

Ball laughed then said, "Look, seriously, I'm headed to Ohio right now in a Maserati so I'll be there in six hours, like I said. So just have your sexy little ass ready."

He ended the call. When he reached 14th Street, he jumped on the highway heading towards Arlington, Virginia. Ball didn't mind getting money in DC but he preferred to get it out of town. He'd be where no one knew him. There would be less chance of his name getting hot, especially when he already had to worry about a possible warrant for his arrest for that police officer's death; he was named as the number one suspect in that.

He turned up the music and Kingdawud's voice erupted through the speakers.

(Chorus)

Let's ride doing 165 in a 740I where the skinny niggas die

Nigga let's ride doing 165 in a 740I, can't be afraid to die

Nigga let's ride doing 205 in a 740I where the skinny niggas die

(Verse 1)

O you don't give a fuck about me

Then fuck you and your family

Professionally spittin poisonous profanity vanity

Hell god damn it to me tried to conquer my insanity

Never too insane to cop a plea, Wa Alaikum Salaam Ahki

Never a thing that I though you would see

These cowards ain't never gonna stop AG

When my hands holdin heat I'm poppin on easy never stopped on freeze

I got however much now these niggas need to get skied

I'm foreign to laws like I was born over seas

Gun smoke will be the last damned thing that you breath

AK will be the last damned thing that you see

Kill em all! Leaving nobody to blame it on me

Legendary, I'm famous homie

Nobody can understand me I'm lon-lay

Evidently, I'm starvin I'm bone-nay

Never ever trust the phony, they can't clone me

They can't blow me

None of ya'll niggas will ever know me

Debted in blood that's what you owe me

All by my lone-lay

Alllllll   byeeeeeeeee   my   lone layyyyyyyyyyyyyyy

I come creepin

Catch you chiefin

Leaven you bleed-nnnnnnnnnnnn

Leave you bleed-nnnnnnnnnnnnnnnnnnnnn

Let's ride doing 165 in a 749I where the skinny niggas die

The music had Ball in a trance, but instead of focusing on the picture that Kingdawud was painting, he

324

continued to think about Tiffany, his one and only true love.

Back in the fifth grade, while on a school fieldtrip, he had met Tiffany, who had also been on a fieldtrip with her school. Tiffany, who was from Ohio, couldn't travel to see Ball and he, who also had no form of transportation besides the Greyhound, was unable to see her as much as he would have liked. So instead of their relationship ever becoming physical, as they both would have liked, it turned them into best friends. Tiffany was the only person who knew everything about him, good and bad.

He cut the music down and picked up his phone. He dialed her number.

"So, you're here already," she asked, smiling, making Ball smile as well.

"Naw, not yet but I just wanted to know what you are wearing."

"Nothing. I'm completely naked with my hand

"Nothing. I'm completely naked with my hand between my thighs, waiting on you to talk dirty to me," she said, playing along with him. "Man, we not about to do this now because you might crash before you can make it here," she said, causing him to laugh.

"If I die it'll be your fault."

She giggled then said, "I love you Derrick. Make it here safe."

"I will," he said, then ended the call.

He changed CDs and pushed play. Again, Kingdawud's voice came through the speaker's crystal clear.

Verse 1
What rules who's playing a game?
The streets respected a lot of men until they started snitchin
If you couldn't handle the heat you shouldn't have been whippin up in the kitchen
To be gangsters we made a decision
Now we gotta stick wit it

326

Honor's the only thing that separates most men
from their women
Saying you can handle life, it's easy to say until
you get such a sentence
Now life as you knew it is over and you left with
the choices of bein
And everything that could have been in your life
is finished
All nightmares and bad dream plus horrible
visions
All it takes is one mistake and your whole life
can be finished
And we all make mistakes so every one of us is
slippin
Stop the beat, now listen
This gangster life is very vicious and prisons are
places that most of your loved ones won't visit
If you committed to a life of crime you better
understand that part of your business
It'll have you looking at niggas crazy in all of
your pictures
Don't take this personal but ain't no love
This here is all about the riches

327

Razor wire sitting over top of forty-five-foot fences

Got me wonderin should I keep dreamin or chase down my visions

Cause in my visions I see giants being demolished by midgets while trapped in hell for sinnin

What's the difference between a broke man and a genie who granted too many wishes?

Ten-year-old boys with nines, standin out in the trenches

They wish that they could go play

But their enemies and their hunger games won't go away

So it's to Allah we pray

Watchin as our homies all around us get blown away

Know that in this life they call a game everyone gets to go out in a blaze

Chapter 14

In an orange-colored A6 Quattro, Omar drove right out of the dealership lot and up Benning Road Southeast. Once he was past the Masjid on E Street, he made a right into Simple City.

Simple City had received its name from the *Washington Post,* that said it was the simplest place of all Washington DC to get killed, raped, or robbed in. Simple City was infested with abandoned apartment buildings that killers and drug dealers turned into life of the living dead's headquarters.

O drove his car into the City and made a left. He headed up a hill where four abandoned apartments sat apart from the rest of the decrepit buildings that made up the City. He backed into the building parking lot which allowed him to be able to see anyone and everything that came in or out of the neighborhood. He watched as men who all stood around in black leather coats and black jeans served dope fiends and crackheads without a care in the world about being seen by the police; they knew the cops wouldn't dare come into their neighborhood unless they came with all hands-on deck.

Omar looked at his watch and when he looked up, the green trash truck was entering the City right on time. He watched as it approached two dumpsters in the lot. When the truck stopped, two men who had been riding in the back of the truck jumped off and entered each of the six buildings. Each time they came out of a building they carried several huge black trash bags. To anyone who didn't know, the bags were full of money, not trash. The men tossed the bags into the back of the truck and then jumped in. The truck backed out of the alley, never even emptying the dumpsters.

The truck made a right out of the cul de sac. Once it had passed the buildings that Omar was watching; he drove to the main street and pulled out behind the truck. When the truck reached the top of the street, four black Yukons swerved in front of it, blocking it in. Several armed men wearing masks emerged and pointed their weapons at the two men and the driver of the trash truck. They stood, frozen.

"What the fuck is this about," asked the driver, whose name was Walter, as he rolled down his window.

"Be quiet before you lose your life over nothing," said the masked man closest to him.

He pointed his weapon in Walter's face so close that it was inches from touching his lip. Omar went around the trash truck and pulled up next to the front of it. He got out and walked to the driver's side door. He climbed in and asked, "What's up Walter?"

"You scared the hell out of me," Walter said, smiling.

"Yeah, I just wanted to let you know that you should never get too comfortable carrying around my money. I'm always having you watched and followed. Also, you guys seemed to be giving my money up without a fight, which is disappointing, to say the least."

Turning to face the man standing closest to him, Omar said, "Give them some weapons."

Another man got out of the Yukon closest to them; he had a black duffle bag. He crossed to Omar and handed him the bag. Omar took it and stuck it through the window of the truck to Walter.

"Protect my money better or you and your two sons will lose your lives next time."

O jumped from the truck and went back to his car. He got in as the men who had emerged from the trucks did the same. In seconds, they were gone, as if they had never been there in the first place.

Omar had trucks like that one all over the city and he couldn't chance having anyone else watching them, as he frequently took the pleasure in doing it himself.

Chapter 15

Lil Greg had built up an empire out of what had been no more than a nickel-and-dime weed strip. He sat on the hood of his candy apple red Corvette convertible with a disturbing look on his face. He watched angrily as young thugs stood around doing nothing. Some of them even sold pieces of wax or cut up peppermints as crack. All the cocaine connections that were accessible to him were all dead or locked up.

Before he had transformed Wellington Place into a million-dollar strip, it was a lonely place to be. Its gangsters were some of, if not the, cruddiest in the entire city of DC. It didn't take long for them to start killing off and robbing all of their connects. When Lil Greg came home, after a five-year stretch in Lorton Penitentiary, he found the hood right back in the same shape he had once taken it out of.

Across from him on the curb of the main street, there stood a large crowd of his men and other men who were just from the neighborhood. They were drinking 40-

ounce Steel Reserves and smoking weed, while laughing as hoodrats flaunted their bodies in front of them.

"Mean, man what the fuck is so funny," Lil Greg said.

He had been sipping from his own forty-ounce Steel Reserve. He tossed it over near the crowd. The bottle burst into pieces and some of the beer flew up on the crowd.

"Ya'll don't see this shit," he said, waving his hands around in the air as he looked over the entire neighborhood that was Wellington Park. "You muthafuckas think this shit is some type of joke, haw. We went from champagne to shit and from fucking models for free, to tricking hoodrats."

His right-hand man Buggs looked through the crowd as somebody started laughing. Lil Greg crossed the street to the man who had dared to laugh.

"You see something funny," he yelled in the face of the man who was twice his size.

"Man, fuck that, Ima eat no matter who I gotta rob, steal from, or kill," said the man whose name was Elmo.

"Yeah, that's everybody's mentality around here and I'm a start dropping you whore ass niggas like it ain't nothing," Lil Greg said, nearly spitting in Elmo's face.

"Lil Greg, you not the only nigga around here who got murders up under his belt. Shit, the whole time you was gone other niggas had to defend this hood, so you can't tell me shit when it comes to the Park!"

Lil Greg looked at Buggs then he looked back at Elmo, who never saw him pull the Glock 17 from his waist. Lil Greg pushed the barrel of the pistol into Elmo's chest and squeezed the trigger. The sound of the seven rapid shots caused the entire hood that had been running rampant to freeze. They all just watched as Elmo's body fell backwards to the ground. Lil Greg looked around the neighborhood with a mug on.

"Anybody else wanna test my forty," he asked, looking around at all the blank faces. "The fucking games stop right here. It ain't gonna be no more selling demos and jumping pipe heads for laughs. If Ima starve, ya'll gonna die."

Buggs walked through the crowd and grabbed Lil Greg's arm. "Look, let me holler at you."

Lil Greg walked across the grassy hill and into the alley with Buggs.

"So what's up? And this better be important, B."

"Man, look, we dealing with a bunch of wild bandits who can't be controlled, even by death. While you was down Lorton, I seen generations change and I know that these niggers are different than we were. I gotta plan that can make us rich, if you down with it."

"So what's the plan?"

"Look, I got a few lil broads on the other side of the bridge who told me that even the pipe heads around

Kentucky Courts be selling weight," Buggs said. "We can go take that whole hood over in no time and let these niggas round here help us or stay around here and starve."

"Kentucky Courts, haw," Lil Greg said, rubbing his chin.

"Yeah, nigga, Kentucky Courts."

"So who be around there?"

"Man, I don't know but it ain't no killers we respect so let's go ahead and move in. What do you think?"

A smile came over Lil Greg's face and he and Buggs left the alley and returned to his car.

Chapter 16

For some reason, Madball hadn't realized that Cleveland was just another ghetto on the face of the earth. When he entered the city, the first thing he saw was a massive but torn poster of Lebron James. It looked abandoned, like the rest of the city. He drove across the bridge and passed Cleveland's baseball stadium on his right. As he drove down the dark and dreary abandoned street, he wondered to himself why anyone would want to live inside of the city of Cleveland, Ohio.

He looked at the huge slave like houses on both sides of the street, looking as if they had been abandoned like the rest of the city. In silence, he rode, looking at the poorly designed streets that made up Cleveland. Every street he passed was empty. Even the stores he passed were either closed or appeared to him as if they should have been. It wasn't until he reached Superior Avenue that he saw people, and lots of them.

What appeared to be more than a thousand people stood packed on Superior Avenue, which was a very long road. It reminded him of Second and P weed strip in Southwest DC. A few young boys placed their hands up to their mouths as if they were smoking. That was the signal to him that they were selling weed. He smiled. No sooner had he passed Superior Avenue than Cleveland turned back into a ghost town. As he drove down the street, he looked for more people, but didn't see a soul.

He drove up under a bridge and through a traffic light that seemed out of place. That's when he saw a huge green sign that read, *Welcome to East Cleveland.* He looked up at the light at the street sign and saw it was Euclid Street. To his right, he spotted a club with a long line of people standing out in front. On the opposite side of the street was another club with a line longer than the first.

"Nowhere got action," he said, smiling and looking over at what appeared to be a pack of hookers who looked low budget.

He stared at signs on the side of the buildings, *$250 per month for our five-bedroom apartments,* and he was shocked. Even a hole in the wall in DC had higher rent

339

than $250. He came up to a gas station where two men stood in the parking lot trying to sell t-shirts and CDs. He pulled up in front of the store and got out, and then he walked to the doors of the store.

"Ay, man, nice car," one of the boys said, smiling at him.

"Thanks. Here goes a hundred dollars for ya'll to split," he said.

He reached into his pocket and took out a knot of money.

"Thanks, man," the other two boys said, quickly gathering around him.

He gave them each a fifty-dollar bill and said, "That's for ya'll to watch my car and this is for ya'll to split."

He handed the oldest of the boys a hundred-dollar bill. The boys looked at the money as if they had never seen money before. Ball pushed open the glass door and entered the store. He grabbed a small blue cooler, some Hydroxyzine and a bottle of Isotol, and then walked to the counter.

"Do you need anything else," the cashier asked, smiling at him.

She was an old while woman who appeared to be missing all of her front teeth. She rang up the items and placed them in a paper bag.

"Two packs of Backwoods cigars in the silver pack," Ball said.

He pulled three hundred dollar bills off the knot of money in his hand. The cashier dropped the two bags of cigars into his bag. He handed her the money and said, "Keep whatever change that's left."

"Thank you kindly," the cashier said.

She smiled again and watched him walk towards the front door and leave. He returned to his car and set the bag on the backseat. He took out the Hydroxyzine and read the back of the label, and then he tossed the bottle on the seat behind him. He started the car, left the parking lot, and turned again onto Euclid Street. Once there, he grabbed his phone from the passenger seat and dialed Tiffany's number.

She was in the bathroom getting ready to take a bath, but took off running when she heard the phone ringing. She reached her room and ran to jump on the bed, then reached over to the window seat where the phone was.

"Hello," she said, smiling. "Boy just keep coming, you're almost here. I'm in my bra and panties so let me finish getting ready for you."

"Tell me what you just said about me being almost there and to keep coming when I'm between your thighs tonight," he said, smiling, as well.

He tried to imagine her lying half naked on the bed with the phone in her hand.

"Shut up, boy. I gotta go because it's cold in this room and my nipples are starting to get hard," she said.

She smiled and hung up the phone, knowing she was teasing him.

After tossing the phone on the bed, Tiffany stood and looked in her mirror at her thighs and booty. *Wow, he's gonna fall in love,* she said to herself. She watched her booty shake as she went to the door. With every step, she admired how the pink and blue silk panties were full with her luscious cheeks that were free of any blemish. She ran down the hallway and back to the bathroom. She closed the door and finished getting undressed. She stepped out of her underwear and stepped into the warm water that waited for her in the tub.

She took her time and sat down in the water until her whole body was submerged. Then she took a sponge and bottle of Creamy Heaven body wash and began washing her feet. She worked her way up her thighs and once she reached the diamond between her legs, she gently caressed and cleansed her kitty. She touched her clitoris and began to feel a tingle shooting up her thighs and back, thinking of Derrick making love to her.

Oh my god, she said to herself, pulling her hands away. She continued washing her flat midsection and her breasts, then her neck. After washing her face, she rinsed the soap off her body and stood up. She grabbed a towel and stepped out of the tub; the water ran down her body between her thighs. She quickly dried herself and began admiring herself again in the full-length mirror on the wall across from her. *How could a man not want that,* she thought to herself, as she looked over every inch of her five-foot, six-inch flawless frame that was very well put together.

When her eyes reached the bottom of her stomach, she stared at the star-shaped birthmark over top of her silky black pubic hair adorning her diamond. She took hold of her breasts and lifted them, wondering if he would like them. She turned and looked at her voluptuous booty, spreading her thighs. She palmed her left cheek and wondered if he would believe that she was soft. *Whatever I am, I'm yours,* she said, smiling and looking at her tiny feet.

She crossed to the sink and opened the cabinet above it. She looked at the bottles of body oils, searching for the one she thought would impress Derrick the most. She chose Wet Flowers and closed the cabinet. She turned back to the tub and put one of her legs up on the edge. Spreading her thighs, she began massaging the oil into her thighs and between her legs. She oiled her feet and then caressed her juicy cheeks. She applied oil to her arms and hands, as well.

Then she squeezed more of the Wet Flowers into her palms and rubbed them together so the oil spread evenly. She began to caress her breasts, then her neck. She took her purple and pink Victoria's Secret panties off the toilet seat and slipped into them. They hugged her snuggly. When she turned to look at herself in the mirror, she laughed. Her booty was so big that the fabric of the panties nearly disappeared. She turned to look back down to her kitty. The fabric made her treasure box look like the diamond it was. She quickly slipped on her bra and then stepped into the purple and pink Fendi jeans that had been on the toilet seat.

She heard the horn blowing and moved faster. She pulled the jeans up over her booty, even though she had a hard time making them fit and fastening them. She took her pink, glittered Fendi body shirt and pulled it on over hear head. She tucked the bottom into her jeans. She slid the Versace black stilettos on and quickly left the bathroom.

She kept going down the hallway to the front door. She stepped on the first step of the stairs and walked down into the living room. When she reached the front door, what she saw made her hesitate about going out to the porch, but she did anyway. When the screen door opened, her grandmother, who was standing at the gate talking to Derrick, turned and looked at her.

"So, what time are you bringing her back," she asked Derrick, looking once more at Tiffany.

"Ma, Ma, I'll be ok," she said, walking to the gate where Derrick stood, smiling from ear to ear.

He scanned her entire body and, once he looked up the second time, his eyes stopped and rested on the voluptuous diamond between her legs. He admired how the jeans tore away at her, as if struggling with her diamond for space. Her entire body tingled as he stared at her and she tried to be conservative in front of her grandmother. She could not restrain herself any longer. She ran to him and jumped into his arms. He held her and smiled, saying,

"You smell so good." He tried to keep himself from getting hard from the heat of her vagina against his midsection.

"Good choice of color," he said, carrying her to the Maserati. He set her down on the hood, and then pulled a tiny black box from the right pocket of his jacket.

"What is it," she asked, smiling as he handed it to her. She opened it without hesitation and what she saw inside nearly made her cry.

"Don't cry," he said, kissing her face as she lowered her head. "Do you like it," he asked, taking hold of her head.

"I love it," she said, looking up at him with tears in her eyes."

He removed the pink gold Haptajodel and Cartier wrist watch from the little box and placed it on her wrist. Then he kissed her. She hugged his neck and wept against his chest. He held her tightly to him.

"Come on, let's go," he said, lifting her down from the hood.

He walked her to the passenger side door, opened it for her, and when she looked inside, she blushed and covered her mouth.

"I see you haven't forgotten my favorite color," she said, picking up the two-dozen pink and yellow long-stemmed roses.

Before she sat down, she took off her shoes to keep from stepping on the pink and yellow rose petals he had spread all over the floor. She stepped inside the car and rested her bare feet on the soft, silky petals. Ball closed her door and went around to the other side of the car. He jumped in. Closing the door, he looked behind him to say good bye to Tiffany's grandmother, who was still standing on the porch watching them. She waved good bye to them. Ball shifted to drive and pulled away from the curb and drove down the street.

"So are you going to stay with me all night," he asked, looking at Tiffany.

She nodded her head yes.

"Well look, Ima get the room in the Ritz Carlton next to the stadium for, like, four days. Can you stay with me that long?"

"Yes," she said, batting her huge green eyes at him and running her hands between her thighs. "If I'm so beautiful to you, what stopped you from coming to get me all those years, or coming down here to be with me," she asked, looking away from him.

He didn't know how to answer her, so he didn't, but said, "Look, Tiff, I need your help on something. I got twenty-five kilos of cocaine that Ima try to sell before I leave here. If I can sell them for more than what they go for in DC, you and I can make some money."

She remained silent, still disturbed at his not answering her question.

"Come on, Tiff, this is important to me," he said, placing his hand on her neck.

"Am I important to you," she asked, looking at him with a tear in her eye.

"You already know you are," he said, grabbing her hand and kissing it."

"Well prove it then," she said looking deep into his eyes.

"Tiff listen, please. I need you to help me do this for us. If everything goes right, I'll give you $25,000."

"You just don't know what to say to me; you been broke as long as we've known each other, so you know it's not the money I want."

"So what do you want," he asked, as he made a right and pulled up alongside the Ritz.

"You," she said, as a tear rolled down her right cheek.

"Tiff, please don't do this right now. WE gonna be together forever and you know that."

"Give me the phone," she said, holding out her hand.

She put the pone to her ear and listened as it rang. On the fourth ring, her cousin J-Diggs answered. "Brother, this is your baby sis. My boyfriend Derrick from DC just came down and he has twenty-five virgin white girls with him. He wanna know if you or your friends would be interested in dating outside of ya'll's race."

Ball just stared at her in amazement as she listened to whatever J-Diggs was saying. She looked at him and asked, "Are they old enough, because him and his homies say they ain't no pedophiles."

"Tell him they can't get no younger than thirty-two."

"He said they gonna have to be no older than thirty for him to take them out," she told Ball.

"Well they thirty then," Ball said, looking at the valet who stood at Tiffany's door. "Tell him to meet us around 11 am tomorrow in the mall and to bring his paper cause these broads wanna go shopping."

"He said he's bringing a model scout with him and if his model scout approves of them, then he might take them shopping," Tiff told Ball.

"Ok brother, I'll talk to you later," she said, then ended the call.

Ball grabbed the lever under his seat, popping the trunk. Then he opened his door and stepped out of the car. He walked to the trunk. The valet opened the door for Tiffany; he admired her beauty as he breathed in her perfume. Ball pulled the two rolling Louis Viton suitcases out of the trunk and walked to the front of the Ritz, where Tiffany was waiting for him.

"Damn, you don't see me standing here?" He mugging on the valet, who couldn't seem to stop looking at Tiffany.

The man turned and looked away as another valet came outside.

"The key is in the armrest," Ball told him. "So all you have to do is place your thumb on the key slot to start it."

He placed his arm around Tiffany's thin waist and they entered the hotel and walked to the Concierge's desk.

"Here, pay for this room," Ball said, handing Tiffany a stack of hundred dollar bills he had pulled out of his pocket.

The stack of money was neatly wrapped, as if it had just come off the press. She took the money and quickly placed it in her pocket, which could barely hold anything, let alone two thousand dollars in hundred-dollar bills. She pulled a grey debit card from the back pocket of her jeans and passed it to the woman behind the counter.

"Yes, I would like a room on the top floor and please make damn sure it is facing the Ohio River on the stadium side."

"Yes ma'am," the woman said, typing some information into the computer in front of her.

"Also, please make sure that we have a bar and plenty of Do Not Disturb signs," Tiff said, looking at Ball with a smile on her face.

He blushed while holding the elevator door open as he waited for her.

"That will be $3,200, miss," the woman said, looking up from her computer at Tiffany.

Tiffany handed the woman her card and, as she scanned it, Tiffany moved her hips and legs in a way that allowed Derrick to see the diamond in between her legs pulling at the fabric of her jeans. He became hard instantly and she knew it. She licked her lips and pretended not to see him staring at her. She turned back around and stood on tiptoe, making her butt move slightly. He continued to stare at her as his blood rushed to his groin.

"Ok, there you are," the woman said, handing the debit card to Tiffany.

"Thank you," Tiffany said, placing the card back in her pocket.

She walked towards Derrick in the sexiest walk she could muster up. She passed him and entered the empty elevator car; he followed her and the doors closed behind him. He let go of the luggage and scooped her up into his arms. She wrapped her luscious thighs around him. They began kissing passionately, fondling each other's bodies. He reached under her leg and palmed her ass as she moaned from the strength and passion of his caress. She took hold of his shirt and lifted it over his head, and then she began kissing his chest. She grabbed the front of his pants, and as she undid his belt and reached her hands down to take hold of his hard, the elevator doors opened.

An older couple stood facing the elevator, with a little girl who seemed to be their granddaughter. They all stared in shock, which made Tiffany smile. She grabbed Derick's hand and he let her down then took hold of the luggage. Without hesitation, they rushed out of the elevator and down the hallway to their suite.

Once inside, they dropped everything and went at it again. This time, he lifted her by palming her ass and she wrapped her thighs around him and began to undo her pants. He reached the bed and laid her down gently, then climbed over top of her.

As she tugged to take his pants down, she did, and he tried his best to take hers down as well. Before long, their clothes were flying in every direction all over the room. When they both were finally naked, they paused for a moment and just stared at each other.

Her body was beautiful in every way; there was not a mark on her perfect caramel brown mocha skin. He kissed her neck as their fingers interlocked. He worked his way down her body, kissing her ever so gently. When he reached her belly button, he admired the circle-shaped moles she had above her pussy hairs. He continued kissing his way down her body and when he reached her diamond, which smelled like wet flowers and heavenly cream, he parted her lips and began to taste her, ever so gently. She closed her eyes and began to moan. She palmed his head and he caressed every inch of her with his tongue and lips. As she moaned, she called his name gently. He used his tongue to caress the pink inside of her. He felt her entire body shaking and before long she began to gush forth into his mouth, only causing him to suck her more passionately than before.

As she orgasmed, she looked down at him, wanting him inside of her. She grabbed his head and pulled at him. He began to rise. He kissed his way back up to her face and they began to kiss passionately. She took hold of his hard staff and caressed her outer moisture with it. She placed his hand on her tiny hole and he began to push. Although he continued to push, he was unable to enter her. He looked into her eyes and saw that she was frightened.

"Are you ok," he asked as he stopped trying to enter her.

"Yes, I'm ok," she said, sounding like she was in pain.

"Look, we don't have to do this if you don't want to."

She lowered her head, causing him to take her hand into his hand. He touched her face with his free hand and lifted her head.

"Look at me," he said. She looked at him and he could see that she was afraid.

"Are you a virgin," he asked, as he frowned up his face. Without answering him, she just nodded her head to say yes.

"Look, Tiffany, we don't have to do this if you don't want to."

"No, it's okay. All my life I waited for this moment with you. I used to dream about us being together like this," she said.

She opened her wet warm lips as she had spread her legs for him. He looked down at her and instantly became hard again. He took hold of himself and placed the head of his shaft between her lips. They were so soft that he almost came with the first touch. He moved her hand, interlocking her fingers inside of his, causing her tight vagina walls to collapse around him.

He found her hole and pushed and pushed and pushed, as she bit at his neck. After several tries, he finally entered her. Slowly, he began to push deeper until he was completely inside of her. He reached around and palmed her luscious, soft, warm ass and slid out of her slowly. He repeated this several times, until he found himself having to release. He began kissing her. Just as he came, she did, as well. They both lay still, holding each other while listening to the racing rhythm of each other's heart. As he lay in her arms, she caressed his back with her soft hands; he became hard again inside her.

"Do you wanna do it again," he asked.

"Yes," she said, spreading her thighs for him, as wide apart as she was able. He pulled himself out of her and turned her over. He got on top of her; she lay flat on her stomach, looking into the mirror on the dresser. She watched him spread her cheeks apart and enter her again. She instantly began to orgasm.

He was gentler than he had been the first time. He kissed her back and neck while telling her he loved her and asking if she was ok. For the first time in his life, he was making love to a woman he truly loved and who truly loved him back.

After they both came again for the third time, he looked down at her and just smiled. He scooped her up into his arms and held her as long as she would let him. Around midnight, they both woke up in each other's arms. She looked at him and smiled. He pulled himself out of her and walked across the room and out to the balcony, in the frigid air. Standing naked, he looked up at the moon then he looked down at the river and watched the moon's reflection make love to the waves. She walked out onto the balcony behind him and wrapped her arms around his waist. She rested her face against his back, making him smile. At that moment, he felt complete.

"Do you really love me," she asked, caressing his chest.

"I've always loved you, Tiffany," he said, turning to face her.

"So take me with you," she said, tears welling in her eyes.

"Look, tonight has been the happiest night of my life. When I'm with you I feel completely safe, but I don't always feel that you are safe with me," Ball said.

"Don't say that," she said, crying and placing her head against his chest.

He inhaled, and then exhaled deeply holding her tight to him. He knew that he had hurt a lot of men and that one day all the bad that he had done would come back to haunt him. He knew that one day, the family of somebody he had killed would want their lick back. He feared that if she was near him when it happened, she would be hurt because of him. He believed he would never be able to live with that.

"Let's just share tonight and enjoy it, as if it's our last night on earth together," he said, then kissed her forehead. "Now come on, let's get our naked butts inside before we both catch a cold and not be able to spend another healthy minute together.

She smiled as he took her hand. They left the balcony and went back into their room. Once inside, she went to the phone, dialed out, and ordered room service.

As she told the concierge what she wanted, Ball went to his luggage. He took hold of both suitcases and dragged them into the bathroom. He closed the door behind him. He cut the water on in the tub and cut on the hot water in the sink, as well. He fumbled around in the cabinets below the sink until he found a dryer. He plugged it in and set it next to the closet.

He removed the tiny cooler he bought and took out the hydroxyzine. He placed a little water in the bathroom trash can then poured the entire bottle of the hydroxyzine into it. He mixed it around with his hands until it turned doughy, and then he grabbed a roll of trash bags from under the sink. He began opening them, one by one, spreading them across the entire floor. Once the floor was covered with the bags, he unzipped the suitcase and began taking out the bricks of compressed powder cocaine and laying them on the floor too.

With a sharp knife, Ball cut open the packages of cocaine and poured them into a plastic trash bag he had tripled up. He laid the trash bag at his feet and began dumping the powder cocaine out of the packages into the bag. Once he had emptied all twenty-five of the bricks, he used the bottom of the trash can to crush the hard pieces until all of the white substance was powdery smooth.

He held the bag open carefully and took hold of the trash can. Then he began pouring the water mixed with hydroxyzine into the bag. Once he had poured all the mixture into the bag, he tied the top of the bag and began mashing the mixture with the powder cocaine. He repeated this motion for several minutes until he was satisfied the mixture was thoroughly done.

He took one of the suitcases and pulled out the digital scale. He placed the cooler on top of the scale and zeroed out its weight. Then he untied the trash bag, and using his hand, began scooping out the cocaine mixture. He carefully watched the scale and when its weight reached 1000 grams, he took the cooler off the scale and pressed down the cocaine mixture until it was compressed to the size of the cooler.

Next, he grabbed the dryer, turned it on, and pointed it down at the cooler. After five minutes of applying hot air, he turned off the dryer and set it aside. He grabbed the side of the bag, lifting the compressed brick of cocaine out of the cooler. He repeated this process over and over until he had thirty 1000-gram bricks lined up neatly across the bathroom floor. He turned the heat on in the bathroom, then he washed his hands in the sink. When his hands were completely clean, he opened the bathroom door, stepped out, and closed the door behind him.

Tiffany, now wearing a burgundy robe, was standing at the door, paying the waiter for the food he had delivered. She turned and smiled at the sight of Derrick behind her.

"Thank you," she said, taking her debit card and the receipt from the waiter. She closed the door and smiled again as she approached Derrick. She jumped into his arms again and began kissing him. As soon as she placed her hands around his neck, she began to feel him getting hard.

"So, I guess you want dessert first," she said, smiling.

H opened her robe revealing here huge well-rounded breasts with firm pinkish-brown nipples protruding. He looked at her thighs and the tiny patch of fur that adorned her diamond, and that made him lick his lips. She allowed the robe to fall to the floor as he palmed her ass and felt the heat from her treasure chest warming his fingers. He felt his fingers becoming wet as her juices flowed forth. While kissing her lips passionately, he carried her to the second bed in the room, but before he could lay her down, she pushed him back on the bed and got on top of him.

As his shaft stood erect, she took hold of it and began caressing it with her hands. She lifted herself up, allowing him to see the pure pink inside of here, and then she gently placed herself down on him. As he entered her, she tried not to scream, but the pain was overwhelming. She could feel every inch of him as he entered deeper and deeper, making it hard for her to breathe at first. He pulled her down to him and began kissing her. As they kissed, she moved herself up and down on him until he exploded inside her.

He didn't want to stop, because he knew that she hadn't reached her climax, so he closed his eyes and forced himself to stay hard. He felt so good, being inside her; her insides felt so good to him, that he didn't want to be finished making love to her. He caressed her soft skin with his hands and as he did so, he began to grow hard again. He pulled her down on top of him and flipped her over, without taking himself out of her. He palmed her left thigh with his hand while using his right hand to push her legs farther apart. He began to ram himself in and out of her as she moaned and screamed, begging for him to make her cum. Again, he flipped her over to her back and continued to thrust in and out of her, until they both came, falling to sleep in each other's arms.

Chapter 17

J-Digg, carrying a small leather briefcase, looked at his watch as he entered the lobby of the Ritz Carlton and continued walking until he reached the mall at the bottom of the hotel. He reached into his pocket, pulled out his phone and called Ball. The phone rang twelve times without an answer. He began to leave, but he knew they must be in the shower or still asleep. He walked to the K-Jewelers, where he saw a very pretty, tall, dark-skinned woman with long, silky hair, strolling the floor. He cleared his throat and entered the store, heading straight towards the woman.

"May I help you," she asked, smiling.

"You already have," he said, looking her up and down and making her blush.

"Are you looking for anything in particular?" He licked his lips, looked her straight in the eyes and said,

"You."

She put her hands on her hips and looked around to make sure none of her co-workers were watching them. Then she said,

"Thank you."

"So can I take you out to eat," he asked as he looked down at the black leather pumps she was wearing.

"I don't even know your name," she said.

"I'll just call you 'Gorgeous,' and you can call me whatever you want and whenever you want." She blushed again and walked behind the jewelry case, where she worked. He slowly followed her.

"You wouldn't have to work so hard if I was your man," he said, looking at her well-manicured nails. "So what is your commission on each sale?"

"I get 2% on whatever jewelry we sell, so it's really nothing."

He looked into the glass case beneath his hands and scanned the watches spread out on the shelves below. His eyes rested on a Urwerk UR-2025, which had a price tag of $120,000.

"Do you have that in blue steel," he asked looking up into her eyes.

"Yes, but the blue steel is more expensive. Instead of $170,000 you'd be spending close to three hundred thousand.

"That's it," he said, and grabbed her hand, making her look around.

"Here, put it on my Visa black card and make sure that you get yourself that diamond tennis bracelet," he said, pointing to a Cartier princess cut platinum bracelet that held five carats of canary diamonds.

She took his card to the cash register and scanned it, and then she rang up both items. She handed back his card. She printed out the receipt and picked up a pen near the register. She wrote down her house phone, cell phone, work phone, mother's phone, and her address, then passed the receipt to him.

"Well, I guess I will be taking you out tonight."

"What's wrong with taking me out right now," she asked, smiling at him.

"You gotta work and I gotta work, so we'll catch up with each other once we are both off," he said.

Smiling, she said, "Well, if you wanna wait for tonight, then that's cool, but I just made a year's worth of commission, so I can take off right now, if you'd like."

He smiled then lowered his Cartier shades so she could see his eyes.

Chapter 18

Viola Rashawn Burgess was one of the sexiest and most successful women in the metropolitan area, but her downfall was her attraction to bad boys. Big Bruce, her baby father of 10 years, was known throughout DC for selling tons of cocaine. Everybody in DC, Maryland, and Virginia believed that Viola was helping Bruce launder all of the money he made through her twelve beauty shops, but they had no way to prove it.

"There her sexy ass go right there," Bookie said as she got out of the money green C155 she had driven.

He watched her as she straightened her beige knee length Versace skirt that matched her beaver skin Ferragamo pumps.

"Man, I wanna piece of that," Pops said, licking his lips.

As she walked towards the front of the store, they all admired how her huge, soft booty caressed every inch of the back of her skirt, making it seem alive.

"Man, look, ya'll can get the money but Ima get a piece of Mrs. Viola," Bookie said.

He watched her closely as she entered the shop, letting the door close behind her.

"Do what you want but if we don't get that money, Lil Greg is gonna be mad as hell. He said his inside source's girl saw her put the money in the safe under the sink last night."

"Whose money is it anyway," Pops asked.

"Ours," Buggs said, turning around in his seat to look at Pop.

"Naw nigga, for real, who do we gotta worry about coming after us if everything goes wrong,"

"Bruce's nephew Lean and Omar from around the Gardens. They both some skirts so they ain't gonna be coming after nobody. Them Bama ass niggas scared of their own damned shadows," said Buggs, making Pops and Bookie laugh.

"Yeah, once I have my way with Mrs. Viola, their Big Bruce is gonna be after me and I don't give a damn because a woman like that is worth having to kill over," Bugg said, smiling.

He opened his door and said, "Come on, ya'll, let's go.

With a fifteen-shot Ruger in his hand he crossed the street and headed around to the back of the shop. Both Bookie and Pops went to the front door and began knocking. They waited, but Mrs. Viola didn't come to answer the door. Pops began banging on the door and then he heard Mrs. Viola's voice over the speaker next to him.

"We are not open yet, so come back in two hours," she said.

"Shit," he said, stomping his foot on the pavement. "Come on let's head around back," he said, turning to head around to the back of the shop.

"Nigga," Bookie said. "Stay here or come through the front."

"Fuck Buggs and fuck you too. I'm going around back so either you coming or not?"

When they were halfway around toward the back of the shop, they heard a huge blast sounding just like a gun shot. The sound rang out four times then it stopped.

"Shit, come on," Bookie said, running to the back door.

When they reached it, it was already open. Buggs had shot off the lock and stormed inside.

"Come on, we gotta get in there," Bookie said as he entered the shop.

When Viola saw Buggs shooting at her door, she ran to her office. Hearing all the shots, she stopped, panicked. When she saw him enter the shop, she ran towards the steps, but he ran after her. She made it to the top of the steps with him right on her heels. Just as he reached out to grab her, he heard the back door open. He stopped in his tracks and she made it to her office, where she closed and locked the door behind her and tried to catch her breath.

Buggs began to smile from ear to ear. He took the combination for the safe that Lean's girlfriend had given him, and entered the code. The door to the safe soon opened and his smile grew bigger. He took a black nylon gym bag from his pocket, opened it, and began placing the bricks of cocaine from the safe into the bag.

Mrs. Viola, who knew if she called the police that she would also be arrested, reached under her desk and grabbed the twelve-gauge Franchi Spa that was loaded with over fourteen rounds. She unlocked the door and left her office. With the huge gun in her hands, she went down the stairs; Bookie and Pops, who were trashing her shop, never even saw her sneak up on them. She raised the Franchi Spa, pointed it in their direction, and fired. The blast from the buck shot rounds tore through Bookie's chest and sliced Pop's back wide open. She then fired five shots at once and the blood from their bodies and their burning flesh spattered the walls of her shop. Then she spun around and fired at Buggs, but he dove to the floor, clutching the gym bag in his right hand.

Buggs had to let go of the bag to grab his gun; he didn't want to do that, especially after seeing that several kilos of cocaine and nearly all of the cash he had put in the bag fall out when he hit the floor. He reached for his weapon that was at the small of his back, but he didn't dare raise his head, making it an easy target for the Franchi.

"Shit," he said, as she fired at the sink above his head.

She hit one of the plumbing lines and water sprayed all over him. He looked at the A Kick 47 lying on the floor by the safe, where he had left it. He wanted to grab it but knew that if he did he would instantly be chopped apart by the Franchi Spa Mrs. Viola seemed to keep firing. He tried counting her shots but he knew that a Franchi Spa could hold up to fifty shots. He did what he thought was the best thing to do. He raised his weapon and fired it in the air, and Mrs. Viola ducked behind one of the couches. When she did, Buggs took off running for the back door. He didn't stop until he was back inside the van and was pulling away from the curb.

Chapter 19

At exactly 11:15 am, Tiffany woke to the sound of Derrick's phone vibrating across the nightstand next to her. She reached over and grabbed the phone, saying,

"Hello. Hold on just a second."

She grabbed Derrick's arm and shook him but he didn't wake up, so she grabbed his penis, which was rock hard. He opened his eyes with a smile on his face.

"For a minute, I thought I was dreaming," he said, looking into her eyes.

"I'll always be right next to you, if you like," she said, smiling and handing him the phone.

"Who is this," he said. "Yeah, what's up Dutch." Ball listened as Dutch told him about his cousin Whitey, from around 21st and Maryland Avenue, speaking to Buggs. And Buggs was bragging about how he, Pops and Bookie had robbed Lean and Omar for more than sixteen bricks of uncut cocaine.

"Alright, Amir," Ball said, calling Dutch by his Muslim attribute. "I'll handle it soon as I get back to DC. I appreciate you calling," he said and ended the call.

He looked at the screen on his phone and said, "Shit," then he jumped out of bed. "Come on, we gotta go. Your cousin called me five times."

"All that sex made me tired," Tiffany said. She went into the bathroom and turned on the shower. She dropped her robe and stepped in the tub. Water ran down her body and between her luscious thighs. When Ball walked in and saw how the water ran down her body, he immediately wanted her. He stepped into the tub behind her and bent her over.

He could feel the heat from her vagina, as if it were all over him. Her moist lips seemed to beckon him to enter them, so he caressed her flower with his hand, spreading her legs apart with his fingers. Then he slid himself into her. She was so wet and warm inside, so wet and gushing, that after five strokes he began to cum.

"Finished already," she said, looking back at him with her huge innocent eyes.

He grew hard again. He wanted to finish what he had started but he didn't want J-Diggs, who he figures was already mad as hell, to leave.

"You're so warm and wet that I couldn't help it," he said, pulling himself out of her. He picked up a sponge and began cleaning between her legs.

"You make me feel like a little girl when you do that," she said, smiling.

As he lathered her with soap and cleansed and caressed her whole body, she took a soapy washrag and did the same to him. They both rinsed off and got out of the shower, then hurried and got dressed.

In less than ten minutes, Ball had tossed all the kilos into the luggage and was walking out the door right behind

Tiffany. He admired the way her hips swung as she walked. Everything about her was sexy. Every time he looked at her, he wanted to strip her naked and make love to her.

They entered the elevator and rode down to the bottom floor where the mall was.

"Come on, I'm sure I know where he might be," she said, taking Derrick's hand.

They crossed the lobby and entered the very loud and crowded mall.

"How are you gonna find him with these people in here," he said.

He reached in his pocket for his phone but he had left it on the bed.

"Damn, I forgot my phone."

"I said don't worry," she said.

Tiffany pulled Derrick down the aisles, past the huge crowd that crossed back and forth by them in every direction. Just as they reached the front of K Jewelers, J-Diggs was exiting the store.

"There you are," Tiffany said, hugging her cousin.

"What's up baby girl," he said, kissing her forehead.

"This is my man Derrick who I told you about," she said, looking at Ball.

He stuck out his hand to shake J-Diggs' hand, but J-Diggs just mugged on him telling Tiffany to come on. They made their way to the escalator and stepped on, taking it down to the food court which was even more crowded than the rest of the mall.

"Here, Tiff, go get us something to eat." J-Diggs handed her three crisp hundred-dollar bills. Without question, she worked her way from the two men towards the Roasted Caribbean chicken grill.

"Have a seat," J-Diggs said, pointing to the table. They sat across from one another.

"Sorry I'm late," Ball said.

J-Diggs raised his hand to silence him, saying, "What you did is something that gets men life sentences on a humbug. While I was sitting around waiting on you to get out of some pussy, I could have been robbed or apprehended by the police and it would have been your fault."

He removed the glasses from his eyes and set them down on the table in front of him. Then he leaned across it so he was closer to Ball.

"You'll lose a lot of money chasing your dick, but you'll never lose a woman chasing money, that I guarantee you," he said.

He put his right-hand palm down on the table; a small black leather suitcase was cuffed to his hand.

"So where is your stuff?"

384

"Right here," Ball said, sliding one of the suitcases beside J-Diggs' leg.

J-Diggs unzipped the bag and reached inside of it as Ball looked around to see if they were being watched. J-Diggs opened the case he had set on the table and removed a tiny valve of liquid.

"You gonna do that right here," Ball asked nervously.

"Why not," J-Diggs said, opening the vial.

"So where's your tester? Is he coming?" Ball asked. He continued to look around the food court.

"When you act nervous, people tend to think you got something to hide. And that's when they start watching your moves, so relax," J-Digg said. He raised back up from the suitcase. He took the little vial and shook it.

"So you're not gonna get somebody to test this shit to see if it's proper," Ball asked.

With a disturbed look on his face, J-Diggs looked Ball straight in the eyes and said, "You didn't really think I was gonna bring some geekin ass fiend off the block to test over four million dollars' worth of coke for me, did you?"

He placed the vial on the table in front of him. He looked at the color of the liquid which was light blue, and then he slid the briefcase from beside his foot to Ball.

"This is the only tester I use," he said, pushing the vial across the table. Ball picked it up and looked at it.

"That's what the DEA drug chemists use to test the level of cocaine in crack or cocaine base. You should invest in one if you really gonna be selling drugs. Matter of fact, you can have that one," J-Diggs said.

He stood up and Ball opened the briefcase. He looked at the money inside, neatly stacked rows of freshly pressed hundred-dollar bills. Each had a paper wrapper on it that showed $1000.

"This is eight hundred thousand," Ball asked, still looking at the money.

"Man, how long have you been doing this," J-Diggs asked, grabbing the other luggage.

"Naw, it just look small, that's all," Ball said, shutting the case.

J-Diggs shook his head and said, "I guess you was expecting a huge black trash bag full of wrinkled bills that crackheads and dope fiends wiped their asses with."

"Hey it's five more in there," Balls added, watching J-Diggs start to walk off.

"Tell Baby Tiff to bring you to my spot off Kells around 2:30 pm cause I brought money for twenty-five not thirty."

"Yeah, my bad," Ball said, placing his hand on the briefcase full of money.

"You keep making stupid mistakes like the ones you've been making all day. You won't last more than another week in the streets," J-Diggs said, walking deeper into the crowd.

"Two-thirty, not 2:35 or 2:40, but two-thirty," he said as he continued moving through the crowd. Ball watched him as he exited them all next to the stadium. Soon as he was out of the mall, Tiffany walked back to the table with their food.

"So did everything go ok," she asked, sitting down next to Ball.

"Yeah, everything went cool. He wants you to bring me to his spot on Kells so he can pay me for the other five."

"I guess he was mad when you said something about thirty instead of the twenty-five, he was expecting to get, haw?"

"Yeah, somewhat but all in all he was cool as hell," Ball lied.

He grabbed a roasted chicken breast and sank his teeth into it. As he chewed, he added the amount of money he had made. At twenty a brick, L's cut would be exactly $500,000, which was a half million dollars. Lean and Omar who were getting $5000 off each key would see $125,000. He had made exactly $125,000 as well, which was both Lean and Omar's cut together. The thought of it made him smile but he was still salty that L was getting all of the money when he ain't take none of the risks.

What the hell do I care, he thought to himself, knowing that at $30,000 a key he had at least another $150,000 coming to him. As he and Tiffany sat eating, he ran the figures through his head over and over again. When they finished eating, as promised, he gave her twenty-five thousand dollars instead of fifteen thousand. They spent the remainder of their time shopping and waiting until 2:30pm rolled around.

Chapter 20

As Go-Go, who wore his orange DC Jail jumpsuit proudly, walked out the front door of the jail. He was smiling ear to ear and cussing out the guards who had opened the door for him.

"If your ass come back, we gonna whip you real bad and toss you in North One's hole," the guards yelled.

"Ya'll can kiss my ass. I ain't never coming back,"

He continued walking towards the Stadium Armory train station. He nearly ran down the escalator stairs. When he reached the toll booth, he stopped and looked at the security guard and grabbed hold of the front of his jail jumpsuit.

"Go ahead," the security guard told him. The guard knew well that everybody who got released from DC Jail didn't have a dime. Go-Go hopped over the rail and went down another set of stairs. The train he was waiting for pulled up in front of the station. After it came to a stop, the doors opened and he got on. He looked at the huge map of the train's route. When he saw that Potomac Gardens, his old stomping grounds, was the next stop, his heart began to flutter. He looked at the map again thinking to himself, how long it would take him to get to Petworth Station.

The train stopped and people got off and headed up the platform. Go-Go paused for a minute, and then he got off the train, as well.

I can catch a ride from around the Gardens, he told himself.

He went up the steps to Pennsylvania Avenue. The closer he got to the Gardens, the more nervous he became. Go-Go thought about his two beautiful daughters and his mother; he had promised her he'd come straight home once he was released. He hadn't told anyone his release date in order to keep them from trying to pick him up. He called himself surprising them, but deep down inside he knew his true intentions had more to do with the cocaine addiction he had been struggling with for more than six years.

Go-Go, who had once been one of the most notorious stick-up kids Uptown, had started smoking cocaine when he was unable to take advantage of the killers on the Southeast side of DC, the way he was able to handle the guys he grew up with Uptown. After being shot five times around Trinidad Street Northeast, he started smoking crack. Making his way towards 1430 Projects, he thought about the promises he had made to his family over the last twenty-three months when he had been locked in DC Jail.

Just one more taste and then I'm going straight home, he told himself.

As he bent the corner and his eye fell upon Potomac Gardens, he realized that nothing had changed, not even the fences that sat around the entire projects. He came to 13th and K Street, a block away from the notorious 1000 Building, he spotted Silvia, a woman who had been foxy back in her day.

"Yo Silvia, what's up," he said, walking to her. Silvia, who had a large crowd of customers all around her, didn't see or hear him. He watched her continue to serve the fiends what they wanted. He watched her selling hundred-dollar slabs, eight balls, and working fifty's and wondered how a crack whore like her could have come up with so much work. That shit must be fake, he thought, but he knew better. The killers around the Gardens didn't go for nobody messing up their clientele and anyone that got caught or was assumed to be selling demos was as good as dead. He waited until the last couple that had approached her got back into their car and pulled off. The he walked to her.

"Damn Baby, you doing real good," he said, smiling at her.

"Go-Go," she said. She smiled as she jumped into his arms and wrapped her legs around him. She kissed him on the lips as he let her back down to the ground.

"So what's up baby? I need a blast," he said as he looked at her purse.

"I got you baby, but I can't smoke too much because I'm working right now."

"Come on, let's go to the abandoned building where we used to do it at," she said, smiling at him.

She walked off in front of him. He looked down at her dusty soiled jeans but even though he hadn't had a woman in two years, he couldn't see himself hitting it. She had lost so much weight that he could barely see an imprint of her booty in the back of the jeans she wore. They crossed the street and disappeared behind some buildings and into the alley. They continued until they came upon a row of buildings whose windows were boarded up. He grabbed hold of the plywood that sat over the window at the corner of the building and pulled it back, allowing her to slip through, then he followed. They made their way through the dark, damp, moldy building and into the kitchen, where there was the most light.

She reached into her bra and pulled out a glass pipe which she quickly filled with a piece of the crack. She handed the pipe to him and he placed it in his mouth. He inhaled as she held the flame of her lighter to it. Go-Go was high as hell. He gave her the pipe and began to look on the floor. He searched around for pieces of crack that he or someone else might have dropped years or decades ago, while Silvia re-stuffed the pipe and began to set a flame to it.

Before long, they both were standing around, geeked out of their minds. While he searched the ground for pieces of crack, she kept peeking out from behind the plywood nailed over the window in the kitchen. He looked at her and finally became hard, which caused him to undo his pants and place himself in his hands. She went to him and dropped down to her knees. She began giving him head. He sat up against the sink, watching her as her head went back and forth as she swallowed him.

"Come here," he said, lifting her up.

He undid her pants and when he saw her body he was pleased. She looked much better under her clothes than she did in them. He pulled her panties down and lifted her up onto his staff. When he entered her, he immediately began to cum.

"Damn baby, you finished already," she said, caressing his back.

He looked over at her purse as she climbed off him and pulled her panties and pants back up. He walked to her purse and grabbed it; she turned and saw him.

"What the hell are you doing," she asked. She walked toward him but when she reached him, he hit her with two quick punches that knocked her out cold. He then sat on the floor next to her and opened package after package of the crack, smoking it as if it might disappear.

After three hours, he had finally run through an eighth of a key of crack. He looked down at Silvia and then he climbed out the kitchen window and walked back onto the streets. He headed towards 1000 Building; as he reached the end of the alley that ran behind it, he saw three youngsters who appeared to be no older than ten.

"What's up Unk," one of the boys said to him.

"We got that real live crack that'll knock dust off your old ass," one of the other boys said, pulling his hand out of his pocket and opening it Go-Go looked down at the tiny bags of crack that amounted to 25 rocks. He struck the boy while swinging on the others who ran. He grabbed the small baggies off the ground and took off running.

The two other boys who had run came out of the alley with their weapons and opened fire at him. The bullets from the two semi-automatic rifles and the hand gun tore pieces of brick off the wall of the building in the alley. Several of them hit the frames and windows of nearby cars, shattering the glass. Go-Go ducked behind one of the cars and crawled low to the ground until he reached the alley. He rose to his feet and sprinted towards the abandoned building where he had left Silvia. Once he reached the window, he looked behind him then climbed in and disappeared behind the plywood that covered it.

Lil Ron Ron got up from the ground and stumbled as he tried to gain his balance.

"Come on," Chapelle said.

397

He and Lil Ron Ron and Junior ran through the alley and headed towards 1000. Once they reached the gate where Cutt, Wild Joe, Loco, Rico and Whiteboy Brian were standing, they stopped.

"Who the hell was doing all of that shooting," Rico asked, looking at Junior.

"Pipe head Go-Go just knocked Lil Ron Ron out and robbed him. We tried to air his ass out but he took off running."

"And ya'll ain't run after him," Whiteboy Brian asked, his ear lobes sagging from the weight of his canary diamond studs.

"Man, that pipe head ass nigga took off like Carl Lewis at the Olympics," Lil Ron Ron said, holding his jaw.

"Ya'll better go get that sucka ass nigga and don't come back around here until he dead or ya'll locked up for killing him," said Wild Joe. Go-Go paced back and forth in the boarded-up building and wondered

398

if he was gonna make it out of Southeast alive. He knew the young'uns had got more troops to aid them and he also knew that they were probably standing right outside the building. He placed the last piece of crack he had into his pipe and used Silvia's lighter to fire it up. He inhaled as long as he could. Without breathing out, he began pacing again, back and forth in the kitchen.

He looked at Silvia, who was still lying in the same spot, knocked out cold. He knelt beside her and started checking her socks. He removed her shoes and checked under the soles. That's when he found the bundle of hundred-dollar bills. He quickly counted them and placed them in his pocket. He checked her other shoe and found five grams of crack crumbs. Then he checked the pulse in Silvia's neck to see if she was still alive. After feeling her pulse, he stood up and went to the window.

Go-Go carefully slid out the window and down to the ground. He looked around for any signs of danger, and then he began to walk quickly with the five grams of coke cuffed inside his hand as it swung. He began relaxing a little, once he reached the end of the alley and could see the McDonalds on Pennsylvania Avenue. As he stepped in the street, he heard gunfire erupt behind him and he went down; three bullets had hit in.

He crawled across the ground behind a car and hid behind it as bullets tore apart the car and the ground around it. He heard Chapelle tell the others to come on and that's when he took off running. As he reached Pennsylvania Avenue, Junior fired at him and one of the bullets tore into his thigh, knocking him back into the street. He took off his shoes and stood up, and then he ran through the oncoming traffic. The boys stopped chasing him when he got to the other side of Pennsylvania Avenue, just in case the police were watching.

"Please help! Please help," Go-Go said, bleeding heavily.

The people who saw him from the parking lot of the gas station quickly moved away from him, fearing for their own lives. He went to a pay phone, lifted the receiver to his ear, and then dialed zero.

"Yes, operator, can you allow me to make a collect call to 202-952-7343," he asked.

The operator patched him through. When he heard his daughter Parida say hello, his heart fluttered.

"Hi baby, Daddy loves you," he said. He watched his blood flow to the ground and puddle around his feet.

"Ay, Go-Go," Lil Ron Ron called out to him. When Go-Go turned around, Ron Ron opened fire on him with a HK MR556; it almost tore him in half. Ron Ron, Chappelle and Junior took off running back across Pennsylvania Avenue.

Flukes and Charel, two tricks, walked to Go-Go who was shaking and on his last nerve signals. Flukes knelt down and grabbed his hand, trying to get the five grams of crack he had cuffed in it. He wouldn't let go. He looked up at her, shaking and with blood pouring from his mouth.

"Come on, let it go, Go-Go. You can't take it with you man," Flukes said.

He opened his hand and took his last breath.

Chapter 21

"You hear that," Buggs asked, looking back down Pennsylvania Avenue. "They always gettin it in on this side of town," he said then puffed on the cigar between his fingers.

"Look, nigga, just stay focused on why we are around here. When I turn this car around and hit brakes, I want you to hop out and give it to everybody in sight," Lil Greg said as he turned down into Kentucky Courts.

Buggs placed the 223 rifle in his lap. He looked in his rear view to see if Baby Boy and Grouper were still behind them. They were. Lil Greg drove down to the end of the block and hit a U turn. He went back down the street towards where Baby Boy was on the side of the street hollering at a yellow bone. Lil Greg slammed on the brakes and flung his door open. He got out of the car with the DDM4V Y assault rifle in his hands. He and Buggs opened fire on everybody standing around outside, as Baby Boy and Grouper got out of their car and opened fire, as well.

Since they had caught the gangsters off guard and standing on the side of the road and in front of Kentucky Courts buildings, Lil Greg and Buggs had little to no resistance to stop them as they moved towards the buildings. Lil Greg looked around and noticed that more than fifteen people were lying on the ground badly wounded or dead. He continued towards the steps of the building until someone on the roof opened fire with a 1919A6 mounted on a tripod.

The A6 tore apart the ground around his feet so he dove to the ground and crawled. Both Baby Boy and Grouper weren't so lucky. The A6 tore them both to shreds as Lil Greg and Buggs watched. Seeing the damage the A6 was doing, they retreated towards the car. They had intended to get inside of the stash house where they learned Omar had over a half million dollars.

The A6 continued firing, tearing away the ground near their feet. The spray of bullets hit the Cadillac they had used and tore the engine out of it. Then the gunfire tore off the roof, as well. That caused Buggs and Lil Greg to run through a nearby alley. The A6 was on them like a heat-seeking missile, tearing brick after brick from the wall. The firing continued until they made it out of the cut and over to the other side of Pennsylvania Avenue. Buggs, who was out of breath, stopped for air while Lil Greg laughed and continued to run. As soon as he noticed Buggs was no longer with him, he stopped.

"Hurry your fat ass up," he said, taunting Buggs. Sweating bullets and still out of breath, Buggs caught up with him.

"We need to find a car," Lil Greg said, going into the parking lot of the Safeway grocery store.

"Come on, I got us a ride," he said, making his way into the parking lot where he saw a couple loading their groceries into their car. He lifted his weapon and said,

"I'd hate to kill you for nothing."

The man tossed him the keys and grabbed the woman standing beside him. Lil Greg passed them and went to the driver side, while Buggs said boo, taunting the couple as he made his way to the passenger side. They got in, closed the doors, started the car, and Lil Greg raced out of the lot.

"They'll give that block up and they'll be glad to give it up when I finish with them," Lil Greg said.

He steered with his knee. He checked his weapon, making sure it still had ammo in the clip. Buggs pushed play on the CD player and Kingdawud's voice blasted out of the speakers.

"I see that we jacked a gangster," Buggs said. Both he and Lil Gregg laughed and nodded their heads to the music.

Verse 1

If I die today it won't just be another day or another death
The ghetto streets gon honor me for the medal on my chest
Bullets burnin holes in my body, war wounds in my flesh
An ounce of og kush daily to keep me from going crazy.
This life is a bitch and the streets, my father, look how they both raised me.

Lean had been sitting in a lawn chair on the roof of 1000 Building but he jumped to his feet and said, "What the fuck is that?"

He and his hitman OG Josh from around Trinidad Avenue crossed to the edge of the building and looked below; they could see everything from K Street to as far away as Arthur Capers.

"Those shots sound like they coming from up Kentucky Courts," said OG Josh.

"Hand me my phone, Sunny Bee," Lean said, reaching out his hand to his right-hand man who passed him his cell. Lean called downstairs to Ronnel, who was in charge of his security.

"What's up boss," Ronnel answered.

"Call up the courts and see what's going on up there."

"I already did boss. The gangsters just got their asses handed to them. They said Lil Greg from around

407

the park, and his man Buggs came through and hit the strip with some heavy work."

His jaw clenched tight, Lean asked, "Are they sure it was them?"

"His man Baby Boy and Grouper lay chopped up all over the block and gangsters said he couldn't get to his car because the can opener hit it. So when they checked it, they found his phone inside of it. So to answer your question, yeah, they sure it was him."

"Fuck! Fuck! Fuck," Lean said, kicking the gravel on the rooftop. "This muthafucker has got to die. He's gonna die, I said! I want him dead and I want his balls cut off and placed in his mouth after his head is decapitated from his body. I want that head delivered to his mother and I want his spinal cord delivered to me!"

"It's for you," OG Josh said, passing his phone to Lean. He took the phone and raised it to his ear.

"Who the fuck is this," he yelled into the phone. Hearing Ball's voice, he calmed down.

"I don't give a damn who he grew up with, I'm having him killed."

Lean got quiet, and then he said, "Ok but you better handle this as soon as you get back." He ended the call and handed the phone back to OG Josh.

"What did he say," Sunny Bee asked.

"He's saying not to kill Greg. He said for me to have Buggs killed to send Lil Greg a message but he specifically said not to kill Lil Greg."

Chapter 22

"Is everything alright baby," Tiffany asked, as she turned right onto Kells Avenue. She passed several huge houses that all appeared to be abandoned.

"Damn, this place is a ghost town," Ball said, looking around at the empty houses.

"All of those houses belong to J. He bought every house on the block in order to make sure that no neighbors could spy on him or his crew. Now are you gonna tell me what's going on," she said as she pulled up to the second from last house on the street.

"A good friend of my childhood days is in trouble and I'm just trying to save his life."

"Ok then," she said. She smiled at Ball and they got out of the car. He walked to where she was standing and took her hand. They walked across the grass into the yard and reached the front door. It was opened by a man holding an assault rifle.

410

"Go on back," he said, nodding his head towards the living room.

Tiffany and Ball walked across the living room floor and headed into the kitchen, where another armed man told them to go down into the basement. They reached the basement door, opened it, and carefully descended the steps. The basement was dark and cold.

"Why the hell is it so cold down here," Ball asked.

He pulled Tiffany close to keep her warm. When they entered the basement, they saw tiny flickers of candles throughout the room. Another gunman ordered them to keep straight and they did. When they came to a bend in the basement that took them around the corner, Ball noticed there was a small crack in the doorway of one of the rooms. He looked through the crack and what he saw astonished him. In what appeared to be a warehouse, beautiful naked women stood counting what appeared to be different colored Ecstasy pills.

"Come on," Tiffany said when she saw all the naked women.

They continued walking until they reached another section of the basement that looked as if it was a new addition to the house that the zoning board knew nothing about.

"Here, put these on," another armed guard said, handing them both cotton masks to cover their noses and mouths.

Ball began to get nervous as he smelled a familiar scent in the air. It was the smell of PCP or several of the chemicals that were used to make it. The guard led them into a warehouse where men in black hoodies stood with weapons, watching three other men in lab coats mix what appeared to be PCP.

"Is that what I think it is," Ball asked Tiffany in a whisper only she could hear.

She shrugged her shoulders and remained quiet. Just then, J-Diggs walked out of a room accompanied by a fourth man who wore a white lab coat. He and the man finished talking then shook hands and parted ways. J-Diggs looked up and saw Ball and Tiffany. He smiled as he quickly made his way to where they stood.

"Hey, baby," he said, hugging Tiffany. He looked at Ball and reached in his pocket for a manila envelope.

"Here's your money for the other five. That stuff was good and according to my boys who run my crack strips, everything is already gone," he said, smiling.

"Can I talk to you about something," Ball asked, looking down at the manila envelope in J-Diggs' hand.

"Baby, do you mind," Ball asked Tiffany. She took the hint and went over to the four chemists, who stood observing their creation.

"Look, if it's not a problem, I would rather you pay me with half of the PCP and another half of the Ecstasy,"

"O, you saw that, did you? You wasn't supposed to see that," J-Diggs said, looking at his bodyguard. "Look, I rather keep my money so I'm sure we can work something out."

He put his arm around Ball's neck. Nodding his head towards Tiffany, he said,

"Look at her. Her father got killed when she was two and her mother, my sister, ran out on her when she got addicted to crack. I raised her as if she was my own and me and her are so close that she considers me to be more of a brother or a cousin, instead of an uncle.

"I'm her father, her mother, her uncle, her cousin, and her protector, so if you have ill intentions for her, I suggest you let her go real fast and never turn back. Do you understand me?"

Ball nodded his head and tried to swallow. As he looked at Tiffany, he said, "I think I love her just as much as you."

"Good, then we have no problem. I'll have my men load the stuff you wanted into the side panels and gas tank of your car. Just remember to fill up every quarter mile. Ok?"

"Ok," Ball said, as J-Diggs patted him on the back.

"Ya'll go out through the back door and hurry up and get her out of here before she becomes unable to bear you any kids."

As J-Diggs stepped away, Tiffany walked back to Ball. "Come on, let's get out of here," he said. He took her hand and they walked down the hallway until they reached the back door. They exited into the back yard and watched as J's men stripped down the Gran Turismo. They filled it back up with huge packages of powder PCP, which was more concentrated than the liquid and the Ecstasy pills.

"Now that you got your money, are you ready to go home," Ball said as he looked at Tiffany. She looked up into his eyes and began to cry.

415

"What's wrong," he asked.

"You really gonna leave me," she asked.

"I would never do that, but since I'm taking you with me, you gotta understand that DC is full of my enemies, so you won't be seen with me. Ever. And I don't want you going into the city unless you really, really have to."

She smiled and jumped into his arms and he swung her around.

Chapter 23

Tinkerbell was about as lovely a woman as any. Since a very young age, she earned the name Tinkerbell for being so enchanting. Her looks were so unreal that people began to say that she was as well. The name Tinkerbell, which was a character out of a fantasy world, was befitting to her, to say the least.

She drove her hot pink Audi A8 up Martin Luther King Boulevard and then pulled into the parking lot of Big K Liquor Store at the bottom of Naylor Road, in southeast DC.

She stepped out of the Audi wearing spaghetti strap wrap around Moschino stilettos. Every person in the area nearby turned their heads to look. As she walked, her hips swung, so her two perfect thighs constricted and made the black and pink Moschino dress she wore hug every curve of her body with perfection. The dress stopped right above her knees, allowing everyone to see her flawless, long, caramel-creamed legs that were to die for. She removed her black Surrotal Mustakenn shades, revealing her powder blue eyes. Her beautiful, tiny, creamy brown face looked as if it had never been touched by air.

Tinkerbell was perfect and she knew it. Weighing a little less than one hundred and fourteen pounds, all body, it was damned near impossible for any man with a pair of eyes not to notice her. Tinker Bell had many nicknames, which ranged from Jewel to Star, but Lean and Omar called her the Kiss of Death. That was the name their Uncle Charles, who raised her, gave to her when he discovered her talent for ending the lives of men as quick as she stole and broke their hearts.

At least he had the Kiss of Death on his side, Lean thought to himself as he also thought about how lucky a man thought he was to love her.

Up twelve blocks from where Tink was standing, the stolen black Denali carrying Buggs and Lil Greg exited Alabama Avenue, passed Savannah Terrace, and headed in the direction of Hope Village Halfway House. They drove past Langston Lane and up past Woodland. That's when Buggs told Lil Greg to pull to the side of the road.

Three boys who had been standing in the alley nearly raced to the truck. With each of their hands full of dime bags of weed, they bum rushed Buggs, trying to get him to buy their weed.

"Who got that loud pack," Buggs asked, referring to the loud smell of the mid-grade or hydro.

"I got that right here," one of the boys said, laughing as the other two stepped off and made their way to the cut.

"Shorty, let me get five bags for forty," Buggs said, pulling out his money.

"Nigga, yeah right, you got over a thousand dollars in your hand and you wanna try to short change me. Forget it," the boy said, closing his hand.

He turned to walk away and Buggs said, "O yeah main man? You gonna turn your back to a gangster like that?"

The boy, whose name was Butta, turned around

with a mug on his face and said, "You need to get the fuck back in your truck before you get that mutha fucker flipped over, slim."

"This ain't your block. This Woodland Zoo." Before Buggs could reach for the Glock 9 at the small of his back, Lil Greg stuck his weapon out of the window and fired, causing Buggs to duck. Six shots hit Butta, knocking his chest wide open.

The boys who were in the alley pulled their weapons and started firing at the truck, but their caliber hand guns were no match for the assault rifle that Lil Greg was firing. They both went down in the alley, hard like a sack of potatoes. Buggs pulled his gun and fired on the men who ran towards them as he ran for the vehicle.

He had to dive through the window to keep from being hit. As the truck drove away, bullets from the A-Kick that somebody in the alley was firing tore holes in the side of his door, missing him only by inches. Lil Greg laughed as he sped down Naylor Road, while looking behind him to see if the men had decided to come after them. When they reached High Street, and he didn't see any vehicles behind them, he slowed down.

The truck had been shot up pretty badly and smoke began to pour out from the engine. Lil Greg pulled into the parking lot of Big K Liquor Store. Buggs stepped out of the truck and looked at the damage the gunshots had done to his side of the car. That's when he spotted Tinkerbell coming back across MLK from the Clara Muhammad school. Buggs completely forgot about almost being killed or just having been in a raging gun battle. He crossed the street and walked to where she was headed then walked right to her.

"I must be dreaming and I need you to pinch me," he said, looking into her blue eyes.

She ignored him and headed across the street back towards the liquor store.

"Did I say something wrong or is a booger in my nose," he asked her, as he followed her. Without answering him, she kept walking towards her car.

"What are you, some type of fairy tale being," he asked.

That's when she turned around and looked at him, nearly causing him to melt. She said, "I don't know you and this city is full of a bunch of creeps and scumbag rapists and killers."

"Well I'm not one of them," Buggs said, closing his leather coat to keep her from seeing the handle of his gun.

She had already seen the gun when he was headed across the street. She acted as if she didn't see the gun on his waist and walked off in front of him, making sure he saw all of her curves, which left men mesmerized. As she reached her car and opened the door, Buggs just stared in amazement.

"You all of it, ain't you," he said walking to her door as she shut it behind her.

"Look," he said, knocking on the window.

She rolled down her window and said, "Boy, are you crazy or something? Why won't you leave me the hell alone?"

"I don't know why, but I do know that if I do, I'll regret this day for the rest of my life on earth. For some reason, I feel like you complete me. It's like we were together in another life."

She shook her head and looked at him as if he sounded crazy.

"I know all of this sounds crazy as hell but I know for a fact that what I'm saying is coming from my heart, not the big or little head. What will it hurt you to give me a chance to prove myself?"

"Well look," she said, uncrossing her legs as he watched, hoping to see her panties. "Since you're so persistent, I will allow you to take me out on one date in order to prove yourself, but if you mess up, just like a fairy tale, I'll disappear out of your real world forever," she said, handing him one of the business cards she had in her sun visor.

"You work for the United States, haw." She smiled, then said, "Well don't assume that ever sexy black woman that you come across is an uneducated hood rat looking for a drug dealer to take care of her. Now, if you don't mind, I have to go."

He watched as she rolled up her window and pulled out of the parking lot. When she had disappeared, he went back to where Lil Greg stood watching a pipe head work under the hood of the truck.

"I see your sucka for love ass finally pulled a top flight model type, haw fat boy."

Buggs smiled and held up her card for him to see. "I'm done," the skinny filthy old man said, closing the hood.

"Here," Buggs said, handing him a fifty-dollar bill as Lil Greg jumped inside the truck and started it up again.

The engine didn't smoke and it was no longer making a clinking sound.

"Thank God for the crackheads. What in the world would us gangsters do without them," Lil Greg said as he pulled away from the curb.

He made a right through the light, then a sharp left, they continued straight until they came upon Suitland Parkway train station. They then made another left and headed past the empty hill where Stratford Woods projects used to be. Lil Greg turned left and headed up the hill. He didn't stop again until they were inside Wellington Park.

After they parked, they both got out of the truck and walked towards their vehicles parked on the hill.

"Where you going," Lil Greg asked, stopping shy of pulling his black Crown Victoria's door open.

"I'm about to get up with baby, you just seen me talking to," Buggs said, jumping into the burgundy Yukon.

"Tender dick ass nigga, I thought you was sticking close to me for the rest of the night," Lil Greg said.

"Man, if you ain't about five-five, with thick hips and powdery blue eyes, you ain't my date for tonight," Buggs said, smiling and closing the truck door behind him.

"Yeah be careful nigga because pussy will kill you faster than a speeding bullet."

"I'll make sure I remember that, Lil one," Buggs said.

He started up his truck and pulled off and moved up the hill as Lil Greg just watched him. *I hope you know what you're doing,* Lil Greg said to himself, and then he jumped inside his car.

"Where are you now," Buggs asked, with his cell phone to his ear. "I know you said call you later but I miss you now," he said, smiling. "Let me take you out to dinner and then we can walk along the shore of the Potomac."

He listened a moment, then said, "Alright, cool. I'll meet you on Florida Avenue, down from Florida Park. Just park your car over there and I'll have my lil man Junior watch it. Right now, I'm headed up to Georgetown to go buy me an outfit. Would you like me to buy you something as well?"

He listened a moment, then said, "Alright, cool. Then I'll pick you up something to match what I'm wearing anyways. What's your size?"

She told him her size, then Buggs said, "Ok, ok I won't push it but, in an hour, I'll pick you up on Florida Avenue, so be ready."

He was laughing as he ended the call. He drove up Georgetown and jumped out in front of the Ermenegildo Zegda shop. He went inside and told the cashier to give him the white silk tow piece Ermenegildo Zegda suit from the mannequin on display. While the clerk tallied his suit, he picked out some brown leather buck hide Bottega square toed loafers. Once he was fully dressed, he looked more like a college football player than a gangster who killed people and sold drugs for a living.

"She gonna love me," he said, looking at himself in the full-length mirror.

He left the shop after telling the clerk to put everything on his tab. Then he jumped back into his truck, which he had double parked, blocking the street. He headed towards Florida Avenue.

When he reached Florida Park, he looked around for the pink A8. When he didn't see it, he began to panic. He grabbed his phone, dialed, and waited for her to answer.

"Where are you," he asked.

"You just drove right past me. Park right there and walk back down. Ima drive us in the new Aston Martin truck I just bought," she said, then ended the call.

He looked behind him and saw the money green Aston Martin truck parked about eight cars down from him on the other side of the street. That made him smile. He told himself he had a winner and pulled into the parking space outside of Khartum Sudanese Restaurant. He parked his truck, turned off the engine and got out.

He looked down at his shoes, knowing that he looked like a million bucks. After locking the door, he walked down the street. Once he was directly across from where she was parked, he ran to the other side of the street and stopped at her door. As he smiled, she told him to get in on the passenger side. He took his time walking around the truck, admiring it.

He reached the passenger side door, opened it and got in the vehicle.

"Wow, this jont is new," he said as he looked around at all the plastic that was still on the seats. "Why didn't you have the dealer take the plastic off the dashboard, at least?"

"This why," OG Josh said, raising up from behind the seat with a calico. He shot Buggs in the back of the head five times, blowing his brains all over the dashboard.

"O and Lean said to make it look real messy so that it will make the Washington Post front page news," OG Josh said, looking down at Buggs' lifeless body.

Tink put the vehicle in drive and headed towards the bridge that most senators and congress people in DC took, leading up to the embassies on Massachusetts and Connecticut Avenues. When the truck was half way across the bridge, Josh opened the door and pushed Buggs' body out onto the road. Lean knew that murders in DC never made the paper unless a child got killed who was white, or a body was found in the heartland of congress country. While Buggs' body was sitting out on the lonely bridge waiting to be discovered by morning traffic, Lil Greg sat on the couch watching "Cops"; while his baby brother Tag sat behind him, waiting on Madball, who had paid him $30,000 to assassinate his own brother, sat watching the screen of his phone. Little did Lil Greg know, but money was a thing that would make his own brother, who he raised with his own hands, kill him in cold blood.

After nearly twelve and a half hours of nonstop driving, Tiffany reached over and shook Ball awake.

"Baby we are here," she said.

Hearing that, Ball sat up in his seat. He looked out of

his window and saw River Terrace across form him and Nannie Helen Burroughs Road to his right.

"Make the right, right here," he said. She turned and headed down Division Avenue. He really didn't want anyone seeing her, but it was too late now. As they got closer to 50th Street and Lincoln Heights, he picked up his phone and called L.

"Brother, where are you," he asked.

"Good, stay right there. I'll be there in like five minutes," he said.

The call ended before Ball could tell L not to come. They continued up the hill past the church in Lincoln Heights and Ball looked over at Tiffany to see if she was ok. He asked,

"Are you ok?"

"Yes, I'm fine," she said, smiling at him.

But as soon as they were up in Lincoln Heights and she

saw the hundreds of people who slow-walked back and forth, or just stood out on the curb, or were in the alleys, and filled up every inch of them, she began to get a little frightened.

"Is this where you grew up," she asked.

"Yeah, something like that," he said. "Pull right over."

She pulled to the side of the road where a group of what appeared to be killers stood, huddled up in black. All of their eyes were bloodshot red and some of them wore masks to conceal their faces. He told her to get out of the car with him. She followed him hesitantly. He could see the fear in her eyes and when he grabbed her hand, he felt her trembling.

"Look, you're with me, so don't worry," he said as he crossed the street and headed to the alley that was crowded with people."

"Ball, what's up, baby," an older gentleman yelled down from the catwalk that separated the building.

"What's up, Uncle Guy," Ball said, smiling as he made his way deeper into the cut with Tiffany by his side.

Everyone stared at her as she passed them. Her beauty was appealing, which made it hard not to look at her. When they were deep in the alley, Ball spotted L. He was standing in the middle of a crowd of gangsters wearing all black, while he wore a white chinchilla coat and white Atlanta Falcons ball cap. L raised his hand, motioning for Ball to come to him. The thick crowd parted as best it could to allow them to get to the middle of the circle which was heavily guarded.

Inside the circle L knew he was absolutely safe from any harm, even from being taken into custody by the police themselves.

"What's up, lil brother," he said, putting his arm around Ball's neck and hugging him."

"Here," Ball told him as he handed L the

briefcase that J-Diggs had given him.

"What's this," L asked, shaking it.

"That's $625,000 that's what Lean and Omar owe you, and a little more."

"How the hell do you know what they owe me," L asked looking Tiffany up and down.

"Let's just say that's the streets take. Now if you don't want the money, I can take it back," Ball said.

He reached for the briefcase. L looked at him and said, "There's no chance of you getting this back and you know it," which made both of them smile.

"Last time I checked, you was supposed to be deep in the daylight."

"I am deep in DC," Ball said, smiling."

"Naw, nigga deep in the country of North Carolina," L said, looking over at Tiffany, who was so

434

ravishingly beautiful that he had trouble keeping his eyes off her. Reaching his hand to her, L asked Tiffany,

"How are you doing, beautiful?"

She gave him her hand and L said to Ball, "I see you finally got your baby from Ohio."

Tiffany batted her eyes at Ball, who said, "Yeah, whatever, Kevin. I got you something else."

Ball reached into his inner coat pocket and pulled out a small bag about the size that most street hustlers used to put dime bags of weed in. He handed it to L, who looked at its contents and asked,

"Where the hell you get these?"

"If I tell you that, I gotta kill you," Ball said, smiling.

"If you don't tell me, you gonna have to worry about me killing you," L said, grabbing his brother around the neck and wrestling him.

"Alright! Alright," Ball said, laughing.

"I got a man out of state who be looking out for me. How much can you get them for?"

"Four dollars apiece," Ball lied. He knew that if he told L the truth, he would have his brother trying to take over what he considered to be his come up.

"Do you have any idea what a woman will do for these little bad boys," he said, looking through the alley at Chanel, the only woman in Lincoln Heights that considered herself too good for him.

"Look, I'm about to change my number later on today, so I'll email the new one to you later on tonight."

"Why? Your stuff hot?"

"Naw, nigga, your little cousin's hot. They keep riding around the city in Maseratis and Bentley coupes, expecting not to be seen by the Feds."

Tiffany looked at Ball, who couldn't help but smile. L

had no idea that he was riding around in a Maserati.

"How did you get up here anyway," L asked.

"We caught the train," Ball quickly answered.

"Yeah, I'd of caught a train to the end of the earth to get something that fine next to me," L said, causing Tiffany to blush.

"Here," Ball said, reaching inside his coat. He removed the left arm sleeve and pulled the Calico off his shoulder, then handed it to L.

"Damn, where the hell did you get this?"

"I just came from down Fayetteville, where there's an army base called Fort Bragg close by."

"Nigga I know where Fort Bragg is," L said, frowning up his face while still admiring the high-powered assault pistol. "I get guns by the crates for the low."

"Yeah, we'll talk about that but I'm more interested in these," he said, shaking the small bag of pills.

"Look, I don't want Lean and Omar handling shit for me anymore. They making shit too hot. The other day, seven people got killed around Kentucky Courts, and every day since then, at least one person has been getting killed."

"I need you to tell them that as soon as they pay me the rest of the money, they owe me that we finished. They gonna have to find a new connect, cause in all these years of being out in the streets, I ain't never made the mistake of getting myself investigated by the Feds."

"They owe you for them sixteen bricks they got robbed for, don't they?"

"And how the hell do you know that?"

"I know all the killers and cruddy niggas, so all information comes right back to me."

"Yeah, well you better make sure you ain't have nothing to do with that shit, cause me and Bruce got some steps on the head of whoever did it."

"Get cha money back killer. I already got that handled."

"O yeah, I forgot that you good at killing up the whole city just to build your legacy. Look, I ain't about to be associated with no murderous, homicidal, psychopathic maniac."

"Look, big bro, I got this. Just chill and I'll have the money Lean and O owes you tomorrow morning; that's a promise."

"Cool, that's what's up. I'll email you my new number tonight and tell Lean and O I said the Feds are watching them, so they might wanna fall back for a while."

"Now, if you excuse me, I think I got a hot date," L said, looking through the alley at Chanel.

Tiffany and Ball laughed as they watched him make his way through the cut. They left the alley too and went back to the car. As Ball got in, he heard L yelling, at him, which caused him to smile. He stepped on the gas and sped down 50th Street before L could cuss him out.

"Look, I got Yolanda B, who is one of the best realtors® in the area, to take us house shopping tomorrow morning, but tonight we are gonna stay in a hotel out in Maryland. Ok?"

Tiffany nodded her head then laid it down on his thigh. "You tried to trick me," she said, closing her eyes and falling asleep.

Ball just looked at her as she rested peacefully. After fifteen minutes of driving, he pulled into the parking lot of the Four Seasons hotel. Without waking her, he lifted her head up and slid out of his seat, then gently laid her head back down. He went inside and reserved a suite, then came out to the car and scooped her up into his arms and carried her across the parking lot and up the steps to the room.

He laid her down on the bed and then removed her clothes. He tucked her under the covers and kissed her forehead. He got up from the bed and crossed the floor to the door, making sure he let it shut quietly behind him. He ran down the steps and back through the parking lot to the car. He got inside, started it up, and headed back to DC.

When he passed Iverson Mall, he picked up his cell phone and called Omar, telling him to get Lean and meet him in twenty minutes, in the graveyard behind Robinson Place. He ended the call and without stopping, drove down Suitland Parkway, past the Legend nightclub. He then turned right and headed up past Wallah Place. In less than ten minutes, he was pulling into Robinson Place, where his old girlfriend Keisha lived. When he pulled into the parking lot behind the building, he saw Lean and Omar, sitting on the hoods of their cars. He pulled up next to them and got out.

"What's up," they asked him.

"Come on, let's get in the graveyard, then we'll talk," he said, walking to the gate into the graveyard.

"You the only wild muthafucker living who likes to chill in graveyards."

"It ain't the dead you should worry about, it's the living," Ball said, taking a seat on a tombstone.

"Look, I talked to L and he said he changed his numbers because ya'll hot as fish grease right how. He'd rather I collect his money from ya'll and give it to him."

"Whatever, nigga. Cousin don't want your wild ass nowhere near what we got going on."

"Ok, call him up if you don't believe me."

Omar pulled out his phone and called L's number. The operator cut in, saying the number he was trying to reach had been disconnected.

"Shit," Omar said, ending the call.

"Ya'll still owe him money from them sixteen bricks ya'll got robbed for, which is something like $320,000. I sold all twenty-five bricks that was in the trunk and I took the $125,000 of your two shares and gave that to L. So now ya'll just owe him a step and $75,000."

"Yeah, and how the hell we gonna get him that when we ain't got no other drug connect," asked Lean.

"Nigga, ya'll got me," Ball said.

"Ima have Lil Greg give me back the sixteen bricks and since he wants Kentucky Courts so bad, Ima let him have it."

"Are you fucking crazy? We can't trust that shiesty-ass, cruddy, son of a bitch for nothing."

"Look man, killers think alike. As long as the beasts in the jungle are fed properly, we don't have to worry about them preying on our flock. Don't worry. I got this," he said, standing up. "L said to tell ya'll that the Feds are watching ya'll as well, so get rid of them flashy ass cars and lay back. I'll handle all of the dirty work and both of ya'll will be eating better with me than ya'll would have been eating with him anyway."

443

Both Lean and Omar had skeptical looks on their faces because they both knew they couldn't trust Ball, unless it was with their lives.

"Look, nigga, I ain't on no crude time shit no more. Ya'll my family and Ima always honor my blood, no matter what. We gonna eat, so stop looking stupid and just lay back"

Ball started to leave the graveyard. He bumped Omar on his way out and asked,

"I haven't cheated you so far, have I?"

Chapter 24

After he left the graveyard, Ball went straight to Wellington Park, where he knew that Lil Greg was, based on his inside source. There were two men on the roof of the building across from where Lil Greg and his headhunters were, ready to open fire with their assault rifles if anything went wrong.

He pulled his car down to the end of the alley, parked and got out. As he looked around the neighborhood, he saw red cherries burning in the dark alleys between the buildings; that let him know that he was being watched. With his hands in his pockets, he walked to the building and didn't stop until he reached the front door and pulled it open.

Lil Greg was one of the first people he saw. In front of him, about thirty or so of his men stood. Another twenty men stood in the hallway of the building stretching as far as his eyeballs could see.

'You got the damned Balls to be coming up in here like you ain't afraid to die or incapable of being killed," Lil Greg said, getting to his feet.

"I came in peace," Ball said, looking over the crowd of men who all looked at him as if they were ready to attack him at any second.

"Look, I'm here to talk business."

"What business?"

"This business of killing my best friend and homie," Lil Greg said.

He frowned up his face and reached around to the small of his back. He pulled a Glock 17 around to the front and aimed it at Ball. As he pointed his weapon, the other men pulled out their weapons and pointed them, as well. Ball counted more than forty-five guns and he laughed.

While removing his hands from his pockets, he said, "O shit, that nigga got two grenades," somebody in the crowd yelled, seeing that Ball was holding two grenades with their pins pulled out.

"I don't fear death but I bet a bunch of you cowards don't wanna die. Either we can talk like men or I can go Taliban on you bitch ass niggas and paint the whole Wellington Park with ya'll blood. So what's it going to be," he asked, looking Lil Greg deep in his eyes.

"Lower ya'll weapons," Lil Greg said, shaking his head.

"I thought so. Now listen to this. You and your man took sixteen bricks from my cousins' spot. I want it back or either the money, by tomorrow or there will be no deal. Also, I want the hands of both Pops and Bookie sent to me around Potomac Gardens with the money."

"And what's in it for me," Lil Greg asked.

"I'll let you and your team have Kentucky Courts which is a million dollar a day strip."

447

"Shit, we already took the Courts, so that ain't offering shit," Lil Greg shot back.

"I ain't finished," Ball said. He gritted his teeth as he looked over the faces of the men who appeared to be scared to death of him accidently releasing the grenades.

"In my pocket is a fifty-thousand-dollar advance for you, Lil Greg. Come get it." he said. He nodded his head over towards the man closest to him and the man went to Ball. He carefully placed his hand in Ball's jacket and grabbed the envelope. He passed it to Lil Greg, who opened it and looked over the money.

"Ok, what else," he asked.

"Well, Ecstasy goes for ten dollars a pill. They sell it for twenty dollars on every strip in this city, so you'll be getting them at half price; and I'll front you a hundred thousand in cocaine, pills, and PCP, just as soon as I get the hands of Bookie, Pops, and the money or sixteen bricks back. A kilo of cocaine goes for twenty-eight thousand in the city. Ima let you and your

448

team get them for twenty-five even. So do we have a deal, or what?"

"What about the PCP? We can sell that around here all day," one of Lil Greg's men said.

"An ounce of swamp water goes for six hundred a bottle. I'll let ya'll get it for three hundred," Ball said.

"Shit, I'm game," the man said, looking at Lil Greg to see if he had his approval.

"Tomorrow at 7am sharp, you have the drugs or the money and all four of their hands."

Ball nodded his head and began to back out of the building. He said, "That's what's up," he said. He made it back to his car and he carefully placed the pins back into the grenades. He started the car, put it in drive, and drove off.

Chapter 25

Just as he said, at 7am the next day, a box full of money and the hands of Pops and Bookie were delivered to him. Lil Greg had even taken the initiative to cut their tongues out of their mouths. Ball laughed when he saw them.

He called Yolanda B and told her he was on his way. He returned to the hotel to pick up Tiffany. When he reached the room, he saw she was still sleeping. He pulled the covers off of her, revealing her naked body. He immediately became hard. He stripped off his clothes and climbed into the bed behind her. As his hands palmed her cheeks, spreading them apart, she woke up, startled. When she saw it was him, she smiled and lifted up her right thigh to make it easier for him to enter her.

As he went inside her, he moaned and grabbed her soft right breast. He began to stroke in and out of her as she reached back and palmed his ass, throwing herself back on him. He was amazed that she was sexing him back, but he was pleased. They went at it for nearly an hour

450

before they both finally came. Then they jumped in the shower and washed up.

"I got you some new clothes," he said, pointing to three huge bags on the floor beside the bed.

With her luscious booty jumping up and down, she went to the bags and dumped them out onto the bed.

"O my god, Baby," you did good," she said, covering her mouth.

She grabbed a dark blue silk Bottega Veneta blouse off the bed and put it on without putting on a bra, which made her nipples visible. Then she slipped on the matching skirt and suede Chanel pumps. She began placing all the shoes and clothes back into the Neiman Marcus bags.

"Here's lunch, Ball said, taking off the plastic top of the Boston Rotisserie container of chicken. She went to him and bit into the piece of breast that he had in his hand.

"Ummm, it tastes good," she said as she walked to the door.

He grabbed her bags and followed behind her. They reached the car and while starting it, she said, "I'll drive." She pulled out of the parking lot and headed towards Calvert County, Maryland.

"How do you even know where we are going?"

"You left the number of the Realtor® on the nightstand, so I called her and set up my own open house," she said, smiling. "We are going to live in Maryland?"

"I don't care where we live, as long as I'm with you," Ball said, as he took her hand and kissed it.

They drove through the countryside of Maryland for about forty-five minutes. Then they came to a gated community called King Ranch Estates. Tiffany pulled up to the security booth and let down her window.

"Yes, may I help you," the guard asked, smiling

452

at her.

"Yeah, you can help me; stop staring at my wife like that," Ball said, mugging up the man.

"Baby, stop," Tiffany said, smiling at him. She turned her attention back to the guard and said Mrs. Yolanda B was expecting them for an open house. The guard opened the gate and they drove in. As they drove past the guard post, Ball said,

"I like the ring of your new name," making her smile.

They drove through King Ranch Estates admiring the huge mansions that sat far back from the street. Some of them were completely hidden behind acres of trees.

"Here we are," she said, turning into a long driveway until reaching the black Lexus that had been parked there.

They looked around for the house but couldn't see it because of the surrounding forest.

"Damn, the house must be in the woods," Ball said.

Tiffany pulled up behind Yolanda's car and parked. They got out of the car and walked up the driveway past the Lexus. They soon saw a massive four-level house in the woods, with a lake behind it.

"Wow, baby, this is lovely," Tiffany said as she stepped on the porch.

"Yeah, this is stunning," Ball said, looking at the four white round pillars that held up the roof of the porch over the patio.

They reached the door, which was made of solid cherry wood and granite. They rang the bell twice and after about three minutes, Yolanda B. opened the door with a smile on her face.

"Welcome, welcome," she said, hugging Tiffany.

As they entered the home, Tiffany looked back at Ball and said, "This house is so big you can get lost inside of it."

He was admiring the house but he had something else on his mind that had him glowing inside. He thought about the deal he had made with J-Diggs for the Ecstasy and PCP. J-Diggs had given him each ounce of PCP for $75 and had sold him each pill for $25. That meant he would make over four million dollars in profit, not including the $175,000, less the twenty-five he gave Tiffany and the fifty he gave Lil Greg. He smiled to himself, knowing that he was a millionaire at the age of nineteen.

They made their way through the den that was connected to the living room and continued forward until they came to a second den. It was decorated in shell pink with Asian calligraphy sketched on the ceiling. The entire floor was covered with a white Persian rug that looked as new as the ornaments and expensive artifacts decorating the room. In the far-right corner of the room sat a mahogany grandfather clock imported from the Balkan Sea region. The two white leather recliners matched the white leather sofa that took up the space across the room from the fireplace.

As they passed through the second den, they came to a set of redwood and oak stairs that spiraled to the ceiling and up to the fourth floor. To the left of the stairway was a massive office adjoining a game room with two pool tables and an air hockey table. To the far left of the game room was a miniature bowling alley with just two lanes.

They continued walking and reached the middle of the house where the kitchen was located, across from a huge laundry room with four washers and six dryers. Behind the kitchen was a nursery that led to the garage. As they passed the doors leading out to the garage and the inside parking lot for two, they came to a door made of glass stained with a red tint.

"Where does that go," Tiffany asked when she reached the door.

"Down here is your basement," Yolanda said, opening the door.

They walked down the carpeted stairway leading to the basement. On seeing it, Tiffany was ecstatic. The basement floor was covered in sky blue carpet stretching from one wall to the next; directly in the middle, sat a 50-inch television. Beside that was another huge fireplace. There were four black leather and beige couches spaced throughout the room.

They continued the tour, rounding a corner and suddenly seeing the glass bar, another laundry room and two bathrooms with three additional bedrooms.

"This is very lovely," Tiffany said, hugging Ball and smiling.

"How much did you say the owner wanted for this house," he asked.

"Seven hundred fifty," Yolanda said, checking the folder with the listing,

"Get them to go down to $680,000 and I'll give you $75,000 down today in cash and the rest in a week's time."

Mrs. Yolanda pulled one of her business cards from the pocket of her business suit. She took out her phone and called the owner, then explained Ball's proposal. She ended the call and turned to Ball and Tiffany, smiling.

"He said yes," she told them, which made Tiffany jump up and down.

"I'm glad you're happy. Now let's see the rest of the house, because I'm dying to see how much house there is in a million-dollar house," Ball said.

They walked through the basement and went up to the second floor. They then looked at the third and fourth floor, the majority of which was the master bedroom and two bathrooms attached to a nursery.

"You'll really love this," Mrs. Yolanda B said.

She crossed the master bedroom floor to windows set apart from everything and exactly in the middle of the room. She pushed open the shades and grabbed the two gold latches in the middle of the window frame. With a twist, she pushed them and the windows opened like doors, giving a view of the huge wooden balcony. Both Tiffany and Ball crossed the room and walked onto the balcony. They had a complete view of the lake behind the house.

"Now that's what I call a view," Ball said, hugging Tiffany.

She kissed his mouth and he just held her while they looked over the lake that seemed to stretch around the woods and disappear to the right and left.

"Here," Ball said, handing his car key to Mrs. Yolanda. "The money is in the trunk of my car in a black leather case. Just makes sure my name is not on the contract anywhere."

He looked at Tiffany, who had started to cry. "Go with her, baby," he said, releasing Tiffany from his arms.

She followed Mrs. Yolanda downstairs to the car. After counting the money, she and Tiffany sat at the kitchen table and signed the buyer's contract.

Chapter 26

Ball was sitting on an empire that even his great-grandfather would have been proud of. Instead of buying his drugs from his uncle, he began taking trips down to Colon, Panama, where he was getting kilos for as little as $2,000 each. He used beautiful women who danced in one of his strip clubs to transport the drugs back inside of them, so none of them ever got caught smuggling through customs. He had bought Tiffany, who was now his wife, a string of beauty salons and a developing company; which served the purpose of cleaning his dirty money and that of a select few of his comrades. Ball had so much property and money that he didn't need to sell drugs any longer, but for some reason, the power that came with controlling the streets was something he was too ignorant to give up.

To celebrate the birth of his third son, he decided to throw a party and invite the "Who's Who" of DC's successful society. More than fifty celebrities and sports stars came to the Tunnel of Heaven night club off New York Avenue to show respect for Ball's accomplishments. As he sat in the VIP section of the Tunnel that was completely surrounded by bullet proof glass, he stared down at the A-list guests who were dancing, partying, and drinking like there was no tomorrow.

"We did big things, huh boss," Lil Greg said, sitting down on the couch next to Ball.

"Didn't I tell you I was gonna make us rich," Ball said, smiling.

"Yeah, and I never doubted you," Lil Greg said, reaching to his right for the bottle of Dom Perignon and taking a sip.

"Look at that, baby," he said, turning to the pregnant Tiffany sitting at his left.

He pointed down at the mayor of DC who was dancing with one of the Redskin football players. Tiffany smiled and said,

"I don't think Ima stay too long, baby, because

461

I'm tired."

"Go home whenever you feel like it," Ball said kissing her forehead.

Tiffany stood up and said, "Congratulations, my king and happy birthday," and kissed him on the forehead.

Zulu and another of his men escorted her out of the VIP and out of the club, as Ball sat watching her from the couch where he sat. Lean, Omar and Sunnybee were standing near the bullet proof glass, where women danced all over them and they drank and smoked cigars packed with Kush.

He smiled, happy to see his family enjoying themselves. He was happy that he was able to fulfill his promise to everyone and make himself very rich while in the process of doing it.

"Ay, Lil Greg, didn't you tell that nigga Vamron from the Cripset not to let you catch him in DC ever again," Omar yelled over the music.

"Yeah, that's what I told him and he ain't been back since," he answered, mugging.

"Like hell he ain't been back since. There he go with some bad ass chocolate drop," Lean said, pointing down to the dance floor.

Lil Greg stood and crossed over to the glass. When he saw Vamron, his blood began to boil. Looking at Ball, he said, "I guess he think DC won't be the last place on earth he's gonna end up dying in."

Ball, who was enjoying himself too much, didn't want anything stupid to mess up his night, especially with all of the VIPs standing around in his club. He thought about how he had ordered Lil Greg to start extorting all of the rappers and singers who wanted to be safe when they came to perform in the Murder Capitol and he thought of how all of them had paid, but Vamron.

"Go throw him out of his own party," Ball said, looking at Lil Greg.

Smiling back, Lil Greg and Zulu left the VIP where they

463

had been, and crossed the hallway where another VIP room had been rented by Vamron. His security tried to stop Lil Greg and Zulu from entering the room, until they produced their weapons and pointed them in his face. They ordered him to get to the floor. He complied and they proceeded into the VIP room. Vamron was fondling the breast of a woman who sat on his lap. His boys stood up and Zulu pointed his weapon at them. He told them if they moved, they were all dead.

"Getcha silly ass up," Lil Greg said, grabbing Vamron's collar and forcing him to his feet. The woman screamed and Lil Greg said to her, "Keep screamin and Ima let you hear how loud this Desert Eagle can scream. He pointed the weapon in her face. She curled up on the couch and got quiet.

"Come on, clown," Lil Greg said, pushing Vamron towards the door.

He took him across the hall to Ball.

"May I offer you a drink?" Ball asked, grabbing a bottle of Dom Perignon from the bucket of ice where it

464

had been chilling.

"Naw, I'm good," Vamron said with an attitude.

"First you refuse to pay the small protection fee I offered you, now you wanna be disrespectful and refuse my hospitality," Ball said as he poured out some of the Dom Perignon onto Vamron's grey suede shoes.

"What the fuck, B," he said as he moved his feet.

"In this city we pour out liquor for dead niggas," Ball said, standing up from the couch.

He got up in Vamron's face so close that they were almost kissing, and he said,

"You wanted to play this game, remember? The price I asked you for is less than you pay for your body guard. Now you gonna need body guards for all of your family members who stay right where I can reach them.

"You rapper punks start believing in your own raps and then ya'll start to think ya'll gangsters for real,

465

but ya'll not, and don't ever forget that.

"You see, Vamron, I know everywhere that you're gonna be for the next four years in advance, because your whole life is an open book. What you don't know is this: At any minute, I can have some killer who's out in the crowd blow your head clean off while you're on stage. You don't know who we are or when we will come for you but we know exactly where you'll be every night of the year. So do you really think you are being smart to refuse the offer that I gave you as a token of my appreciation?"

Vamron just stood, speechless, and looked into Ball's eyes.

"I don't even want your money any more. Now it's your life I want, Ball told him. "I can promise you this, homie. You won't make it out of this city alive this time. Get this filthy piece of shit out of my sight."

Lil Greg smacked Vamron across the back of the head with the Desert Eagle, nearly knocking him out. He grabbed his arm and he and Dizzy, another of Ball's

466

men, escorted Vamron and his entire entourage out of the Tunnel.

Once outside the club, Vamron made his way to the gated fence around the area where his Pepsi blue Lamborghini was parked. The valet pulled his car around. Vamron jumped in and sped away without waiting for his entourage.

When he reached the light at the bottom of New York Avenue, Vamron stopped and checked his rear view to see if anyone had followed him. Not even one car was on the street behind or in front of him.

Zulu radioed to Chappelle and Lil Ron Ron, who sat in the parking lot of Gallaudet University. He told them the make of the car that Vamron was driving and ordered them to kill him. Then he ended the call.

"There he go, right there," Chappelle said, cocking the M31 with a drum roll clip in its belly carrying 71 rounds. "Slide up beside him and Ima crush his skull in."

Ron Ron coasted up to Vamron in the Viper he was driving, but instead of pulling up along the side, he pulled in front. He hopped out of the Viper and pointed his gun at Vamron.

"Don't move, nigga! Don't you dare move," Ron Ron said as he neared the car.

"What the hell are you doing," Chappelle asked, seeing he couldn't get off a good shot without hitting Ron Ron, as well.

"What it look like I'm doing, nigga. Ima rob this nigga then kill him."

Vamron ducked, threw the Lamborghini in reverse and stepped on the gas. Ron Ron opened fire.

"Watch out," Chappelle yelled, trying to get a clear shot, but failing.

In less than three seconds, the Lamborghini had disappeared from sight.

"Damn, he got away. That bitch ass nigga just got away," Ron Ron yelled as he came back to the car.

"Don't even think about catchin that Lambo in this piece of shit," Chappelle said, He looked at Lil Ron Ron as if he wanted to shoot him himself.

Shaking his head, he said, "You missed, slim. Now we both dead for it."

"Man, this is a CV Viper. We can catch him in this," Ron Ron said, stepping on the gas.

The car flew up the street but there was no sight of the Lamborghini or Vamron anywhere.

"Shit," he said, punching the middle of the steering wheel.

"Look man, drop me off around Seventh and Minnesota so I can holla at my mother before Ball sends Lil Gregg and Zulu to kill the both of us."

"Damn, I really fucked up, didn't I!" Ron Ron

said as he drove down Benning Road.

When they reached the crossing where Minnesota Avenue and Benning met, two Yukons were parked in the middle of the street, blocking the way.

"Damn, that's them right there," Chappelle said.

He hopped out of the Viper and took off running, but the gunfire from the 1919 A6s in the hands of the six gunmen who had exited the Yukons chopped him down before he could take five steps.

Ron Ron knew he would be next to die, so instead of going any further, he put the car in reverse and began to fly down the street backwards. Out of nowhere, a sixteen-wheeler came flying up behind him and crushed and rolled the Viper, killing Ron Ron instantly.

The Sixth District Police Station, less than a block from where the 1919's exploded, sent twelve units to meet the confrontation. As soon as Ball's men saw the police cruisers, they turned their weapons around and opened fire on them, as well.

Police cars crashed on the sidewalk, while others flipped over on getting hit with the powerful impact of the A6's gun spray. Ball's men continued to fire until every last one of the cruisers had stopped moving. They jumped in their vehicles and took off.

When they turned on Minnesota Avenue, more police cars swerved in front of them, causing them to stop. They tried backing up, but the police had them boxed in. The men hopped out of the trucks and opened fire, while officers who dared to stand toe to toe with them fired back. After a fierce gun battle that raged on for ten minutes, the police took cover and prayed for back-up. Ball's men made their way back into their vehicles and began driving through the city like madmen. With the "no fly zone" over the area, there was nothing the police could do but let them get away, Scot free.

Chapter 27

DC's mayor, who was under great pressure from the President of the United States and Congress, walked to the podium where several news cameras and reporters waited for him to explain how ten officers had been killed in a single night. He climbed the steps and spoke into the microphone.

"Ladies and gentlemen of this great city and around the world, I am here before you today to speak about a tragedy that has shocked our entire nation. Ten of our officers were gunned down last night by villains and/or gangsters who live within this city. They kill as if it's their God-given right and talent to do so.

"Yes, they have killed before but I am here to tell you that they will not kill again. As of 8:30 tonight, the entire city will be under curfew and anyone caught outside, whether children or adults, will be tossed in jail. I have already spoken with DC's police chief. Effective immediately, we will be implementing what we call "all hands-on deck.

"If anyone is caught in a neighborhood where they are not on a lease to any of the dwellings in that neighborhood, they will be detained and locked up for trespassing.

"We intend to have all hands-on deck do a sweep throughout the entire city; they have already started around Linda Pollen and the Valley Green neighborhoods, as we speak.

"If you are caught without any form of identification anywhere in the city of DC, you will be sent to jail.

"Ladies and gentlemen, our city, this Nation's Capital, is and has been the Murder Capital of this great Nation for three consecutive years and I, with the help of Congress and the President of the United States, will change that. As of today, DC is considered a city under siege!

"I repeat," the mayor said, looking straight into the cameras, "Washington DC, our Nation's Capital, is a city under siege!"

The mayor turned and walked away. The news reporters tried their best to question him, but to no avail.

Ball, Lean and Omar were so terrified of being ratted out that they began to send a chilling fear of death throughout the city and clearly sent the message, "keep your mouth shut."

Any and everybody that the police had randomly picked up for questioning was killed soon after they were released. This caused the hustlers on the street to open fire on the police when they jumped out on them.

"Man, this shit is getting crazy," said Whiteflint, a certified gangster in the streets of DC.

He passed a roadblock of Stanton Road as he continued toward home around 10th Place. Before he could turn onto Robinson Place, two DC police cruisers jumped behind him. They cut on their lights and over their loud speaker, ordered him to pull over. Whiteflint, who usually carried a gun everywhere, pulled over knowing he had nothing on him that could get him arrested. He gathered his registration, license and title for his car and put them on his lap. Then he waited for the officers to approach the car.

Both officers had left their car as soon as two more cruisers arrived to back them up. Before the first two officers could reach Whiteflint's car, the other four officers were out of their cruisers and heading towards his vehicle, as well.

"May I help you, gentlemen," Whiteflint asked, smiling and rolling down his window.

One officer pulled a flashlight from his belt and swung it into the car, striking Whiteflint in the head. He continued to beat him as the other officers joined in. They dragged Whiteflint from his car and beat him even more, once he was on the ground.

After cuffing his hands behind him, they threw him in the back of one of the cruisers and took him to the 7th District Police Station on Alabama Avenue. As he sat on a bench in a cell and was bleeding to death, the officers drilled him with questions he couldn't even understand. Once they realized he wasn't gonna say anything, or that his jaw was broken, preventing him from talking, they took him out to one of their cars. They drove him through the city, looking for somewhere to dump him off so that his death wouldn't be on their hands. When they reached Montana Avenue Northeast, they circled around the back of the street and pushed him out beside a dumpster and drove off. A homeless man who had been trying to get some rest after a heavy night of drinking, saw Whiteflint lying on the ground and bleeding. He got up from where he had been sitting and walked to the man. After checking Whiteflint's pulse to make sure he was still alive, he quickly helped him up and they went to an abandoned building behind them. The homeless man took Whiteflint inside and laid him down. He removed Whiteflint's clothes to see how badly he was hurt and where he was hurt too.

The old man, who knew that Whiteflint had been beaten within an inch of his life, hurried out of the building and ran to the corner store where he bummed for money. When he had enough, he bought food and medicine for the man he'd found. He rushed back to the building and began trying his best to patch up Whiteflint and bring him back to life.

Chapter 28

Ball sat in the front row of the MCI Center, beside his wife Tiffany and their three sons, Daquan, Delaun, and Deneticus, waiting and watching for Bradley Staten to walk across the graduation stage. The entire family was proud of Brad, who had graduated at the top of his class with honors. He was the first Staten male ever to get a full academic scholarship to college. As Bradley's name was called, the entire auditorium erupted into cheers; everyone rose to their feet. They clapped for him and he smiled as he walked across the stage. He stopped in the center of the stage and the principal of Fletcher Johnson High School gave him his certificate.

"Mr. Staten, this entire city is proud of you. You have not only graduated at the top of your class, but you also have graduated at the top of this city. Because of that, Georgetown University has offered you a full academic scholarship."

The crowd erupted in cheers again. The principal, whose name was Mr. Skinner, shook Bradley's hand and said,

"I'd like to thank you, young man, for being so outstanding."

Bradley took off his graduation cap and threw it into the crowd in front of him as everyone cheered again. Principal Skinner asked, "Do you have anything you would like to say, Mr. Staten?"

Reluctantly, Brad stepped to the microphone and said, "I'd like to thank my mother for staying on top of me; I'd like to thank my best friend, brother and the guy who's been my dad when we both didn't have a dad, my brother Derrick."

Ball sat in his seat and was nearly brought to tears as he looked up and saw his baby brother on the stage and smiling at him.

Here it was at sixteen years old his baby brother was headed to Georgetown University on an academic scholarship. There was nothing anyone could have told him that would have made his night better than it already was.

Chapter 29

Several weeks passed since the police beat him within an inch of his life. With the help of the old man, who nursed him back to health, Whiteflint was able to stand on his own two feet again.

"Thank you," he said, hugging the man whose name he didn't even know. "I'll never forget you," he said shedding a tear over the old man's shoulder.

Then he released him and left the building. As he walked down Montana Avenue, he began to feel as if life for him had a different purpose. He reached in his pocket and smiled when he found three $20 bills. He thought about how he had cussed at bums on the street when they asked for change; how he had looked down on them and the drug users of the city. He had considered them the lowest life people of the world.

The few weeks when the old man took care of him, the man whose name he didn't even know; he had formed a new outlook on the way he looked at and judged other people, especially bums and drug users. The homeless man made sure he ate every day. He would listen to that man as he told stories about when he was in Vietnam and how he had started using heroin to cope with having killed so many innocent people.

Whiteflint thought of the man who saved his live as he flagged down a cab.

"Take me around 10th Place," he said as he got in the back seat.

He pulled out the three $20 bills and handed them to the driver. Again, he thought about the old man who could have been his own father. After fifteen minutes of driving through the city, the cab finally pulled up to Building 812 on 10th Street Southeast. Whiteflint slammed the cab door shut and started walking to his building, where a crowd of thugs and hood rats stood, dressed in black.

"What's up, ya'll," he said, looking over the faces of the young men and women who admired him.

None of them said a word to him.

"What's up Lil Calvin," he said, patting the head of a small boy who pulled away from him with disdain. He looked around at all of the people who were mugging on him as he frowned his face up and tried to understand what the problem was. He just shook his head and moved through the crowd and into the building. He climbed the steps in pain, as his leg that hadn't healed all the way began to ache. After climbing the six flights, he finally came to the apartment that he shared with his wife and kids. He knocked on the door in pain. As he got ready to knock again, the door opened and his wife Evette hugged him.

"Aw," she screamed out in pain, letting him go. She looked him over and said, "Oh my god you're hurt."

She helped him inside as his daughter Icest ran to him, screaming "Daddy." She hugged his leg and Evette said for her to watch out because her daddy was hurt. His son, Demoyia, who sat on the couch and looked at him with a mug on his face, got up and went in another room. Evette took him to the bathroom and helped him undress while she ran him some bathwater. She yelled at Icest to get her some medicine and other things.

The bathroom door opened and Icest walked in with her arms full of medicine and other things, which she put down on the floor beside her mother. She looked at her father and when she saw all of the cuts and bruises on his body, she ran and hugged him. She started to cry.

"It's alright baby girl. I'm alright," he said hugging and kissing her.

Demoiya walked to the bathroom door and looked inside, but didn't go in.

"Come here, son," Whiteflint said, looking at him.

"I ain't coming to you," Demoiya said, frowning his face up.

"Demoiya, don't you dare talk to your father that way," Evette said, raising her voice.

"That nigga ain't my father. I ain't no son of no rat bastard."

With that, everything became silent. Demoiya stepped away. With tears in his eyes, Whiteflint looked at Evette and asked,

"What did he say?"'

"Nothing baby, nothing, He's just angry."

"What did my son just call me," he asked slowly.

Evette looked away from him and released his hand.

"The police said that you have been working with them and that's why you haven't been home," she said, shedding a tear.

He stood up and walked towards the door, as Evette screamed his name.

"Baby, please no! Please no," she cried, falling to the floor.

Whiteflint walked to the closet next to the door. He opened it and grabbed a green duffle bag. Inside the duffel bag was an HK MR556, a Klick 47 and a M16 carbine with a collapsible stock.

"No, Daddy, no," Icest yelled, crying and reaching out for her father.

He had opened the door and walked out of the apartment. He continued walking, down the steps, until he reached the front of the building. Outside, everybody that had dissed him was still standing. With watery, bloodshot, red eyes, he stared over the faces of all the individuals who felt afraid. After all the work he had put in, and all the people he helped, people had been so quick to discredit him, instead of the contrary. Right then he realized that what he had lived and was willing to die for all of his life, was no more than a mere illusion.

He pushed his way through the crowd and went across the street to his car. He jumped inside, started it up and drove down the street to the 7th District Police Station. He pulled to the curb and parked. He removed the assault rifles from the bag and strapped them around his arms. He opened his door, got out, and headed towards the entrance of the station.

With both weapons in his hands, he walked through the front door. Once inside, he opened fire on everyone there. Officers and desks were flipped over and had slumped to the ground. The walls were spattered with bullet holes as far as the eye could see. Nothing nor nobody dared to move, in fear of being fired on by the high-powered assault rifles.

Whiteflint headed to the stairs and climbed them, firing randomly at any and everybody, until he was gunned down himself. He laid on the floor with the two assault rifles in his hands and another strapped across his back. The only thing he could think of was the old man who had saved his life.

Chapter 30

"Catch me! Catch me," Najla said, smiling and running through the parking lot of Iverson Mall, near the carnival grounds and the festival that was going on.

Bradley, who was in love with her, didn't know how to tell her or approach her father about marrying her, since she was Muslim and he was Christian. He ran behind her, childishly, through the crowd of people who stood around or moved about the parking lot, enjoying the festivities. He caught up to her near the Ferris wheel and she began to laugh.

"You run like an old woman, Brad," she said, taunting him.

He looked in her reddish-brown eyes, which always made him feel as if he was dreaming.

"Hey punk, you soft ass nigga. What are you doing with that fine ass woman?," he heard a voice say, making him turn around.

A mob of teenagers with dreds and cornrows stood behind him, holding bats and bottles.

"Come on, Bradley, let it go," Najla said, grabbing his hand.

They began walking away but a few of the boys ran in front of them, preventing them from leaving.

"Look man, we don't want any trouble, so just leave us alone," Bradley said.

"It's too late for that you dumb ass nigga. You on the wrong side of town now," said one of the boys as he stepped up into Brad's face.

"Brad, no," Najla said, pulling at him. He looked at her, thinking she was so beautiful and innocent.

"Fuck that bitch, B," one of the boys said.

"Grab her ass," another boy standing behind them said.

The boy who had got in Brad's face reached his hand to grab Najla. That's when Brad hit him. The punch was so powerful that it knocked the boy to the ground, out cold. Brad had been pushed around all of his life. Suddenly he felt the rage inside of him that made him wanna kill every last one of the boys who had insulted him and the woman he wanted to marry. He knew that the men in his family would never allow anyone to disrespect him and he was no longer gonna allow it, either. He grabbed another of the boys, taking his bat, and began beating another boy with it. Najla cried and begged him to stop. He continued to beat the boy and when the other boys tried to stop him, he turned on them, beating them as well.

As he saw himself winning over the large crowd of thugs, he began to feel as if his brothers and cousins were watching him and smiling, proud of him at that very moment. He heard Najla screaming no, no, but then he felt his body drifting down to the ground. Another shot was fired from the tiny .22 caliber, and entered the back of his head, killing him instantly. The crowd took off running and so did everyone else in the parking lot, except for Najla, who sat on the ground, crying as she held Brad's head in her lap.

"No! No! No! Nooooo," she screamed, but it was too late. Bradley was dead.

Chapter 31

Bar, who stood up top of the dumpster in the middle of Potomac Gardens, laughed as two dope fiends fought over a bindle of heroin that one of his men had thrown up in the air. He laughed so hard that it nearly brought him to tears. As he looked on, he noticed Tebetha and Butterfly, who both had their hair all over their heads and looked wild, as if they had just woken up or finished fighting.

What the hell, he thought to himself, wondering why the two women who wouldn't even be caught dead without their nails and hair done, would come outside looking the way they looked. Then he burst into laughter.

"Ya'll look wild," he said, holding his stomach. He looked over at Butterfly and noticed that she was crying. Then he looked at Tebetha and saw the sad look on her face, too.

"What the hell's wrong with ya'll," he asked as he hopped down from the dumpster.

"Your brother, your brother's dead," cried Butterfly.

He looked into her eyes and shook his head. L had finally got what he had coming, he thought. He had been shot more than two different times, so Ball knew that eventually the streets which he loved so much would kill him. He grabbed both of his sisters, pulling them into his arms and hugging them.

"Kevin died doing what he loved best, so don't be sad," he said, kissing Tebetha on her forehead.

"No Derrick," Tebetha said, dropping to her knees. "They killed Brad," she said, sobbing.

He wasn't sure he had heard her right but his chest began to get tight and he found it hard to breathe.

"Butter, who got killed," he asked, with tears in his eyes.

"They killed Bradley, Derrick," she said, as tears flowed down her cheeks.

491

The news hit him like a ton of bricks. For a moment, everything seemed to go blank. He began to walk off in a state of numbness, headed nowhere. He traveled through the corridor and walked out of the Gardens, heading towards Pennsylvania Avenue. A million thoughts were running through his head but no thought in particular meant anything at that moment. He reached Pennsylvania Avenue and walked right into traffic, as cars beeped their horns while swerving to keep from hitting him. He continued walking, with no regard for his own life or safety at all. The purest thing he had in life had been taken from him and at that moment, nothing else even mattered. He wanted to believe that there was some mistake in what Butter had said but he knew that he had heard her clearly.

All of a sudden, he dropped to his knees, put his hands over his face and began to cry. He stayed in the parking lot of the gas station and cried, as he felt a pain he had never felt before, tearing away at him. For a moment, he didn't even know where he was or who he was. The world just seemed all together obsolete to him. He didn't even hear the car pull up behind him and when he felt the hand on his shoulder he almost didn't even look up.

"Come on brother. Come on," Lean said, lifting him to his feet.

They held each other and cried for a while, and then they got into Lean's car and drove off.

Chapter 32

Three months and two weeks later:

In retaliation for his little brother's death, Ball began killing everyone that had ever disrespected or opposed him. The murder rate in the city jumped up sky high. Even the murder rate in Maryland sky-rocketed, as men from DC took out their anger of starving on every male in Maryland. Ball had caused a drought on the street and nobody was eating at all anymore.

With no drugs to sell, the gangsters had nothing to do but ride around, listening to Dirty Cide recording artists, and looking for houses to break into, or people to kill or kidnap.

The once beautiful Chocolate City had turned into the cruddiest, deadliest place in America. No one was safe from anyone else.

So many murders were being committed that the feds began taking charge of the investigations that the metro police had begun. Everything in DC was going federal, from crack pipe possession, to possession of a dime bag of weed. The feds knew that Ball and his crew had something to do with 90% of all the murders in DC and the surrounding states. They wanted him but couldn't find anyone stupid enough to testify against Ball. To make him panic, the feds snatched up Lil Gregg and Zulu, who was on camera killing more than twelve people. When that didn't work, they snatched up Omar, with a warrant for several murders.

Interrogation Room 555, building in Northwest DC

"Man, ya'll pigs gonna let me call my lawyer or what," Omar asked, mugging on the four FBI detectives sitting at the table in front of him.

"If you're not guilty of anything, I don't see why you need a lawyer, Mr. Staten," said the only black agent in the room as he opened a folder on the table in front of him.

"So, Mr. Omar Jajel Staten, this man here is your cousin, right" the agent said as he slid several pictures of Ball in front of him.

"I've never seen that guy in my fucking life," O said, looking away.

"Well, for somebody who doesn't' know him, you sure are in a lot of photographs with him," the agent said, placing several more pictures of Omar and Ball standing together on the block, in the club, and just in other random spots.

"Here's something you need to know about Mr. Staten," said Baker, the agent in the middle as he loosened his tie. "We don't usually get involved unless we got our man by the balls," he said, smiling.

He reached into his pocket and produced a tiny recorder which he placed on the table. He pushed "play," and, as it played, he could hear himself talking about four hundred keys he had sold for Ball. The look on Omar's face told the feds everything they needed to know.

"So I guess that's not you on that recording either, just like that's not you in those pictures, right?"

"Man, that's nothing. I was just talking reckless to some girl, trying to get her to fuck me by impressing her," Omar said, mugging on the agent.

"Look, Omar, we have been following you for the last seventy-two hours and we know that you went to pick up some guns that we believe were used in the murder of several people in Uptown. We have a warrant to raid the storage you got off Georgia Avenue and the three houses that you own," said the detective as he placed the two warrants in front of Omar so he could see them.

"We also got a warrant to conduct a search on Maple Avenue, where Derrick Staten lives with his wife and kids, thanks to you."

"You see, Omar, we have been tapping your phone for quite some time and we have also put recording devices in and under every car you drive. So let's stop bullshitting each other, because on April the

3rd, you went to Maple Avenue to meet Derrick and soon after that, you met with our confidential informant and sold him forty automatic weapons and thirty keys of heroin."

The more the agents talked, the more Omar realized that they weren't bluffing him for sure. All the information they presented him was accurate down to a "t."

"Ok, so ya'll say ya'll know of this shit, so why the hell not just lock me up? Why the hell are ya'll still talking," he asked.

His question made the agents look around the table at each other.

"Look, Mr. Staten, you pretty smart, so we don't really have to tell you this, but we will. We know that you're a nobody in all of this, and quite frankly, we don't even want you. We want him," the agent said, pointing to the picture of Madball on the table.

"With or without your help, we are gonna get him. Don't forget that we've been watching both of you, so we know that he has a certain amount of money you dropped off over his mother's house yesterday that he is supposed to pick up. Her having that money in her house is enough to indict here for money laundering, which carries 10 to 30 years.

"How will your cousin feel about you if we lock up his mother because of something you said or did," the agent asked.

"Man, look, I want my fucking lawyer," Omar said, looking up at the ceiling.

"Trust me, Mr. Staten, this is a federal charge so no lawyer can get you out of the mandatory minimum sentence of life that a Continuing Enterprise charge carries. But you know that, because you father is doing life in the feds, isn't he?"

"So what the fuck do ya'll want from me," Omar yelled at the top of his voice.

"Nobody knows that we locked you up, so you can still help us and help yourself at the same time. We have already spoken to the District Attorney who has agreed to let you go today for your cooperation.

"All we want from you is to get your cousin Derrick to admit to being the guy pulling all the strings on Tahoe."

"Hell no, that's impossible," Omar said, shaking his head.

"Why is it impossible," asked one of the agents.

"Because he's been shot twice so he doesn't trust people around him. He sometimes makes you change out of all your clothes and put on one of those Muslim garbs so he is sure that no one has a wire or a weapon on them."

"That's really clever," the agent said, looking to his right.

"Ok forget the wire taps, we'll give you money to purchase drugs directly from him."

"I told ya'll, he doesn't sell drugs."

"Well you better hope like hell he does for your sake," the agent at the right said, as he got up and walked over behind Omar.

"You're free to go," he told Omar as he uncuffed his hands. "Here," he said, handing Omar a business card, "make sure you keep in touch or we'll just come snatch your ass up again."

Omar left the building. He ran down the stairs and across the street, looking behind him to see if he was being followed. He jumped on the train going back the other way. After doing that five times, he felt that he had shaken off any agent that might have been tailing him. He went to the platform of the Anacostia subway station, where he stopped at a pay phone. He placed some change into the phone and called Lean, who he believed the feds knew nothing about.

"Listen real good. I need to be picked up from the train station across from Barry Farms," he said; he hung up and went outside and headed across the street from the train station. He saw a huge pile of leaves and jumped inside them, then covered himself, making sure he could see the front of the train station. When the money green Chrysler 300 that Lean drove pulled up, he hopped out of the leaves and ran to the car. He got in the back seat.

"What the hell is wrong with you? You on PCP or something," Lean asked, looking behind him into the seat.

"Don't look back," Omar said, ducking low. "Look, the feds just let me go."

"What," Lean said, pulling away from the curb.

"Yeah nigga they just let me go. They want me to set up Derrick. They got me on a recording saying a bunch of incriminating things that might send us all to jail."

Omar grabbed a pen and a card he found on the floor of the back seat by his fee and began writing.

"Look, cousin, here's the addresses where I got all of my money. It's over five million in cash at these spots."

"So what the hell you telling me for? You gonna go get it, right?

"Hell naw, nigga, them people on my line real hard and the only reason they agreed to let me go is because I played them into thinking I would help them get Derrick.

"Right now, I'm a ghost and I gotta get out of this city. Then out of the country just as soon as I am able, and that means ten minutes ago."

"So what do you want me to do with all of the money and your property," Lean asked, as he began to come to tears, knowing that this would be the last time that he ever saw Omar again.

"Keep it. Give it away, I don't care. That money and all that material stuff is the last thing on my mind right now. Look, you gotta get somebody to go get that laundry bag out of Linda's house ASAP. It's some cash in there that belongs to Ball and the feds know it's there. If they run in there and find it, they're gonna charge her with laundering money for us all.

"They think I'm helping them so you got time to get everything out her house and all of the other spots," Omar said.

"Promise me that you'll do it," he said as tears ran down his cheeks. "Pull over here and let me out," he said, wiping the tears from his face.

Lean pulled over while he reached into his coat. He grabbed hold of what he had in his inside pocket.

"I love you, O," he said, pulling out a manila envelope full of cash and passing it backwards to him.

"I love you, too," O said, hugging Lean.

He stepped out of the car and disappeared into an alley behind a building. Lean grabbed his phone and called

Ball, who was just leaving his mother who was around Harmony Cemetery, visiting Bradley's grave.

Ball looked at the text message that said something that let him know the end had finally come to his run in the streets.

The message said to meet the caller ASAP, at a place they had agreed to never even step foot in again when they were kids, and to get ghost because he had an extra shadow.

Instead of taking his car, he went into the parking lot and broke into a car and hotwired it. He drove away from the cemetery. The two agents who had been watching him hadn't noticed him because his car hadn't moved. So they continued to watch Mrs. Linda Staten as she cried and moaned in grief about her son.

Ball sped through Maryland until he reached East Gates Projects, which were no more than gutted out, abandoned buildings. He parked the car on top of a hill and got out. He looked down at the "Gates of Hell," where he and his family grew up. The "Gates of Hell" was the last place on earth that he ever wanted to see again, because so much pain and anguish had been put in his life and the lives of his family inside of that place.

At first, he relented about hopping the fence, but then he began to climb until he was on the other side, down in the East Gates Projects, or at least what was left of it. Cautiously, he traveled through the graveyard of buildings until he reached the building where he grew up. He took a deep breath then exhaled, as he walked inside of the gutted-out building that had once been burned to the ground.

When Ball reached the roof of the building, he saw Lean on the far end of it, looking out into the "Gates of Hell."

"Last place either of us wanna be caught dead, haw cousin, Ball said as he crossed the roof to where Lean stood.

Lean turned around and watched Ball come to him until they were side-by-side.

"Things have gotten that bad that we had to come back here, haw cousin," Ball said, placing his hands inside of his pockets.

"Derrick, man, when will you wake up? Things have been that bad since before we left this place. We were so poor, we set out to do something about it to improve the living qualities of our family. By God, we well over superseded that.

"When we were young, we just wanted shoes and a coat so that we didn't have to walk through the streets barefooted and cold, but then…"

"Then I went on a nut and started killing any and everybody, right?"

"Man, Lean, I remember Grandad, your father and my father."

"Yeah and they all dead or doing life in jail, Derrick," Lean said as tears flowed from his eyes. "I saw how the streets respected the killers and I wanted that same respect."

"No matter how bad the people in the streets were, nobody wanted to mess with the guys who were killing like it was nothing."

"I used to dream of being Carson from around K Street, or Toney Fortune and Tufflion Shawn."

"Nobody wanted to mess with those guys because they knew the consequences would be instant death for them and their families."

"Yeah, Derrick, you're right, but look at the outcome of the lives of the men that you just named. They're all dead or doing multiple life sentences in the feds. You lost sight of wanting to get out of the ghetto and started becoming proud of the fact that you were from the ghetto. Then you even tried to run all of the ghettos."

"Man, I wanted my name to last forever. Even niggas who gettin money can't even say their name will last forever, but even though Toney Fortune died broke, everybody in this city and throughout the world know who he was."

"And that shit means what to his daughter and sons who are starving out here in these streets or getting taken advantage of by the same killers he took advantage of," Lean asked. All of this is a vicious illusion, designed to trap us, cousin, and as smart as you are, I know that you know that."

"Well, I'm fucked now. Ain't nothing I can do to take back what I done. I can't bring Brad back and I can't get Big Kevin out of jail and I damned sure can't give none of them people who I killed their lives back, so what can I do to fix it, haw?"

Lean placed his hand on Ball's shoulder and said, "Live, that's what you can do, Live! You proved that you're not to be messed with, now that the killers know that and show the feds the same thing. We can get away but it's gonna take some money to get out of this."

"Damn, that money! What good is a million dollars to a man living off of $320 a month for the rest of his life?"

"Now you talking. Let's shake this spot before we get caught up in the Feds' traps," Lean said, hugging Ball.

Chapter 33

After getting Tiffany and his three sons out of the country, Ball and Lean began to execute their master plan. They created a diversion that had every law officer in Maryland and DC out on the streets trying to control the violence caused by the fourteen hundred kilos of cocaine they promised. To get the drugs, Lean had told the meanest killers from each street that he was giving the cocaine away to the strongest hood. But first they had to show him they were strong enough to handle that type of work, so the killers and thugs began eliminating each other so fast that all the police had to stay out on the streets to help tame the wave of violence.

While all eyes in law enforcement were watching the city, Ball was able to slip out of the country, right under their noses. Once he was gone, Lean put Part Two and the final part of his plan together.

He paid for a man, the same build and height as Ball to redo his entire mouth making his dental structure identical to Ball's. Then he gave the man Ball's GT

Bentley, but before the man got a chance to drive off, Lean shot him in the back of his head and set the car he had doused with gas on fire. He stood watching as it burned to a crisp. Then he stepped off and called his Aunt Linda.

She walked into the morgue to identify the nearly cremated body of her son, while the feds watched her fake faint to the floor. With their prime, number one suspect dead, they stopped the investigation and didn't even bother looking for Omar, because they assumed, he had been killed anyway.

Chapter 34

"Hey, yo muthafucker, what the fuck you doing looking at me like that? Don't you realize I'm a Staten," the young son of Kevin Staten yelled to a man who was walking by the Porsche he sat on. "I said Ima mutha fuckin Staten," he yelled again.

The End

Kingdawud Mujahid Burgess has done it again! His new book Trilogy Unmistaken Reality 1, 2 & 3 looks to give you more stories from the street, beaconing the question, who will take over the family business and who will change their lives for good? This is his fourth published book with a host of others on the way! Look for his next installment of book 2 and 3 coming soon.

www.ingramcontent.com/pod-product-compliance
Lightning Source LLC
Chambersburg PA
CBHW032259020726
47495CB00001B/170